# SAND

*Near every rider on the outfit had at one time or other
got a glimpse of that black horse, and near every one
had figgered on some time or other catching him.*

# SAND

## By
## WILL JAMES

### ILLUSTRATED BY THE AUTHOR

MOUNTAIN PRESS PUBLISHING COMPANY
MISSOULA, MONTANA 1996

Copyright © 1996
The Will James Art Company
Billings, Montana



Library of Congress Cataloging-in-Publication Data

James, Will, 1892–1942.
    Sand / by Will James ; illustrated by the author.
        p.    cm.
    ISBN 0-87842-352-4 (cloth : alk. paper). — ISBN 0-87842-353-2
(pbk. : alk. paper)
    I. Title.
PS3519.A5298S3  1996                                    96-16736
813'.52—dc20                                                 CIP



Printed in the U.S.A. on acid-free recycled paper.

Mountain Press Publishing Company
P. O. Box 2399 • 1301 S. Third Street W.
Missoula, Montana 59806

# PUBLISHER'S NOTE

Will James's books represent an American treasure. His writings and drawings introduced generations of captivated readers to the lifestyle and spirit of the American cowboy and the West. Following James's death in 1942, the reputation of this remarkable artist and writer languished, and nearly all of his twenty-four books went out of print. But in recent years, interest in James's work has surged, due in part to the publication of several biographies and film documentaries, public exhibitions of James's art, and the formation of the Will James Society.

Now, in conjunction with the Will James Art Company of Billings, Montana, Mountain Press Publishing Company is reprinting each of Will James's classic books in handsome cloth and paperback editions. The new editions contain all the original artwork and text, feature an attractive new design, and are printed on acid-free paper to ensure many years of reading pleasure. They will be republished under the name the Tumbleweed Series.

The republication of Will James's books would not have been possible without the help and support of the many fans of Will James. Because all James's books and artwork remain under copyright protection, the Will James Art Company has been instrumental in providing the necessary permissions and furnishing artwork. Special care has been taken to keep each volume in the Tumbleweed Series faithful to the original vision of Will James.

Mountain Press is pleased to make Will James's books available again. Read and enjoy!

*The Will James Society was formed in 1992 as a nonprofit organization dedicated to preserving the memory and works of Will James. The society is one of the primary catalysts behind a growing interest in not only Will James and his work, but also the life and heritage of the working cowboy. For more information on the society, contact:*

Will James Society, P.O. Box 8207, Roswell, NM 88202

# BOOKS BY WILL JAMES

*Cowboys North and South,* 1924

*The Drifting Cowboy,* 1925

*Smoky, the Cowhorse,* 1926

*Cow Country,* 1927

*Sand,* 1929

*Lone Cowboy,* 1930

*Sun Up,* 1931

*Big-Enough,* 1931

*Uncle Bill,* 1932

*All in the Day's Riding,* 1933

*The Three Mustangers,* 1933

*Home Ranch,* 1935

*Young Cowboy,* 1935

*In the Saddle with Uncle Bill,* 1935

*Scorpion,* 1936

*Cowboy in the Making,* 1937

*Flint Spears,* 1938

*Look-See with Uncle Bill,* 1938

*The Will James Cowboy Book,* 1938

*The Dark Horse,* 1939

*Horses I Have Known,* 1940

*My First Horse,* 1940

*The American Cowboy,* 1942

*Will James' Book of Cowboy Stories,* 1951

# ILLUSTRATIONS

*He'd watched 'em catching horse after horse*
*with long flying ropes and riding away time after time.*
~ page 42 ~

*Another thrill was due him, for he'd never rode*
*in a place like that before, not behind the kind of horses that was*
*hooked to that wagon, nor alongside a driver like that cook was.*
~ page 44 ~

*Two bulls was fighting outside the herd a ways.*
~ page 57 ~

*Then something heavy hit him, and he let out a wild holler*
*as he was sent a rolling down over the edge of the bench.*
~ page 59 ~

*The girl would attract the mad cow's attention by*
*waving them tapideros in front of her face, the same way*
*as a bull fighter waves his "muleta" at a charging bull's nose,*
*and the sweep of her horns would only touch tapidero leather.*
~ page 61 ~

*She knowed bucking horses, she knowed good riding,*
*and she watched it all with the same interest that a*
*town girl takes in watching the changes of fashion plates.*
~ page 75 ~

*Afterwards, the cowboy, the best rider in the world, followed along*
*on them grounds and on the same trails of the buffalo and Injun.*
~ page 89 ~

"And besides," the Kid went on, "you ought to set up in your saddle; the way you ride now you're setting on half of your backbone and you'll be getting kidney sores. Why don't you straighten up and get your knees down from under your chin?"
~ page 92 ~

The buckskin played ball for quite a spell with him that way, and then, like as if he was tired of playing, he bounced him up once more and dodged to one side as Tilden came down.
~ page 105 ~

Even the Kid, with his "growing appetite," was always right up to snuff and on time, often saddling his horse with a biscuit still in his mouth.
~ page 109 ~

One of them mean ponies could easy hit a man with a hind hoof even while that man is slipping the bridle over his head.
~ page 115 ~

If a man got up to refill his cup of the black coffee and one of the others setting around hollered "man at the pot," the feller that was up was supposed to go around with the pot and fill all the cups that was held out to him.
~ page 124 ~

"When the cattle begin to come into the country, they say Old Joe 'took on' a few of 'em."
~ page 130 ~

A wet slippery stirrup to step up on such a horse with sure don't go with "safety first" rules either.
~ page 138 ~

*That bronk will buck out a ways and maybe slip and fall, sometimes on the rider, but whatever he does the rider will hang on to him.*
~ page 140 ~

*Rita had asked Moran a lot of questions about this feller Tilden, who he was, where he came from, and so on, and she'd seemed pretty interested.*
~ page 156 ~

*A good joke, in words or action, is the cowboy's staff of life.*
~ page 160 ~

*Old Joe took the lead.*
~ page 179 ~

*When the calf had no more rope to play on he was right on top of Tilden, and there he bucked and bellered some more.*
~ page 184 ~

*The big herds that was handled and the horses that was rode, all made it a mighty serious business, a work where there was room for none but experienced men.*
~ page 187 ~

*And that jump came near being the last one for him and his horse, because his horse, being tired, hadn't been able to clear the gap as he should. His hind feet had struck only crumbling dirt, and it looked for a spell like both would tumble over backwards into mighty deep space.*
~ page 199 ~

*He'd seen the girl twice more that year, once when her and her dad camped at Old Joe's place for a night, and once again by her lonesome on the range where she'd been hunting horses.*
~ page 207 ~

*He was riding one horse and leading two, and the horse*
*he was riding was none less than the little buckskin*
*which had bucked him off so often.*
~ page 212 ~

*No man was ever sure of catching any wild horse till he had*
*his rope on him. Even then the rope might break, and many*
*other things can happen which all has to be chanced on.*
~ page 226 ~

*And sure enough, here he come, as big as life and*
*making a picture that of a sudden made Tilden forget*
*everything else but the want of him.*
~ page 233 ~

*The only person he could see was Moran*
*saddling a horse in the corral.*
~ page 251 ~

*But, when night came on and he hit back for his camp,*
*he seen where all his wondering had been wrong, for a standing*
*there by a fresh-built fire was Old Joe busy mixing something.*
~ page 265 ~

*The blizzard was going on its fourth day.*
~ page 269 ~

*All the cowboys, including Moran, was now busy*
*topping off their ponies for the spring round up.*
~ page 284 ~

*The horse, being wise, was watching.*
~ page 289 ~

*The black stallion had turned.*
*~ page 306 ~*

*And when he turns a fighting bronk into a well broke cow horse,*
*that pony's spirit is just as intact as the day he was caught.*
*~ page 314 ~*

*And as that head appeared above the nine-foot fence at him,*
*and the weight of his body shook the whole corral,*
*Tilden didn't want to see more.*
*~ page 318 ~*

*He does his gentling in the middle of*
*a bare corral or wherever he happens to be.*
*~ page 325 ~*

*A half a second later a heavy timber*
*came up behind him and held him there.*
*~ page 331 ~*

*Tilden turned, starey eyed, and there,*
*to within a few feet of him, was Rita Spencer setting on her horse.*
*~ page 334 ~*

*And there on the porch, and like as if in tune*
*to make that day's happenings perfect, was Rita.*
*~ page 359 ~*

*The black stallion was in the shadow of it.*
*~ page 364 ~*

# A FIRST WORD

I guess this story goes as fiction, but to me it's pretty true, for I knowed such a feller as I'm writing about here. I knowed the girl too. Fact is I am the horse wrangler in this story, the Kid. I was working on the outfit when that feller come along, it was one of the first big outfits I'd ever worked for and I was much of a kid. I sold him his first horse and coached him on his first ride, and the impressions I give as the Kid in this story are the impressions I had at the time.

And being a kid, I didn't realize much when this feller I'm writing about came to the outfit and begin telling me of all that was on his chest, what he'd been and everything. But now, as I try to recall the talks we'd have while I herded the saddle bunch, I get a better inkling of how he might of felt, and so I'm writing of him as I'd see him *now*. The range country he loses or finds himself in, the cow camp and workings he runs into, the wild horses he sees, and the girl he meets are all of now, today.

And, after tallying up, I don't think I'm far off in this story of him, as I see him now. I might not be so correct in telling of his impressions as a city man lost on the big ranges because, after all, I can only write the story from the cowboy's sight of it, but I tried to make up for it there, and one big reason which made me want to tell of him is that he stuck. He was the first grown feller what knowed of easy ways of living who came to the cow country and stuck, the first one *I* ever seen, and the kind of a man you'd least expect, too, for there was nothing to him to stick with, nothing but a rack of bones and a fluttering heart, and he'd come to a world that was all strange and which he was least fitted for.

## Chapter I

Two hundred pairs of ears raised up and pointed to a ridge behind which the setting sun had just disappeared. The two hundred pairs of ears belonged to the remuda* of the Ox Yoke outfit and the eyes of them had spotted an object, a strange object, on top of that ridge and against the sky line.

The horse wrangler who'd just corralled the remuda was tying the rope which made the gate of the rope corral of the round-up camp, when noticing the ponies looking, and a few snorting, he, natural like, looked the direction they did. Even the cowboys at the camp and the foreman and the cook had took up the signal and followed along the line where the horses' ears pointed, and all glimpsed the strange sight.

And a strange sight it was sure enough. The proof of that was the way the horses acted in the rope corral. Another proof was the bunch of cattle, big inquisitive steers a circling around the object and following it up. But what made the object so strange wasn't for what it

* Saddle-horse bunch.

3

was, it was more for the shape it was in, it was afoot, a man, afoot . . .

On account of the long distances, the range country is not much on shoe leather, it's more on the hoof, and a human afoot in the big territories is a sight seldom seen.

"Must be some homesteader that got out of his 'hundred-and-sixty'* and couldn't find it again," says Baldy Otters, the cow foreman, as he seen the outline of the man on the ridge. Wether it was from fear of the cattle that was sort of curious-like following him, or what, the man had topped the ridge on a high lope and kept a going along it at that high speed. Then of a sudden he stopped, like he couldn't believe his eyes. He'd spotted the round-up camp on the creek bottom. On he came again at higher speed than ever waving his arms and hollering for help. The remuda, not used to seeing anybody coming so fast from the open that way and afoot, was near at the point of taking the rope corral with 'em and hitting out. But the stranger wasn't noticing nor caring just then just how much commotion he stirred, he was craving for company, company different than the big sharphorned steers that'd been circling around him and acting like they'd most anytime prod a horn into his ribs just to see what made him tick.

Shirt sleeves a flapping, tore pants dragging and stirring up the dust, the stranger kept a coming. The inquisitive cattle that'd followed him had turned tail

---

* Homestead.

4

at the sight of the camp, but the stranger didn't know that they had, he'd never looked back. Then the foreman, seeing that the coming scare-crow wasn't figgering on slowing down, and not wanting to have the whole remuda breaking thru the rope corral, started on to meet and head off the wild stranger. A couple of the boys went along with him, but before they could get within fifty feet of him the stranger seemed to, all at once, act kind of groggy, his legs begin to wobble, then his arms went limp and he went face down into the buffalo grass.

The foreman wondering, hurried to the stretched out figure, turned him over so he could get plenty of air, and begin fanning him with his hat.

"By golly," says he as he sized up the looks of him and kept a fanning, "I didn't know there was any humans like this. Why just look at that face Bill," he says to one of the boys near him, "it sure don't look like the sun had ever seen it, . . . but," he went on, "I guess the worst that's the matter with him right now is that he's run hisself plum down."

A few more of the riders had come up by then. One of 'em was sent to bring a bucket of fresh water, and with the work of a few and the coaching of a few others they proceeded to bring the stranger back to life.

They worked on him for a good half hour. Dark had come, and wanting to see what effects their work brought on four of the boys packed him towards camp a ways and where the light of the fire would shine on his face.

"He's the hardest feller to bring to I ever seen in my life," says a rider who'd been using his skill on the stranger. "If it was one of you boys in the place of this hombre I'd say it's a case of notifying the folks." Then the rider went on, "I used to know a feller by the name of . . . I forget the name now, well that don't matter,—anyway, that cowboy had a horse fall with him once and rolled plum over the top of him. When I come along to where he layed that feller was in the most twisted position I ever seen a man in. He looked all broke up and mashed in the ground and his scalp was tore half off and hanging over one ear. I straightened him up and just as I was beginning to fan a little air at him he opened his eyes, looked at me a bit and grinned, then made a motion for me to get him up on his feet, and when I did he started singing 'Bury me not on the Lone Prairie.' . . . I helped him get on his horse and . . ."

The rider felt the stranger's arm move and cut the story short. Then he says, "He's coming to at last, I think."

And sure enough, by the flicker of the fire, it was seen that his eyelids begin to quiver and pretty soon they begin to open. A vacant stare was in them eyes but soon enough they cleared some, the cool of the night air and all with none of the boys slacking up on the job gradually brought him to till he near could figger out where he was at.

But the men that was around and looking down at him sort of puzzled him, specially for a brain that was hazy as his. These men looked different than any he'd ever seen, and the light of the flickering fire made 'em seem all the more strange. The big hats they wore and the general outline of 'em along with the "chaperajo" leather that was on their curved legs didn't tally up at all with the outline of any mixed crowd of his knowing, and his trying to figger that out sort of held him back some.

"Well, how're you feeling, Son?" asks Baldy Otters after he'd watched the stranger for a spell. "I expect a cup of coffee would do you good." Then not waiting for an answer he went on to speak to the cook: "Warm up some of that 'condensed panther' you call coffee for this feller, will you, and maybe he'll want a little something to eat after while too."

The sound of the deep strong voice of the foreman, along with the word "eat," which he'd just heard, seemed to bring real life thru the weak length of the stranger, he raised hisself on his elbows and looked around for the man who'd just spoke and about that time he felt two pair of strong arms getting a hold of him and raising him up like he was a feather. . . . There's a feeling on the range that as long as a human can stand up everything is fine no matter how bad a shape that human might be, that goes well with the saying "Never say die."

*The men that was around and looking down at him sort of puzzled him.*

The boys slapped the dust out of his clothes as well as they could with their hands and escorted him to a tarpaulin covered roll of bedding closer to the fire. . . . The bed roll belonged to a cowboy who at the time was at a hospital and waiting for some broken bones to knit. . . . They set him on that bed without unrolling it and, even tho he was some shaky, all hands let loose their holt and left him be. But they stayed close in case he needed help and gathered around the fire, for the early spring night had a considerable chill in it.

That same chill brought the boys to mind, as they noticed the shaky human on the bed roll, that there sure was a scarcity of clothes about him. A few figgered he must of left some place in a hurry, for the thin and tore shirt, the kind that's cut short at the neck so as to add a collar onto, sure didn't look like no protection against open country breezes. The pants which was awful roomy like and had gatherings around the waist (looked like them gatherings was made that way a purpose too) hung on him like a tent. His bony knees showed thru and his ankles to match stuck out from the frazzled edge bottom.

A coat of some kind seemed right then the main necessity and the boys dug one up soon enough, and then they noticed that he also needed a hat, for the night breeze was sure blowing thru that sorel foretop of his. But getting the hat turned out to be a harder proposi-

*There sure was a scarcity of clothes about him.*
*A few figgered he must of left some place in a hurry.*

tion. There was only one rider in the outfit who sported two hats and that hombre was out with the herd, so, there was nothing to do but take the one he'd left at camp—it was his old one but of the kind that never wears out much and with a little blocking would be good as new. They put that on the stranger's head, and then it seemed like there was no more they could do much in the line of clothes. Hot food and drink was the next things to follow up on, and right about then the cook, grumbling as most good round-up cooks do, came along with a steaming pot of coffee and a tin cup.

One of the boys poured a cupful and handed it to the stranger, and right then was seen why that stranger hadn't seemed to cheer up much when the warm coat was put over his shoulders and the hat on his head. That feller was hungry and thirsty, and nothing else had mattered much. He grabbed the hot cup like his life depended on it and took a swallow of the black coffee without ever thinking of how hot it might be. A kind of a surprise look came to his face with that first swallow. Maybe he missed the cream and sugar, but anyway, he drained the first cup, took on a second one, and by the time he got thru with it he was smacking his lips for more. A tin plate full of boiled beef and potatoes mixed was edged in with the third cup, and along about then there came a light to the stranger's eyes which all went to say that he was due to be amongst the living for sometime to come yet, even if his general appearance didn't say so.

Seeing that all was now well with the stranger, the foreman drawed his attention from the tin plate for a spell and told him that whenever he wanted to go to sleep he could crawl in the bed he was setting on. Then him and the boys all left for their beds which was scattered on the ground here and there. Three or four o'clock in the morning comes awful soon to a man who's rode all day, specially when part of the night's sleep is chopped off by an hour or so of nightguard around the herd. As a rule a cowboy hits for his blankets a short time after the sun goes down, but they'd stayed up a little longer that night on account of the stranger, taking care of him, and then hoping afterwards he'd talk some and explain his wild ramblings. But he'd been too weak and fagged out, and all he'd ever said was "thank you" a couple of times when things was brought to him. He'd never even smiled, but that hadn't been expected much—his face didn't look like the kind that'd been lit up that way for a considerable time.

"By golly," says one rider to another as they was both hitting for their blankets. "That feller is sure a revelation on the human race. I never seen a skin the color of his nor how that skin alone can hold them bones together. There's sure nothing else doing it."

"Yep," joins in the other rider. "He's the closest thing to half a man a feller could expect to see, sure must be something powerful wrong with the poor devil."

The stranger set on the bed and went on to finish up all that'd been piled up on the tin plate. Once in a while he'd reach for the coffee pot and fill his tin cup to the brim. He was very busy, so busy that he didn't notice the men had all gone till his plate was slick and clean. Then he looked up and around him and the only company he had was the fire that'd burned down to big hunks of red coals. He gazed at it for a while, and as it is when gazing at an open fire that way, his thoughts went around some, but not too much, just enough to make him feel sort of peaceful and contented, the first time he'd felt that way for many a day.

Off in the distance he heard the beller of many cattle. Once in a while he'd hear a horse nicker and another answer. He heard a rider come into camp and after a while it sounded like three or four rode out, then two or three more rode in. It was the change of shift on nightguard, and there was something about the ringing of their spurs, the quiet noises of this strange range land that was sort of soothing. There was many sounds he couldn't account for but that didn't matter now. He felt safe, his appetite was satisfied, and as, in a hazy way, he listened to the far off goings on around him, he found an attraction in them that kept him from thinking of other things—the many other things he'd often wished he could forget.

The coals of the fire was losing their light when a rider walked up, throwed some more cottonwood limbs on it, and after the flames begin to play along again, offered to help the stranger into his bed, remarking that it was quite a contraption to get into if a feller ain't used to it. The stranger looked up at the cowboy a spell and tried to smile a show of appreciation, but the smile didn't loom up as he'd like to had it, so instead he put his efforts in trying to stand up and get out of the way while the bed was unrolled. He was surprised at the first try that standing up wasn't such a job as he'd figgered it would be. He was pretty stiff and wobbly but he made it, and stepping off a ways he watched the cowboy do the work.

"There it is, stranger," says the rider when he was thru, "hop in and have a good sleep."

The stranger wasn't much for hopping right then but he done a pretty fair job crawling. The ready bed looked mighty good to him all of a sudden, and after the cowboy helped him undress some and pulled the blankets and tarp over him there was nothing more the stranger could wish for. In less than two minutes he was sound asleep.

## Chapter II

The sun was away high when the stranger woke up the next morning, and, outside of the sounds the cook made while tending to his pots, all was quiet. The horse wrangler had long ago took the remuda out to graze, and the cowboys was in the hills, on circle, and combing the neighboring country of cattle, for the spring round-up was on at full swing.

The first thoughts that came to the stranger's mind as his eyes opened was sort of hazy. Even his eyesight was dim, and it took him a long time to figger out what was above him he was staring at. It looked at first like cloudy sky, then afterwards, looking around a little he seen it was a piece of canvas somebody had stretched over his bed so as to keep the sun from shining on him too strong.

It never came to him how thoughtful that was, his mind wasn't working that well, for the nightmare which he'd been thru the last few days had nowheres been lived down yet, not even with the night's rest he'd had. He layed there in his bed while thoughts of all kinds run into one another in that muddled up mind of his. Pretty soon he begins looking around, then a streak of green prairie sod with the sun a shining on it was gazed at a long time, and from then on things begin to come back sort of gradual.

Looking out under the stretched piece of canvas he seen scattered around on that green sod the tarpaulin covered beds of the cowboys, pieces of rope, wheels of a wagon with a rope corral next to it. The sight of that helped some to make him recollect. Then he turned and looked on the other side. The canvas being so low at both sides didn't allow him to see very far, but there, he seen wheels of another wagon, and a man's legs. That man seemed busy going from one cast iron pot to another, and then the breeze carried to him the smell of cooking meat. It was the round-up cook at work fixing up the noon meal.

The sight of that and the smell of the cooking done more to make the stranger realize his whereabouts than all he'd glimpsed at before. He really woke up, and so well that he tried to raise on his elbows. But there was a stiffness along his arms and shoulders and all along his body that made him hesitate to go any farther. He stayed propped up on his elbows for a spell and looked around some more. He knowed where he was at now.

He was thinking hard on the subject and about his coming in on the camp the night before when he heard footsteps on the grass and pretty soon the face of the cook peeked under the canvas cover.

"Well, I see you ain't kicked the bucket yet," says that feller in his natural rough voice.

"No, sir," the stranger finally managed to say. . . . He only had a hint of what the cook had meant.

"How about some coffee?" says the cook, "I guess it wouldn't go bad, would it?"

The stranger was kind of slow figgering out the answer to that, but he did want coffee the worst way, and the cook knowing it went on to get the pot and a tin cup.

"It'll be noon in an hour or so," says the cook as he came back with the coffee," and you can eat then, with the boys, if you want to rest up a little longer."

That struck the stranger fine, hot coffee was the main thing with him right then, and he had it, right within easy reach. Many cupfuls was poured out of the black pot before he put down the tin cup, and he felt better. His mind was clearer. He layed back in the bed and stared at the canvas over his head. Yep! his mind was much clearer, so clear that he begin to think of the many things which'd happened to him the last few days, it seemed months, and all was fairly plain to memory.

He layed there and let his mind back track to the beginning of the last few days' wild rambling, figgering, in that way, to come to the cause of what had started him out on the fast changing events which now left him in a canvas covered bed on the open prairie instead of being between the silk sheets of his own bed and where he belonged.

In a hazy way, he recollected that whatever happened hadn't been none of his doing. He knowed he hadn't planned on it or expected any such like, and the happenings had been so strange and come so fast that up till now he hadn't had the chance to think on the subject.

Going back to the beginning so as to get things straight, he remembered a wild party at some friend's house on the West Coast and not far from his home grounds which was in the city of Seattle. He'd been to many wild parties of that kind and it was hard for a while for him to figger out which one had been the last one. But finally he felt pretty sure of that certain friend's being the last one, the one where he'd received a telegram from his father with orders in it for him to catch the next fast train out and meet him in Chicago. He'd had something for him to do down there.

A short time after receiving the telegram was when the happenings started in. He couldn't remember very clear just what, because at that time he'd been in no shape to realize much, nor for a couple of days afterwards, and all he could get of that time's goings on was very dim recollections.

As usual, he'd been drinking, he remembered that easy enough. He also remembered a lot of noise and laughing. That was usual too. Then he'd received the telegram, he'd read it once without getting much meaning out of it and, not wanting to be bothered, he'd been about to throw it away when a name at the bottom had caught his dim vision. It had been his father's name, and the telegram had been the first he'd heard of him for many weeks.

The tracking down of what went on after that was sort of checked up there, and thoughts of his father occupied his mind for quite a spell. He hadn't seen him for years seemed like, but soon now he'd be with him, and he wondered if his dad would be at all glad to see him, what was left of him, and after all he'd done which wasn't to the good. Many things came to his memory as he layed in the cowboy's bed that wasn't pleasing to think back on, and finally seeing he wasn't getting anything but downhearted sorry feelings with such thoughts he went back to the first subject and to figgering out the how come of the past few days' happenings.

The wild party had been on at full swing, he remembered. There'd been a heap of laughing and hollering. Another drink had been passed around to him and he'd waved it away, he'd wanted to think about the telegram and its meaning. About then he'd heard more laughing and one of the voices close to him had said:

"Get another shot of hop, Corpse, and come to life."

That had brought more laughing and more remarks

and thru it all he'd kept a thinking. . . . He'd long ago got used to be joked and laughed at, for ever since he'd stopped being the life of the party he'd turned out to be the goat, and there'd been many a laugh at his expense. . . .

He'd slumped down in his chair and with the crumpled telegram in his hand went on thinking. One name had kept a repeating itself in his mind and with it had been mixed thoughts of his father, but them thoughts, as strong as they'd come, wasn't to last long, they hadn't had the backing of a clear brain. Soon all had faded away, another drink had been poured down his throat, he'd heard more laughs and more funny remarks about himself and after a while his head had slumped on his shoulder and he'd went to sleep.

He'd slept, he didn't know how long, when he'd been woke up by many hands pulling at him and standing him on his feet. By the noises and many laughs it'd sounded like another joke was about to be pulled off. In a hazy way he'd seen one of the girls holding the telegram he'd received. She'd read it out loud, and then afterwards, amongst more laughs, he'd got the drift that they was all going to take him to the depot and send him to his dad. They'd all seemed to somehow got a lot of fun out of that.

He hadn't held back any or passed no opinion on the subject when he was helped with his coat, half carried into a crowded limousine, and rushed to the train. He hadn't cared when somebody had reached in his pocket and got some money to buy him a ticket with. It all had been sort of like a dream, and sooner or later he'd wake up and find himself in some underground saloon or some such a place where he'd lately been making his home. The compartment on the train, filled with smoke and laughing people, had all sort of fitted with that dream. Then all had been quiet. He'd heard a rumble underneath, a motion that was sort of soothing and he'd went to sleep again.

There'd been a considerable time on the train which he couldn't recall much. The porter had come in often with drinks and special eats which he didn't know he'd ordered. He'd took on the drinks on account of their soothing effect and finally his head had begin to clear some. Then, as the train had rambled on it'd gradually come to him that he was headed for Chicago and to his father. Well, that had been all right, anything would of been all right.

For, even tho his mind had been clearer than it'd been for many a day, he still hadn't been able to realize much. The result of the years he'd spent going from one dive to another, from wild to wilder crowds, couldn't been wiped off in a couple of days. It'd come to him that he was on a train. He'd knowed where he was headed, but so far he hadn't thought why nor how come.

All that was faint memory to him as he layed in the canvas covered bed and tried to figger things out. It all had just as well happened a year before so hard it was to recollect, but filling his cup once more of the black coffee he went at the problem some more.

What puzzled him most was how he happened to be where he was, wherever that was, and then, of a sudden, and as he stared hard at the canvas above him, it sort of shaped itself out. He remembered getting up out of his berth early one morning, he'd felt stuffy and wanted to move around some, he'd dressed, and a while later the train had stopped. More with the idea of moving around than with thoughts of fresh air, he'd went out of his compartment, thru the aisle of the pullman and to an open door with steps leading out.

He'd felt the gravel under his feet as he stepped out of the car. It was still dark but he'd spotted a little building alongside of the track, and being the air had felt good and he'd wanted to limber up he'd walked over to it. He'd sat down by it, and when, what'd seemed to him, just a little while later he looked around, the sun was shining. He'd got up and started to go to his train, but as he'd turned the corner of the building he seen nothing but bare track where the train had been. The train had gone on.

He'd looked at the track for a long time, then at the little building which he'd sat alongside of. He'd looked up and down both ways along the straight steel road and wondered how the train could of gone so quick, or had there been a train after all? . . . The station agent would know. He'd went in the little red building which he'd figgered was some kind of a station, but there'd been nobody in there, just a bare little room with one bench and a stove.

He'd wondered what kind of a place this was that nobody was around. He'd come out again, the sun had got higher and lighted up the land. He'd squinted at that land, not realizing at first, but gradually it'd come to him that this, all around him, sure enough was land, long distances of open prairie, and not a soul nor a break nowheres. Where was everybody, or anybody?

He'd walked away from the building so as to get a better view all around him. His eyes had followed along the straight far away sky line, and then to complete the circle, he'd moved a little to one side to see what the little red building might be keeping from view, and there, seemed like about a quarter of a mile way, he'd spotted another building, the only break in all the landscape around him.

He'd been glad to discover that, for, he'd thought, with buildings so scarce there'd sure be somebody in that one, somebody who'd tell him where he was and what to do—he'd never thought, in the condition he'd been in, that there'd soon be another train along if he'd waited by the track. . . .

*He'd squinted at that land, not realizing at first, but gradually it'd come to him that this, all around him, sure enough was land, long distances of open prairie.*

Figgering that the building he'd just spotted wasn't more than four or five *blocks* away, he'd started acrost the prairie towards it. He'd took off his hat as he'd walked and brushed the dust off of it. Then with his handkerchief he'd kept dusting his coat, and his creased pants had got dusty too, but he'd finally given the dusting up when he looked at his low-cut shoes. He'd decided to wait till he got nearer the house because the dust accumulated faster than he could brush it off.

If he'd only had his cane he could of walked better but he'd left it on the train, and he'd have to get along without it. He'd strutted on and on, and it'd seemed like, before he got very far, that the little house in the distance took one step every time he did, away from him. The four or five blocks he'd figgered the distance to be had turned out to be twice that many, and that had got to bothering him more than the dust or being without his cane. He'd felt that there should been at least taxi service in such out of the way places. He hadn't walked so far for a long time.

But finally it'd got so that the house looked closer to him, and he'd begin to walk faster so it wouldn't get away. . . . When he'd got into the shadow of it and to the one door he'd felt a little tired, and disappointed a whole lot, for the door had been found open, and at a glance he'd seen where there hadn't been a soul lived there for some time.

He'd rested there in the shade of the place for a spell and tried hard to figger ways on how to proceed. There was no use going back to that little red building by the tracks, he'd thought, because there was nobody there either. He'd took off his top coat, for the sun had got high and warm, then he'd look around the big country again, and his hopes had went up, for away off in the distance he'd spotted a few specks which all looked like they might be buildings, maybe the out-skirts of some town. But it'd come to him that if the distance to them specks was as apt to fool a person as the distance to this house had fooled him he sure wouldn't get there for many hours. Anyway, the hopes of reaching some place, where he could talk to some-body would be a heap better than sticking around this vacant house. Besides he'd wanted to get some informa-tion. He wouldn't of knowed just what kind, but he'd wanted it anyway.

He'd started walking again, and towards them specks. He'd walked and walked till he felt as if he'd crossed half the continent, and even tho the specks had seemed to grow bigger and closer, the distance between him and them hadn't shortened like he'd figgered it should. He'd looked for smoke above them specks, any town had smoke, but not seeing any he'd figgered that maybe his vision, which he knowed hadn't been so clear, had sort of failed him.

He'd went on a little faster then, and there'd been no sense of direction as he followed the specks. He'd looked back once to see how far he was from either the little red building by the track or the other place, and there'd been a puzzled look on his face when neither of them could be seen nowheres. He wouldn't of knowed which way to go to find 'em in case he'd wanted to, and so, in that fix the best thing he should do was to *not* lose track of the specks he'd been following. They'd seemed to be his only hope. . . .

He'd covered a lot of distance by then and once in a while he'd begin to rest, but while resting he'd always kept his eye on the specks which he'd figgered to reach sooner or later. High noon had come and the sun being a little hotter right then he'd rested once more. He'd got awful tired and sort of wondered at hisself being able to cover so much territory.

It'd been as he rested that way and wishing he'd had something to drink, he'd got pretty thirsty, that something queer begin to happen amongst them specks which he'd been watching so close. He'd sort of had his suspicions before as to them being buildings but he hadn't dared think they wasn't, not after walking so far, and getting lost, and when he seen them specks get together and *begin to move* was when a mighty hopeless feeling had come over him. He'd about given up and he'd felt awful tired all at once. . . . Being so put out, with no idea which way to go from there, he'd just set and halfways tried to get his thoughts to working.

The specks had got in file by then, one right behind the other, and as he'd tried to think, he'd watched them. They'd seemed to grow in size, and by that he'd sort of got the idea that whatever them specks was, was headed his way. He'd wondered if they could be people, for at a distance like that and coming straight for him they'd looked tall and narrow, but he hadn't wondered long. . . . Soon, the leader of them specks threw up a tail, and playful like begin to jump around and run, the others followed up.

It'd been only a short time after that when there'd been no more guess work as to what them specks was. He'd of a sudden recognized 'em, for he'd seen pictures of them, and jokes in magazines where one of them crethures would be blowing steam out of its nostrils and chasing somebody. He laughed at them jokes himself but he'd sure never expected to see such jokes come to real life, specially with him taking part.

The disappointment he'd felt a short while before had of a sudden been forgot at the sight of the wild rollicking crethures, and a mighty strong feeling of self preservation had took place right then. . . . If they hadn't seen him, he'd thought, there was still hopes. Then, he'd noticed he was right on the trail, or path, as he'd call it, that they was following.

He'd flattened hisself close to the ground and begin crawling. He'd crawled for many yards while his heart beat fit to bust, but a fearful hint that he'd started too late had took a holt of him. A big steer, more wicked looking than any bull he'd ever seen on paper, had come up over a little raise while following the trail and spotted him crawling there, and the others, sort of sensing that something strange was close had soon gathered near the steer, all heads up, and sharp horns a shining.

One wild glance over his shoulder showed him that what he'd feared had come. There was no use crawling any more. He'd got up, and got up a running, and with a fear in him he'd never felt before he'd looked for a place to hide into or climb up onto, but not a tree nor a hole big enough was in sight, nothing but wide, awful wide, and open spaces. . . . If he hadn't been too sacred it would of come to him right then, about another saying he'd often laughed at, "The open spaces," but there'd been no laugh in him right then, the open spaces had seemed awful real and serious like.

He'd run on and kept at it for all he'd been worth, and the cattle, full of curiosity at seeing a human afoot that way and feeling as they generally do at that time of the year was more than up to such tricks as to run with him a spell and beller and play around him. Such tricks hadn't been at all appreciated, and once when a yearling got so close, he'd throwed his top coat at him, his hat

*A big steer, more wicked looking than any bull*
*he'd ever seen on paper, had come up over a little raise*
*while following the trail and spotted him crawling there.*

had been aimed at another, but that hadn't stopped the
curious cattle any, only for a spell. They'd come on all
the more to see what else he'd do.

He'd fell once, twice, and each time he'd got up and
run some more, and when he'd about come to the end
and running secmed no more possible, a great sight had
come to his eyes and made him go again, for just a short

distance ahead it'd seemed that the earth had fell away and like to make room for a creek which run deep in the middle of the big country. There was trees along that creek and the sight of them had given him new life. He'd part rolled and part run down the sudden slope to the creek bottom and soon his hands had felt the friendly trunk of a solid old cottonwood. He'd climbed up it fast as he could, and once perched up on a limb at a safe height, he looked back. . . . The cattle, their fun over with, had trailed up the creek and gone to water.

He'd stayed up in the tree till his lungs quit aching and calling for air, then seeing that no cattle was in sight, he'd come down and took a long drink of the clear creek water. The rest of the afternoon he'd spent on recuperating, and he'd sure needed it, for never in his life had he been so weak and tired out. He'd looked for a place where he'd feel safe going to sleep into, and after a while it'd seemed like he'd found one along a rim-rock that run along the edge of the creek. He'd seen a sort of a cave there and he'd climbed up the rim-rock to it, but soon as he stuck his head over the edge he'd heard a queer rattling buzz and looking where the sound came from he'd seen something coiled up there, something which he hadn't took time to identify from any pictures he'd ever seen, for the sight of that something, wedge-shaped head a swaying on its coiled body, had sent a chill up and down his backbone which had sudden like made him let go of all holds, and with a weak squawk he'd slid down and run back to the old faithful cottonwood.

He'd stood by it for a spell and wild eyed had looked all around him, and when nothing else had seemed to pop up, his wore out nerves and body finally quit on him. His legs buckled up and his body slid along the trunk of the tree to the ground, and there, all in a heap he'd went to sleep.

The whole afternoon had passed on with him a sleeping that way, the sun had gone down, and it hadn't been till the chill of the night begin going thru his indoor clothes that he'd stirred and his eyes opened. After a spell he'd tried to move but he'd been so stiff and sore and weak that it'd seemed impossible. Then, for the first time, he'd felt an empty feeling at the pit of his stomach, a very empty feeling, and his thoughts had turned to something to eat. But them thoughts had soon changed for others. Fear had took holt of him once more. The dark, and the strange sounds that'd come from all around like as if some wild animal was making ready to pounce on him, all had made him forget the empty feeling and thoughts of food.

He'd stood and shivered, too scared and stiff to move, and kept a trying to look thru the dark at whatever he'd imagined was near. Then, by the faint light of the stars, and as he'd watched a clump of bushes on account of twigs he heard cracking in there, he'd seen one then another dark object come out making queer sounds and slowly head his way.

All that his nerves'd had to contend with before had left him in no shape for any more thrills. With that accounted for, and the dim starlight which sort of transformed things, them objects had looked twice their real size. Then, by that same light he'd seen what looked like stiff bristles a shining along the backs of both objects. They'd appeared more than ferocious, and he hadn't waited no longer. He'd got strong again and his stiffness had gone, up the faithful old cottonwood he'd climbed once more, and at the noise he'd made, the two porcupines, also scared, had went back to where they'd come.

Once perched up there on one of the big limbs, it'd seemed like the only safe place. He wouldn't of dared coming down, not on a bet, but as night wore on he'd found it a hard place to get comfortable in, also a hard place to keep from falling out of as his head sunk and his eyes closed once in a while. Then again, the light shirt and two-button coat hadn't been much against the cold which had chilled him to the bone. So adding all, it hadn't been a very comfortable night he'd passed amongst the limbs of the old cottonwood, and when daybreak come it hadn't come a bit too soon, for he'd been at the point of braving any danger rather than stay up there another minute.

With the coming of the new day there'd somehow sprouted up new hopes in him, and new strength. He'd all at once decided to try and get back to the railroad and find the little red building, and stick there till a train come along. Then he'd ride to the nearest station and buy a ticket back to where he'd come. He'd wondered why he hadn't thought of that before instead of straying away as he did.

He'd washed by the creek, drank a little, and trying to forget how empty he felt, he'd started to follow out his intentions, and his intentions had been good, but his sense of direction had been all wrong. He'd started and gone the opposite direction and plum away from the railroad and the little red building he'd so sudden decided to go back to . . . the country acrost the creek had looked just the same to him as that he'd rambled on the day before and anybody would of had a hard time convincing him that it wasn't it.

On he'd went sort of happy that he'd soon be out of this awful country. The stiffness had sort of left him a little as he'd walked, and being there'd been something definite in his mind as he went, it all had helped considerable;—he'd soon be there.

But when the high noon sun beat down on him that day, there'd been, so far, no sign of the little red building nor of railroad tracks. He'd figgered then that he just hadn't walked far enough as yet. Besides, he'd walked slower and rested oftener.

Keeping his coat over his head so as to protect it from the heat of the sun he'd went on, and the further he'd went the more he'd noticed that his steps wasn't so sure, his knees sort of wobbled around, and often he'd felt sort of dizzy and weak. He'd wondered at that, but soon now he'd be seeing the little red building, and that's what'd kept him going. Once or twice he'd thought he'd seen it in the distance, he'd even imagined he seen the telegraph poles along the track. But remembering his experience of the day before he'd stood still and watched, and pretty soon his hopes would dwindle away when the dark speck he'd been watching would be seen to move. And, again remembering his experience of the day before, he'd also given them dark specks an awful wide berth.

The afternoon had wore on over half when a weariness which he couldn't fight away from had took a holt of him. He'd slumped down for a spell a thinking it'd go away but soon he'd forget the little red building and all about his getting there. He'd went to sleep.

The sun had been near tipping the skyline to the west when awful roars and bellers had woke him up, and in a split second he'd jumped up to face a ring of wild eyed cattle surrounding him. They'd happened along and come up to see what'd been laying there. There'd been a lot of howdedos amongst the good feeling herd about it, but when the bundle on the ground had jumped up so sudden the cattle had been near as surprised as he had, but not as scared.

All weariness had gone from him with the sight of the cattle, and his jumping up, breaking the circle as it had, had left him an opening and he hadn't been slow in seeing it. He'd thrown his short coat at the closest and with a cry of fear broke out with all the speed there'd been left in him. But the run wasn't to be as long as the one of the day before, and the cattle had no more than started to trot along with him when he'd topped the edge of another creek bottom, and this time instead of only trees there for protection, there'd been a big camp, many horses and men . . . and shirt sleeves a flapping and hollering for help he'd made for that fast as his weak legs could carry him.

# Chapter III

The first couple of days since the arrival of the stranger at the Ox Yoke round-up camp hadn't cut much figure in happenings, and outside of the cowboys finding out that his name was Gilbert Tilden, and the stranger learning that he was somewheres in Montana, all had been pretty well as usual.

In that time the stranger Tilden had seldom strayed away from his bed. For one thing he hadn't the strength to do that much, and another thing was that his mind was sort of mixed up. There'd been so much happened seemed like and which was all out of the ordinary of what had ever happened to him before. Hardships, to him, had only been a word which he'd read somewheres and with only a weak hint of what that word had meant, and when he'd tasted a little of it in his two days' ramblings it'd all left him to wondering. And thinking back on the subject it'd seemed like a miracle that he'd lived thru the awful experiences.

He'd layed in his bed and blamed himself for foolishly wandering out of the train and more so for wandering from the railroad. If he'd been half a man, he thought, and had kept away from all which had soaked and turned his brain to mush he wouldn't of got into this jack pot, he wouldn't had to go thru the suffering which his wanderings had brought him.

There was many other things which he hated to think back on that wouldn't of happened, if he'd been half a man. Good years of his life, ambitions, health, pride, and all had been sacrificed for pleasure and a high old time. Then, when the time come that pleasure hunting sort of soured on him, and he'd looked around for something worth while to grab on to, he found he hadn't had the strength to grab and hold. He couldn't pull away from the old habits that went with fast life, and every time he'd fell back a little deeper. He'd been like a sapling which had been washed away to drift in the swift current of a river. He'd tried to edge to the side of that swift current and take root along some bank and grow to something, but the still waters had had no hold on him, and soon he'd went the pace again, drifted on, water soaked, to finally sink.

But of a sudden, and without his expecting, it'd seemed as if he'd been jerked out from them swift currents and like as if to lay on a sunny bank for a spell; for even tho he didn't realize it, and all had seemed against him, the last few days' happenings had been the best that could of come his way. What all had struck him as an awful nightmare had really been like a hard blow which had sudden weaned him away from what had been the cause of wrecking him into the poor excuse of a man he was. He'd been pulled away, high and dry, from all and the same which he hadn't had the gumption to fight against.

Then, the few days at the cow camp, while recuperating, had smoothed things off some and helped along a whole lot. In that time he'd hankered very little for what went with the speedy life he'd been used to. The hankering had come once in a while and gone without his trying to figger out what it was he'd hankered for. He'd felt like in a trance, and the cause of that had been the sudden and mighty big change which had come into his life.

Polished floors, marble steps, butlers at high fancy doors, limousines and crowds was all he'd ever knowed. He'd never give a thought that there was anything else much. And, when all of a sudden and without his expecting, he was dropped, seemed like, into the most natural of what all nature puts out, in a big country no human had ever scarred, the big change he'd felt as he'd tried to find his way out had been of the kind that'd made him forget most everything excepting how little he'd amounted to.

The feeling had stayed with him, and even tho it'd been some easier when he struck the cow camp, there was something else there which lived up to the big change he'd experienced. The camp and all that went on in it was mighty strange. He'd watched things from under the stretched canvas that covered his bed and at the sights he'd seen he'd sometimes even wondered if these men and this big country was part of the same which he'd knowed.

He'd seen the cook shovel hot coals in a hole in the ground, seen him put a big black pot in there and surround it with more coals and well over the top. He'd tasted what'd come out of that black pot afterwards and a big surprise had come to him when the taste reminded him some of the meats the white capped chefs used to put out, only this tasted better, and it was cooked and put out so different.

Amongst all that was strange to him, the men had him guessing the most. Them he'd knowed had all been of the kind where each had stood different one from the other and easy to identify. Hardly no two had been alike and there'd been no resemblance no way much. But with these there seemed to be a likeness wether one was short and the other tall, the built and features of 'em evened up pretty well to one, and sizing 'em up, he'd found a heap of difference between 'em and the indoor men he'd knowed. Maybe it was in the kind of clothes they wore. He'd been used to seeing men in creased pants, always wearing a coat and collar, and these wore leather and soft shirts. But the clothes wasn't it so much, these men handled themselves different seemed like. Their walk and the way they carried themselves was strange and as if the ground wasn't for them to step on.

Then there was the life they lived. He'd watched 'em catching horse after horse with long flying ropes and riding away time after time. He'd seen 'em come in after long rides, set on the ground, and with plates on their knees, take on a meal of the day. Seeing 'em eat that way didn't at all remind him of the dinners he'd been to nor the places them dinners had been served at. There was no four walls around, decorated tables, chandeliers above, and starched-front waiters serving things out of silver platters.

All these men done, working, eating, and sleeping, was done under the sky for a roof and the earth for a floor, and their talk, which he'd listen close to as they gathered around the fire of evenings, tallied up well with their strange life. Once in a while there'd be songs come to his ears, songs that was sort of good to listen to with the breeze of the evening. The words or the tune of 'em was nothing like any he'd ever heard before. They'd somehow stir up lots of strange things in him.

With all that going on which was close to Mother Earth and nature there'd come a time when his experiences of landing in the heart of the big range country begin to fade away into what's past. An interest to figger out what he'd happened into had took a holt on him, and strange as all of it had been to him, he'd forgot pretty

*He'd watched 'em catching horse after horse
with long flying ropes and riding away time after time.*

near everything else so he wouldn't miss any of which had stirred that interest.

It'd got so that he'd near figgered it all to be a very worth while experience, and once after he'd got to realizing things pretty well, he'd grinned a little at the thought of telling his friends back home about it. But the grin soon went away, for them friends of his would never appreciate the telling.

It was early one morning when he was woke up and was told that the outfit was moving camp. He'd got up, poured himself some black coffee, and a few minutes afterwards was helped up alongside of the cook on the "chuck wagon" seat.

Another thrill was due him, for he'd never rode in a place like that before, not behind the kind of horses that was hooked to that wagon, nor alongside a driver like that cook was.

The sun wasn't up yet when the cook sort of "throwed his lines away" at his four horse team and started 'em on a lope. The wagon rocked back and forth acrost the rolling country and no road was seen or followed as the outfit lined out for the new camp grounds.

Tilden didn't get to see much of the country as the wagon rambled on;—he was too busy a hanging onto his seat with all the little strength he had, and it wasn't till the team had to slow down in climbing a hill that he had a chance to look around at all.

Another thrill was due him, for he'd never rode in a
place like that before, not behind the kind of horses that was hooked
to that wagon, nor alongside a driver like that cook was.

The sun came up, and going up another hill Tilden had taken the chance to look back at the sunrise. It was the second one he'd ever seen and the first he'd ever appreciated. And there was more than a sunrise back there to look at and admire, there was all what that early sun had to shine and spread its light onto. Back of him, Tilden seen two other wagons which was part of the outfit. Then behind that in a hazy mist of dust came the many saddle horses. Still further back came a big herd of cattle all spreading and grazing towards the new camp grounds.

Looking at all of that in the early morning sunlight, it came to Tilden that he'd never seen as great a sight in his life. And it being so strange, and all with the big territory around, sort of stirred something in him which made him wonder at hisself.

The round-up wagon camped on a wide bench that day, by a spring at the foot of a knoll. From that spot the country around stretched out in level and rolling grass lands for more than the eye could see.

Tilden, after watching the pilot and the wrangler set up camp and the cook lining out his pots and fire, unrolled his bed and stretched out on top of it. He felt like he needed rest mighty bad, for that ride on top of the chuck wagon had furnished him a lot of thrills which he hadn't been able to compete with. It had been wilder than any automobile ride he'd ever took and that's saying a whole lot.

That afternoon, feeling a little rested and stronger, he took it onto himself to walk up on top of the knoll above the spring. He wanted to get a good view of the country he was in, not that he hadn't seen enough of it, but because he'd never seen it before when he felt safe as he did now. He wanted to give it a good look and try to figger out what there was about it that sort of scared him and still called him on.

But the country didn't tell him much when he finally got on the knoll and begin looking at it. One thing he felt was the awful size of it, and maybe that was every-thing. The distance and what was between 'em made him feel about the size of an ant and about as helpless. He'd never felt as insignificant before, and it was a shock to him, for wherever he'd went on his home grounds he'd always felt like he was something. If not big, he'd at least felt above what he'd classed as common level, and somebody sure enough. A crook of his finger had always set things a humming and butlers and waiters and clerks had contested amongst themselves to please him in what-ever he'd wished. Everywhere he'd went amongst the steel canyons of his home territory things had been that way, and cane in his gloved hands, he'd strutted about there, used to all of that, and like a king. Even his friends, as much as they'd got to make a joke of him, had respect for his name and his pocket book, and their clubs and homes had been his by a knock at their doors.

But that day, as he set on the knoll, ragged pants a flapping about his legs, tore shirt a sagging from bony shoulders, there was many things came to him about life which he'd never thought of before. The big country had bared his mind of the fog that'd surrounded it the same as it had bared his frame of his fancy tailored clothes that'd covered it, and he seen himself in the natural without make up, without any of the things which all had went to make him feel that he was somebody. And when it come to tallying up on what there really was to him, he sort of shrunk and he felt a lot like as if any little breeze might dry him up and blow him away, into nothing.

He sat there on the knoll for a long time while he sort of stargazed with half closed eyes at the far away skyline. It was the furthest he'd ever stargazed, and his mind, like his vision, for once clear of the poison fumes and smoke screens that'd cramped it, was free and played along on the same unhindered territory that the vision was taking.

Consequences was, with his mind foot-loose that way and all a working, many thoughts came to the top which up till now had been left undisturbed and to rust. Many new lights on many new subjects was stirred, and even tho some of them had made Tilden shrink as they'd show him up for what he'd been, there was others which showed him what he might be, if he only would.

"If he had a mind to, he could," but he also realized, as he kept a thinking on the subject, that that mind of his couldn't do all the work he wished on it without having something for it to stand on, something to back it, and all of them things he seemed to lack. Seeing himself as he had and summing it all up, he found he had nothing but a wish and a little hope to start with. There was no gumption, no confidence, and no strength.

But maybe, he thought, if he had a mind to, he could keep that wish and little hope alive. If he could gather up a little strength to carry it on as he went, then a little gumption to protect it, and afterwards confidence to go on, then maybe would come a time when he could shed off them weaknesses and stand up above 'em, a man.

There was many ifs, many maybes, and buts, as he went to planning ways of making a stand for himself. But the fact that he was planning, that he'd been able to see himself for what he really was, felt ashamed, and wanted to try to get up, was proof that he'd struck a footing, a bigger footing and more to stand on than he even realized.

The next thing then had been to build up, to start in, where to go, and what to do. He thought of going on to his father soon as he got to the railroad again, and try to be the son his father had wanted him to be; but he soon left that thought aside, for after tallying up on himself as he'd just had, he'd of a sudden felt mighty small and he couldn't bear to think of showing himself to his father's sight. The tailored clothes he could buy would give him a neat front for sure, but he'd need more than that to go to that father of his. Before he'd show himself to him again he'd want to be fit inside as well as outside.

He'd been sort of proud at taking that stand, and again glad that he felt ashamed. He'd never been ashamed of anything before much, and realizing that he had, had made his hopes shoot up some, for there's no pride where there's no shame, he thought, and pride goes in the makings of a man.

He'd of a sudden realized and felt thankful that the train didn't go on with him, that he'd lost himself in this big country, for it came to him that nowhere else than right where he was would he ever been able to think clear enough to reason and realize things. Nowhere else would he ever thought of being unfit, and he felt thankful again that he didn't reach his father's side, for there would of been more shame.

With that to consider, he'd decided there was only one other way for him to go, and that was back there to where he left. He'd go to work at something even if only for the reason of keeping away from what all which had been so close to bogging him down. He'd try to make something of himself so that some day his father might be a little proud of him.

But here he'd checked himself some, and figgering things as they would be, he'd got to wondering, wondering if he really could keep clear of the habits he'd got into back there. It seemed easy out here, but what about when he'd meet some of the old crowds, feeling lonesome and all. . . . And when it had come to a showdown with him he'd figgered that if he only managed to hold his own without trying to make something of himself he'd have all he could do and then some.

Then a fear got a hold of him, what if he couldn't hold on and went back to all he'd got away from? . . . He'd shivered a little at the thought of that, and then it'd come to him that maybe after all right where he was would be the only safe place for him. But he couldn't stay here. This camp he'd stumbled into was no kindergarten camp nor resort, this was a place for busy men, men who could do something. Then again, this country, it was too big for him, he felt too helpless to take care of himself in it. . . .

Them thoughts milled around in his mind for quite a spell and then out of the middle of them one came that hit him right between the eyes and made him flinch. He'd all at once felt cowardly, useless, and ashamed as he realized what little confidence and guts there was in him. He was afraid to go back because of what was back there to draw him away from his good resolutions, and he was afraid to stay where he was because all was so strange here and so big.

Feeling sort of desperate at all that tormented him, he'd got so he blamed his father for some of what he was now going thru. Why hadn't he made something of him instead of letting him go as he had, even if he'd made him prisoner and chained him somewheres. That would of been better than going the pace as he had and he might of come to reason in time to be of some use, where now. . . .

But soon again the blame came back to his own shoulders, for he remembered how his father had time and again tried to reason with him, tried to draw his interest, and even threatened him.

His head was bent over his knees in memory of all of that and for quite a while his thoughts rambled away back, as far back as he could remember and to the time when his mother had smiled her last smile at him. He'd been just a child then, but he remembered her well when she left him and his dad in grief to go over the Blue Ridge that's crossed but once in a lifetime. Home hadn't meant so much to him from then on, his dad had tried to forget by diving into his work and accumulating more millions, and later young Tilden had been allowed to spend any part of them. He wished now he'd never seen a dollar nor ever knowed good tender care, he'd never deserved that.

After a spell he raised his head, stared at the long distances, and there was tears in his eyes, but back of them tears was a light of the kind that's seen in a man's face when he's up and a fighting.

# Chapter IV

The day's work was done and the cowboys was riding up to camp when Tilden, leaning on a willow stick, started to come down the knoll. His steps was slow, for his strength hadn't accumulated very fast, and that body of his, which had been fed more on stimulants than on food, hadn't been up to all that'd been piled on it since he'd struck the range country. The two days' wild ramblings without food and nothing but scares had been more than it could stand. Then, trying to recuperate on all that was strange, on plain camp grub instead of fancy dishes and none of which his stomach had been used to, was sort of slow.

Going up on the knoll had been the furthest he'd strayed from his bed since he came to the Ox Yoke camp, and it seemed like as short as that walk had been that it'd done him good. A little strength had come in them shaky legs of his and his steps was some steadier as he went on his way back to camp.

He'd got to the bottom of the knoll when the shadow of a rider spread out in front of him, and looking to where it came from, he seen Baldy Otters a setting on his horse and like he'd always been there.

"Well, I see you're up and walking around," says that feller.

"Yes, a little." He sort of forced a smile. Then something came to him which he wanted to ask the foreman.

"I've been wondering," he went on, "if there is some way I could get back to the nearest railroad station or town. . . . You've all been very good to me and I don't want to impose on you any more than I have to."

"Well, that's all right," says Baldy, "and I'll see that you get to the railroad somehow. But right now I've got a big herd on my hands and I need every man and rig I have till I get thru moving 'em. In the meantime you better try and get some tallow on your ribs so you can stand the trip."

The foreman rode on to the rope corral and went to unsaddling. "Sometimes," he hollered over to Tilden, "a rig goes by and you could get a ride in that way."

But a few days passed with no chance of that kind showing up. In that time Tilden had tried his best to follow up on Baldy's advice and pile up on tallow. But that hadn't piled up much, not any, seemed like, for, as good as the victuals looked and tasted, there was no appetite that called for such.

But if his appetite failed him, there was something else which had sort of made up for it and come to life, and that was his interest. He'd woke up to the fact, since the day he'd faced himself on the knoll, that there was a whole lot for him to fight for. He'd struck a lead, something to follow and work up to, and he'd grabbed at it with the same thrill that a prospector feels when he finds a long hunted for gold vein. The little there was of him didn't faze him no more. There was enough to start from and build up onto, and all he'd have to do was work and fight and keep his interest alive.

Soon now, most any day, he'd be going back to the country and folks he knowed, amongst all that was good, fair to do middlin', and bad, and he welcomed the fighting he'd have to do to pass up the trails that led the wrong way so as to follow up his lead. Only one thing worried him, and there was the snag, for he wondered sometimes if he'd be strong enough to win. Confidence hadn't come in with the good resolutions he'd made, but maybe he could work up some of that later, and he'd cheer himself up by thinking of the lead he'd found and which he'd try hard to follow.

The new woke up interest which had come to life as a result of that lead was another great help to him. It had made him see and appreciate a lot of things he'd never seen or appreciated before. And all that, he thought, was sure enough a start.

With all that was strange in the life he'd stumbled into at the cow camp he hadn't found it hard to put that interest to work. Every chance he had he'd be at the rope corral and watching the riders rope and saddle their horses. He'd never imagined that a man could take a piece of rope and make it do what these men done with it. Then the saddling and riding of horses, he couldn't see how any man would dare handle and ride such horses the way some of them would fight and buck. He'd never thought a horse could act the way some of 'em did. And far as that goes there was many things he seen done that seemed impossible. It was all a mystery.

It would of been all the more of a mystery if he'd understood the game enough to feel beyond what he seen. But he more than took in all what happened even tho he seen only the surface of the goings on. His fear of missing something often got him into places where it wasn't safe for a man to be. The boys had got to feeling responsible for him, and he'd got so that when he heard one of 'em holler "watch out" he'd jumped as best as he could out of the way and wether it looked like any danger was in sight or not. A glancing hoof had grazed his leg once, and that had been one lesson.

He'd watch the boys ride away and sometimes he wished he could go along, but he felt hopeless to ever be up to such, and he'd go back to his bed to rest up a while. Sometimes he'd lay there till the boys rode in again, and lately he'd got so that soon as they come in he'd be up to eat with 'em, listen to them talk, and watch 'em catch fresh horses afterwards. He liked the evenings best when all gathered around the fire to talk over the events of the day, and even tho most of them talks was past him to understand very well, there was something about 'em that made him do his best to listen and catch on.

One day, feeling stronger than usual, he'd took his willow stick and headed acrost to a wide bench land not over a half a mile from camp. He'd seen the riders bringing cattle there and holding 'em into one big herd. He wanted to see what they was holding them cattle for, and why they was taking some cattle out of the one big herd and chasing 'em into a smaller one. The cowboys was doing a lot of riding around there and it would be very interesting to go over and watch them a while.

He felt no fear of the cattle as he walked on towards 'em, not with all them riders around. Anyway he wouldn't go too close. Two bulls was fighting outside the herd a ways. The strength and action of them more than had him wondering. He came closer, and he no more than got to within good watching distance when, happening to glance to one side, he seen a high-headed, kinked-tail cow being cut out of the big herd and heading his direction.

"That old girl acts mad about something," says one rider to another as he seen the cow line out from the herd.

Two bulls was fighting outside the herd a ways.

"Yep!" says the other grinning, "I guess being turned so often as she has to-day has stirred her fighting spirit."

Tilden squatted in the grass. He knowed the cow hadn't seen him as yet, and that soon a rider would be heading her to the smaller herd. And sure enough, as he'd often watched it done from the camp, a rider fell in behind the cow and like to turn her, but about that time, the critter spotted him out there afoot, and wild eyed came right for him.

Twice she dodged the rider that came to turn her, and every time she made a pass at the horse with her horns, and headed on straight for Tilden. She was bound to take her grudge out on something. Then the rider, who hadn't noticed Tilden there before, turned sort of white at the sight of him. There came sudden thoughts of what that cow would do to him if she ever got near, and right about then some real riding was done, riding of the kind Tilden admired so much. But he missed that. Seeing that the cow had spotted him and meant business he'd quit trying to hide in the tall grass and about that time he was running for all he was worth.

The closest tree or place to hide was at camp. He had no hopes of ever being able to reach that in time, and when right close to his heels he heard the sound of hoofs he felt like his time had come sure enough. Then something heavy hit him, and he let out a wild holler as he was sent a rolling down over the edge of the bench. Any

*Then something heavy hit him, and he let out a wild holler as he was sent a rolling down over the edge of the bench.*

second he was expecting to feel sharp horns tearing thru him, . . . and when he stopped rolling, and looked around there was a wild look in his eyes as he seen the mad cow heading the other way and the rider close to her side. . . . He wondered if he was still alive.

But he didn't wonder about that long. That rider had drawed his attention, and setting there sprawled out on his hands he got to wondering about her, for the rider was a *her*. He'd seen long hair a flying to the breeze and under the wide brimmed hat. He'd seen her riding skirt with long fringe at the bottom, and little boots with little spurs on 'em.

And how she could ride. She'd lean her horse against the side of the fast running range cow and he forgot the scare he'd just had at watching the skill she had in handling the mad critter. Sometimes the cow being crowded too hard would slow down, let the horse go by her and take a jab at him with her horns. But instead of finding horseflesh, them horns of hers would only graze the long "tapideros" that covered the stirrups of the saddle. The girl would attract the cow's attention by waving them tapideros in front of her face the same way as a bull fighter waves his "muleta" at a charging bull's nose, and the sweep of her horns would only touch tapidero leather.

The cow would start running again then, and the girl would go to crowding her once more, for it seemed like that ornery critter had no intentions of being drove back to the smaller herd and where she'd been cut out to go.

In maneuvering around that way, the cow had managed to make a sort of half circle and she was again getting close to where Tilden had sprawled. Tilden was about to begin moving again when he seen the girl do a queer thing. He seen her take her rope, shake out a loop, and not hesitating any, spread that loop over the mad cow's horns.

*The girl would attract the mad cow's attention by waving them tapideros in front of her face, the same way as a bull fighter waves his "muleta" at a charging bull's nose, and the sweep of her horns would only touch tapidero leather.*

That was sure a foolish thing to do, he thought. Why should anyone want to catch such a mean animal? If it was him he'd been glad to let her go and never see her again. Tilden was in no way of knowing that a range rider never lets any animal get away from where it belongs, not if it can be helped. And that cow was going to go back wether she wanted to or not. But even tho Tilden thought it all to be foolish, he felt mighty grateful to the girl, for he'd figgered that she was only trying to save him from them sharp horns.

The girl had no more than throwed her rope on the critter when that animal turned, and swishing her long tail, charged straight for her horse. Tilden held his breath. But that was just what the girl expected the cow would do, and exactly what she wanted her to do. She turned her horse and raced away and gave slack to her rope till the cow stepped well over it. Then she spurred her horse to his best and as the rope tightened up sudden behind the cow's front legs, that critter's head was jerked to her side and she was lifted off the ground to land in a heap and out of wind with her head under her.

The cow had hardly landed and the dust from her fall had just been stirred when Tilden seen the girl leave her horse, seemed like while he was at full run. The cow was drug right to her feet, and quicker than Tilden's eyes could follow, he got a glimpse of the girl, a short rope in her hands. And a little while later the critter was tied down to stay.

Tilden's eyes near popped out in wonder, and again when he seen her reach for the cow's head to take the rope off her horns. And he near started up to help her, for the critter, even down, was bellering her rage and doing her best to jab the arms that reached at her head.

But soon the rope was off, and the girl, going to the good little cowhorse who'd stood there rope's length away, mounted him and jerked the rope from under the cow by the saddle horn.

She coiled up her rope, and as she turned her horse towards Tilden that feller felt a whole lot like digging himself a hole and crawling into it. For at the sight of her coming his way, his look of wonder had sudden changed to one of guilt. He felt to blame for all the trouble and risks she'd took, all thru his ignorance too. He should of knowed better than coming up to a herd afoot the way he had, and then again he must of cut some figures running like he had, hollering bloody murder, and acting so scared.

He was sure no sight for any lady to see anyway, but there was no use trying to hide now. He stood up and acted like he was awful busy slapping the dust off his clothes, and even when from the corner of his eye he got a glimpse of her horse standing there close, he kept on a slapping and like he didn't know she was there.

"I hope you didn't get hurt when my horse run into you."

Tilden acted surprised at hearing a voice, and he looked up. That was the only thing he could do, but queer as it was right then, that was just what he wanted to do, after hearing that voice. It was awful clear and sort of musical like, and the clearness of it he noticed, after he'd looked up, tallied up well with the clearness of her eyes which was smiling at him, a little.

Tilden had always been a pretty bold sort of a feller amongst most of the ladies he'd ever met, but this time, as he looked up at the girl on horseback, he found himself sort of tongue tied. He'd tried to speak and only stuttered, and there was a queer feeling run up and down his backbone which made him awful conscious of himself and what he might do or say. He'd only smiled at her when she spoke and shook his head, like to let her know he'd heard and that he wasn't hurt.

The girl wondered at him not speaking. Maybe he *was* hurt.

"I'm sorry if you are hurt," she says, "but it was the only way to keep that cow from ramming into you. I had to crowd my horse between you and her, and there wasn't much room. . . ."

This wasn't what Tilden had expected, for he felt that if anyone was to blame, he was the one, for being where he didn't belong, and finally he spoke to that effect.

"I think you did a wonderful job, Miss," he says, "and it would have served me right if I had got hurt. As it is, I am only very grateful to you and I'm sorry I've put you to so much trouble."

The girl had kept her eyes on him as he spoke and like as if trying to figger out the strange sight he'd turned out to be. His face was fair enough looking, she thought, if it had a little flesh on it. But he seemed all eyes and she couldn't figger out the look in 'em, like as if he was lost, or had his rope on something he wanted and couldn't hold onto.

She wondered who he was and how he come to be here, for she knowed he sure didn't belong to this country of hers. None of the cowboys had told her about him. Maybe he'd drifted in at the camp some way. And, she thought, that was a good place for him not to stray away from. Then soon again she spoke.

"You better hit back for camp, because soon as the cow cools off a bit I'm going to let her up and drive her back to the herd."

He hesitated, and then he asked. "Can I be of any help?"

The girl wanted to laugh, but she didn't even smile, and reining her horse to a start, said, "No, thank you."

The girl, wondering who he was, had nothing the best of Tilden, for, as he watched her ride away he also wondered, even stronger than she did, who *she* was. He kept a watching for her while going back to camp and he was thinking about her a long time after he got there. He went over his little talk with her, and he wondered why he'd been such a block-head and hadn't seemed able to talk. No woman had ever found him paralyzed that way before. But maybe, he thought, it was on account of her riding in on him at a time like she had. Then again, he'd never figgered on seeing any girls out here, specially a girl like her.

He dug up many reasons which would sort of allow for him acting the way he had, and when he got thru he didn't think it was the girl herself that'd been responsible. He figgered if he'd met her at his home grounds and according to the way he was used to meet girls that he'd been at ease and words would of come natural.

But when, after the work with the herd was thru on the bench, the girl rode in to camp amongst the cowboys, he sudden like forgot to figger out which, between the girl, the place of meeting, and himself had been responsible for his queer way of acting. He'd all at once went blind and he wasn't seeing anybody nor anything but her.

What a picture she made on a horse, he thought, so straight and slim and graceful, and how she handled and rode that horse of hers. He wondered some if she'd look as good afoot, and as he watched her he wasn't disappointed none when she got down off her horse by the rope corral and begin unsaddling.

He figgered it queer as he seen her unsaddle that none of the cowboys offered to do that for her and he got up to help her, but he just went halfways when she turned her horse loose. He was too late. Tilden had no way of knowing that a range rider saddles and unsaddles his or her own horse and that an offer of help at such doings only brings a surprised smile and a "no."

He only wondered all the more at her for going ahead and doing things without looking around for the favors her sex are used to getting. He thought of her roping that mad cow. No girls, and very few men, if any, he ever knowed could of done anything to match that, for even as little as he understood the game, he'd seen that it'd took steady nerves and a powerful lot of skill.

Still, to look at her a standing there on the ground there was nothing about her which would suggest that she was such a hand at the rough game. The face under the big hat was mighty ladylike and its beauty to be admired, and the whole graceful slim length of her was true feminine, with not a flaw nowheres of anything coarse, rough, or manly. Tilden thought, as he watched her coming towards the chuck wagon, that she could just as well been wearing the long robe of a queen as the fringed riding skirt, and stepping on polished marble the same as she walked on the grass covered prairie sod.

The meal at the round-up wagon wasn't as usual that evening. Every cowboy had sneaked away for a spell soon as camp had been reached and felt around between the blankets of their beds for cleaner trousers and shirts. They'd then gathered at the creek and came out of there a while later with faces a shining, hair combed as slick as was possible, and all prepared to do credit to the company that'd rode in amongst 'em.

For the company of ladies was long to be remembered events at the Ox Yoke cow camps. Such events seldom happened, and when they did every rider turned out with his best, even the cook.

Tilden noticed the change of atmosphere, and at the sight of what all took place on account of the girl's presence, turned a wild look over himself wondering what he could do. His ragged clothes showed up all the more in contrast of them the riders had put on, and then, for the shame he felt in being amongst 'em, with the girl maybe noticing him, he started to walk away amongst the willows of the creek. He'd rather, on account of that afternoon's happenings, that she wouldn't see him anyway, and he thought of hiding till she rode on.

He walked on thru the willows and up the creek and came to where he heard a lot of splashing in the water. The Kid, the Ox Yoke horse wrangler, was there and going thru what the others had done. His round sunburned face looked thru the branches at Tilden and he grinned.

"Say," he says, "this water is sure cold ain't it."

Then noticing Tilden's dusty and ragged clothes, he went on.

"Ain't you going to clean up?"

"This is all the clothes I have," says Tilden, "and I'm afraid they can't be made to look any better."

"Hell, I guess I can dig up another clean shirt, and

maybe another pair of pants too." He sized up Tilden. "And I think they'll fit you all right."

That offer was more than welcome and Tilden wasn't slow in accepting, for he wanted to see that girl some more, and in the wrangler's clothes that way he could maybe mingle in amongst the boys without being noticed much.

The Kid took it onto himself not only to fix him up in clean clothes but coached him along in how to wear 'em so he'd look as much like one of the boys as possible. Along with that help he went on to furnish some information as to who the girl was.

"Ain't you ever heard of her?" says the Kid surprised as Tilden asked about her. "Why, she's old Butch Spencer's daughter. Everybody knows Butch. He was the horse-stealingest hombre that ever was at one time, and a gun-fighting fool. He's still packing some bullets under that hide of his and on that account he can't ride anymore. This girl here, Rita, does the riding now, and they say she was the one who made her dad behave before he was ready to. She's a hand too, let me tell you, and a humdinger. I don't reckon there's a better looking girl in the world, and if she wanted to she could have a thousand fellers, but far as I know there's only this bronk peeler Cliff Moran who's with the wagon now. He's 'repping' for her and her dad, and I guess she's come to take home what cattle he's found."

They started walking back towards the chuck wagon, and the Kid talked on as they went. Tilden learned a lot more about Miss Spencer and he didn't have to ask no questions either, for the Kid, surprised as he'd been that he'd never before heard of her, was sure riding high in setting things to rights and telling all he knowed. Everybody sure should know Rita Spencer.

By the time Tilden got within hearing distance of the chuck wagon he felt privileged a whole lot to be within half a mile of such a girl, let alone being where he could see her.

The riders had started eating when the two got there, and all was making the rounds at the pots. Baldy Otters and Cliff Moran was taking it onto themselves to contest in serving the girl with whatever she might want, and busy as she was with all the attention, Tilden felt safe in reaching for plate and cup, filling them, and hightailing it to where he could set and see her without being noticed.

Otters and Moran seemed to've also took it onto themselves to do the honors in entertaining the lady visitor and the conversation went on steady for quite a spell. Then Moran, being a younger man and not up to snuff like Baldy when it come to carrying talk that way, begin to take a back seat and listen like all the others was doing. But came a time when even Baldy begin to fish for words and he finally begin to run dry. He'd asked her about everything seemed like, how her dad was getting along with his bad leg, how many head of steers she would ship this year, the colts she figgered on having broke, and many other things.

"Where's Skip?" the girl asked as Baldy was trying to think of something else to talk about.

There was a stir amongst the circle of riders and one stood up.

"Here I be, Miss Rita," says that feller. He came over closer. "I kind of thought," he went on grinning, "being you appreciate good company, that you'd be looking for me."

The girl smiled at him. "I just wanted to ask you," she says, "if you've seen that black horse lately, the one you said you'd catch for me."

"Well, now, before I answer that question"—he leaned over and squinted at her—"did I sure enough promise to catch that horse for you?"

"Not exactly, but I didn't think you'd be so mean as to keep him all to yourself if you did catch him."

"No, maybe I wouldn't, but if I caught him it'd be most likely that I would, cause you see ma'am, I have no hopes of ever catching that horse much. There's too many out to do that for me to have a chance, and the reason I'm not promising anything is because I'd hate like samhill to have some other gazabo lead him over to you some fine day after I'd done promised to do that same thing myself. But, whoever catches that horse will have to be a powerful early bird, and a wise one, cause that pony sure don't aim to be no man's, nor lady's beast of burden. He's making hisself harder to keep track of than ever, and I'm here to gamble that if any loop is ever throwed at him, it'll be a spilled loop. . . ."

"Have you seen him at all lately?" the girl asked again.

"No, not for two months or more, and then it was only for a second, cause he'd spotted me first and he disappeared in the brakes."

The talk went on some more about the black horse and how he could maybe be caught, but many was dubious as scheme after scheme was dug up which would end that pony's freedom. Tilden was all ears as he listened to what all the riders had to say about the wonders of that horse and how it seemed impossible for anybody to ever catch him. He even forgot to watch the girl in his interest for the stories that was told about that horse.

Them stories reminded him some of one he'd read in a magazine once when he was a kid. Only, the one he'd read had sounded so pretty, these sounded true and real. He remembered when reading that story how he'd wished he could of been the man who'd caught the wonderful horse, a horse almost human, and which had turned so gentle and faithful after he'd been mastered. As a kid, Tilden had liked horses a whole lot, and the liking was coming to life again.

The girl was speaking, and as the sound of her voice came to his ears Tilden's eyes natural like gazed her way.

"I'm offering ten of my best yearlings to anybody who brings me that horse," she was saying, "so Mr. Skip, if your ambitions are that way you better make a hand of yourself."

"I'd be glad to," says Skip, sort of mournful like, "but I've got to chase sway-backed critters for this daggoned outfit. How would Baldy get along without me?"

Baldy laughed and turned to the girl. "You'll have that black horse in your corral some bright morning," he says, then he winked at Skip, "even if I have to run him in myself."

"Ye-e-p," howls Skip. "Let's turn this daggone herd loose now and all go to running wild horses, and may the best man win."

There wasn't a man in the outfit who wouldn't of been mighty glad to follow up Skip's suggestion, but that suggestion was so impossible that it made a good joke, and it brought a laugh that fitted well.

The sun was still an hour high when the Kid brought in the remuda. The night horses was caught, and the girl roped hers and went to saddling. Tilden wondered at her riding away so late in the day, even tho, as the Kid told him, her home was only about ten miles away. It'd be dark long before she got there, he thought, and how could she find her way then. Besides she'd be driving a bunch of cattle too.

But his worries, seemed like, had been for nothing. He seen that the cowboy Moran was also saddling a horse, a mean horse as usual. He watched him ease a leg over the saddle and straighten up and kept his eyes on him as the fighting pony took him on. How he wished he could ride as that cowboy could, specially when he seen how the girl took such an interest in the performance. He felt a sting as he noticed that, for he thought her eyes was on the rider only. But Tilden's own imagination was all that was responsible for that sting, because the girl had eyes for the horse as well as the man. She admired good riding the same as any red blooded folks admires doings of the kind that calls for skill and nerve.

This was part of her every day life in which everybody contested to do better than everybody else, and every time she seen a horse "unwind" she found herself judging and stacking up points for or against the rider. She knowed bucking horses, she knowed good riding, and she watched it all with the same interest that a town girl takes in watching the changes of fashion plates.

With Tilden, the sight of that horse and man a tearing things up gave him an altogether different feeling. The show of ability and confidence of the rider only went to make him feel insignificant, helpless, and useless. Of course, riding wasn't in his line, but seeing one thing done so well brought to mind many other things that

She knowed bucking horses, she knowed good riding,
and she watched it all with the same interest that
a town girl takes in watching the changes of fashion plates.

men done everywhere, and he felt so little and hopeless in ever being able to tally up against such.

Moran reached down on one rein and pulled up the head that'd been bellering its opinion against man and saddle, and with a well placed rowel against the short-ribs of that horse, lined him out from the one spot and set him going for other sods on a long crow-hopping lope. Tilden seen the girl ride alongside of him and he watched the two till they neared the cattle, bunched 'em up, and started on.

The second guard was going out when Moran rode back to camp, but Tilden hadn't heard him, and as it was he'd felt safe for the girl in thinking that she'd at least have a good escort on the way home. The events of the day had pretty well wore him out and when he hit his bed the thoughts from them happenings was all mixed so that he was past trying to straighten 'em out. He'd went to sleep on 'em, and dreamt of a lady in queen's robes with little spurred riding boots showing under the edge.

## Chapter V

Since the girl's visit at the Ox Yoke camp a new subject had sprouted up amongst the riders there, and the talks of the evenings had kept at that subject till it seemed no more could be said about it. The black horse had been that subject—the wild stallion which the girl had asked about.

Near every rider on the outfit had at one time or other got a glimpse of that black horse, and near every one had figgered on some time or other catching him, but he'd been near forgot about on account of the work that'd kept 'em busy, and Miss Spencer had been the one who brought him back to memory and who'd stirred every one of them riders' interest in figgering ways of trying, again, to catch him.

"You see that range of hills over yonder?" Skip had said one day while pointing at some mountains away off in the distance. "Well, he runs at the foot of them, spring and fall. In the summer he goes higher and amongst 'em, but in the winter I don't know where he runs. He seems to disappear."

"Yep, there's something queer about that horse," another rider had said who'd had experiences trying to catch him. "He'll quit his range the minute he spots a rider after him, and go any old place, and he might not come back again for a couple of weeks. You can't relay on a horse of that kind, and you can't set a blind trap for him because you never know which way he's going to run. Then again there's not a horse alive that can take a rider to within roping distance of him."

"I know a feller who'd took after him once," the rider had went on. "He was riding a horse which he'd paid a lot of money for and had imported from somewheres. That pony was tall and lean and mighty fast on anywheres near level ground, but when he got up amongst that black horse's territory it was another story. The black horse was spotted and the chase started, but it'd no more than started when with a wave of his tail the black horse ended it all. He'd disappeared and left that fast horse like he was standing still, and all that was left to show that the black horse had been there sure enough was two little mares he'd been with."

But regardless of how impossible it seemed of anybody ever being able to catch the horse, there'd been scheme after scheme brought up which *might* work. Every rider on the outfit had thought and talked on them schemes till he was blue in the face, for every one of them had hopes of some day catching that horse and riding him up and saying to Rita Spencer, "Here he is."

But that last was a secret with each one of the riders, and according to the way they talked they just wanted the horse awful bad and that was all.

"I *am* sure going to give that pony a fogging soon as the spring round-up is over," Skip had said. He'd laughed, "And if I don't get him there's no use of any of you fellows trying."

As the talks had went on about the black horse, and his wise ways of keeping out of the trap, snares, and loops, there'd been one man amongst the riders who'd listened with wide open ears to all they'd said. That man was out for all the information he could get on that horse, and not a word nor move the riders said or done was missed by him. He wanted to catch that horse too and more so than any of the riders did.

None of the riders had any hint of *him* wanting to get in on the chase, and if they'd knowed of it they'd most likely laughed, for that man who was so serious in catching the black horse was none other than Gilbert Tilden, the boy from the narrow, shut-in, steel canyons of man-made places.

Tilden himself had laughed, when as hearing the boys talk, the idea first struck him, and he'd only wished he could be up to such or anything that seemed so impossible. But as he'd listened to the talk the idea had took root and growed on him;—so did the impossibility of it. It'd finally seemed so impossible as he figgered on the subject that he'd decided it was just the thing he wanted to do,—the impossible.

The first of that had come to him on that day when Moran had fanned the orneriness of the fighting bronk he'd rode that evening when Miss Spencer was at the camp. The way she'd watched had made him wish he could ride and be such an all around cowboy as Moran was, or anything, so long as it was something good, something not everybody could do. Not that he wanted to make a show of himself, but he'd wished he could do something worth while and well, for his own satisfaction.

Like Moran for instance, he knowed that cowboy would of rode that same horse wether the girl or anybody had been around or not. Every horse in his string was a fighter, that was the only kind he rode, and he done it so well.

If he could only flip a rope as any of the boys could, or mount a horse as the girl did, or make biscuits as the cook put out, or anything at all, Tilden would of been mighty pleased. But there was nothing he could do. Not only that, but he'd been in the way of everybody, as much so at his home grounds as at the cow camp. He'd been just something on two legs that'd moved around on the work of others and rolled in luxuries which he'd never turned a hand to deserve.

Every day at the cow camp had brought new things which had often made him realize how little he amounted to as a man. The height of his ability had been limited to flipping a ready made cigarette, manipulate cracked crab, and mix cocktails or such like, and there'd come a time when, as he thought on the subject, he felt he shouldn't be seen amongst men, none at all. That feeling had lasted with him a spell, and then that same feeling finally proved to be the saving of him, for out of it had come another feeling to want to do something, something that would put him on equal with other men.

Then, as the boys had kept a talking of the wild horse was when the idea of catching that horse had come to his mind, a horse which none of these experienced men had been able to catch. The impossibility of it had floored him at first, but for that same reason he'd hung on to it, for the more impossible it seemed, the more he figgered it was the thing he should do. It'd be something which would make up in a way for all he'd *never* done.

Catching that horse would be a heap harder, he'd figgered as he'd thought things over, than going back to the world he knowed and make something of himself in some big financial way. He had the capital to start with if he went back there, and that would be half the battle. Besides he'd be amongst all he was so familiar with and the trail would be pretty well mapped out for him. It'd be near like falling into one of them soft beds at home after the servants had got thru making it ready.

Where here, with all that was plum strange, not a familiar trail nowheres, his helplessness riding him, and figgering on going it all one better by trying to catch such as the wild horse, that all sure enough struck him as bucking up against the impossible. There was nothing he could think of that could be more so, and that's just why he'd decided to try and put it thru, for he felt if he could do that, which he was least fitted to even try, he could do other things afterwards that may be just as hard, things more worth while.

As far as the horse himself was concerned, he was just a horse. Tilden didn't know enough about horses to appreciate such as that black stallion was. All he appreciated was the value of him in how he'd feel by catching such a horse, doing the impossible, and that was beyond any price.

So, that's how come that Tilden, stumbling onto the lead of the black horse, forgot about trying to get back to the railroad and to his home grounds, as his first intentions had been, and one day, when a rig came by which was headed for the railroad, he only used it as a chance to send a telegram by. It was for his father and read, "Finally found a lead, Dad, and decided to stay here and follow it. Don't worry about me." He added his address and handed it to the driver of the rig, who, after reading it, stuffed it carefully in his shirt pocket and drove on.

As the rig disappeared, all of that which he'd left back there seemed all at once very far away, past, and of another life. He belonged to this big country now, it had saved him, pulled him out of the big hole he'd got into, and showed him a lead to follow. He was going to stay in it now and learn to know it while following that lead.

And even tho he had no confidence in being able to accomplish all he'd set out to do, he wasn't going to let that stop him. He had no confidence in being able to do anything anyway, and if he failed it'd be just another failure. But he must not fail, for he knew that if he once put a hand on that pony's hide after going thru whatever he'd have to go thru to catch him, that that confidence he lacked so much of, would shoot all thru him and take a holt to stay. Nothing would be impossible from then on.

As it was now and without that confidence, he'd go to it and do his best. He'd grin at hardships and be game, build up confidence as he went, and work to get that horse like as if his life depended on it. For his life, the makings of him, he felt, really and sure enough depended on some day catching that horse, all by himself and having him all his own.

What he'd do with him after he caught him seemed too far to figger on. It wouldn't matter much what he done with him after that, but once he'd smiled to himself as he thought of how nice it would be if he could tame him and sometime ride over to wherever Miss Spencer lived and maybe give him to her if she wanted him. He'd pictured the look that would be in her eyes as she'd see him riding on that horse, and that picture had stayed with him a long time, so long that he'd forgot he'd have to catch the horse first before such a picture as he'd been seeing could come to life. He'd smiled as he finally realized that and to himself he'd said, "I'll get him."

But "getting him" was going to be a job, more of a job and even more impossible than Tilden could realize. Every chance he had he'd listened to the riders as they'd planned different ways of catching the horse, but even tho them talks had all seemed pretty plain to him, there was many things the riders knowed and took for granted without explaining, which Tilden didn't know, things he'd have to learn thru his own experiences.

Tilden only had a hint of that fact, and even if he'd realized it, that wouldn't of made him hesitate any. It'd only made things more interesting for him on account that it'd just seemed more impossible.

So, feeling that way about it, he went to starting on the steep, rocky, and mighty rough climb to making a hand of himself. By now he was a lot stronger, his bones was covering over some and his appetite had tallied up according. The sun had cracked his lips, peeled his nose and chin, and tanned him up to looking half human.

The big undertaking which he'd decided on only helped him some more, and he kept so busy making a hand of himself that he didn't have time to feel tired no more. He cut some willows one day and chopped 'em for wood for the cook, a big pile of it, and at that job he learned that one kind of wood don't burn so well. "It's green wood," said the cook, "but it'll burn next year if the pack rats don't use it all for tooth picks."

He learned many things from the cook that way which, as he figgered, was all part of his eddication. He learned that potatoes burn when they run dry, that dutch oven lids get hot, that a big fire with high flames is not as good to cook on as a bed of hot coals, and many other things.

The cook stood his help pretty well. That is, well enough that the wrangler wasn't bothered to bring in any more wood and water. Tilden had took that job along with others, and at that, the Kid felt mighty grateful, so grateful that one day he let him get on his best pet horse.

Tilden got a thrill out of that ride. It was the first time he'd got on anything that moved that wasn't on wheels, and feeling that he was being packed around by something alive instead of gas-fed machinery kind of got under his skin and made his blood race. Bridle reins fastened onto a head with brains didn't compare with the steering wheel of a long hooded motor, and even tho handling them reins and making the horse go, turn, or stop was all a puzzle to him, he enjoyed that first ride to the limit, and wished before he was half started that he could go on and ride and ride.

But the Kid had work to do, the remuda was scattering and he'd have to head off the leaders. Tilden heard him call and he watched the Kid get on the horse and ride away, like as if man and horse was one. He wondered how the Kid *steered* his horse so as to make him lope out in one direction, the horse had seemed to know what was wanted of him without any visible hint from the rider, the reins had hung slack and no spurs had touched that horse's sides.

He asked about that soon as the Kid rode back, but the Kid was only puzzled at that question. He'd never thought of that, because to him, riding and handling a horse had come with his raising, it'd been as natural as his breathing.

"I don't know," the Kid answered after thinking on the subject a spell, "I guess that comes with riding."

"Well, if that's the case," Tilden went on, "I wish you would teach me how to ride. I can't seem to be able to steer a horse very well."

"I couldn't teach anybody how to ride," says the Kid, feeling sort of backward about it. "If you want to learn just get on a horse and ride and things'll come to you, if you do enough of it."

But Tilden couldn't see things that way, and he felt like he'd need plenty of coaching before he could get on a horse and ride away in half as good style as the Kid could. Riding is sure what he'd have to know about if he was to ever get within sight of the black stallion, and he'd have to know about that mighty well. Realizing that, Tilden wasn't going to let the Kid get away from him.

Reaching in his pocket he pulled out a roll of bills, peeled one off, and went to hand it to the Kid.

The Kid looked at the bill and he couldn't talk at the sight of it. It was a fifty dollar bill. The biggest he'd ever seen was a twenty and he didn't know there could be so much money in one bill. As he looked at it he got glimpses of the silver mounted spurs he'd wanted so bad the last time he was in town. Then he'd have enough money left to get a good pair of chaps' too. But as much as he wanted to get them spurs and chaps', he didn't feel right in accepting the money. Fifty dollars was a powerful lot, it seemed like, to be a present to him, and he'd never got anything before in his life without he earned it, earned it well.

Tilden was surprised at the stand the Kid had took, for most young fellows he'd ever knowed would never felt backward in accepting any amount of money. He appreciated that, and to make him feel more at ease he thought of another way.

"Well then," he says, "maybe you'll sell me that horse of yours."

"He ain't my horse," says the Kid. "He's a company horse and the company don't sell no horses unless they're shipped out of the state. But," he went on, "I've got one private horse I might sell you. . . ."

"How much will you take for him?"

"We-e-ll," thought the Kid, "I wouldn't take less than . . ."

"I'll give you a hundred dollars for him," says Tilden before the Kid could go any further. Tilden remembered how the Kid had once said that he'd never take less than fifty for the horse, which meant as much as to say that, being it was a big price, he never expected or cared to sell him.

Selling a horse for a big price wasn't like accepting money for nothing. It was more like as if he'd put over a big deal, something to brag to the boys about, but with that price it was agreed that the Kid was to teach Tilden the main points about riding, and that way all was put over well with both parties feeling winners.

Early the next morning, after Tilden had done his usual work around the chuck wagon, him and the Kid both rode behind the remuda to where the ponies would be held to graze. Tilden had borrowed the cook's saddle. The Kid had showed him how to put it on and how to cinch it. And on his horse, the first horse he'd ever owned, Tilden rode on to the grounds where his eddication was to begin.

No better grounds could ever been picked for him to start his eddication on. It was the same grounds that

*Afterwards, the cowboy, the best rider in the world, followed along on them grounds and on the same trails of the buffalo and Injun.*

the buffalo roamed on many years before and the trails they made was still to be seen. Injuns had rode over it on war parties and on hunts. Afterwards, the cowboy, the best rider in the world, followed along on them grounds and on the same trails of the buffalo and Injun, and them was the grounds, with the cowboy, range cattle and horses still roaming over 'em in full swing, where Tilden took his first lessons, not only in riding, but in self reliance, in developing confidence, and guts.

"Go turn that horse back before he gets away," says the Kid to Tilden that afternoon. Tilden got on his horse and started to do as he was ordered, but as he got near the leading horse he sudden like felt himself slipping out of the saddle and the next second he was on the ground. His saddle horse, knowing what to do and without waiting for the feel of the rein, had turned and turned too fast.

That was sure a surprise to Tilden, and after getting up he eyed his horse wondering if he should mount him again, but he didn't wonder long, for soon he heard the Kid hollering at him, and Tilden mounted. The next bunch of horses he went to head off Tilden managed, by main strength, to stick to his horse. He'd learned to turn when his horse did, and that was a beginning.

The next day was pretty well the same for Tilden. Only difference was he felt stiff and sore all over, but when the Kid told him to "come along" he obeyed just like any good pupil obeys a good teacher. He fell off his horse once more that day, and the reason of that was he thought his horse was going to turn one way and instead he'd turned another.

The Kid took him to hand at that.

"Don't forget," he says, "that while you're watching one horse your horse might have his eye on another, and if you don't handle your reins so he'll know which one you're watching, you're both apt to head off separate directions, just like you did now. And besides," the Kid went on, "you ought to set up in your saddle; the way you ride now you're setting on half of your backbone and you'll be getting kidney sores. Why don't you straighten up and get your knees down from under your chin?"

Such talk is what Tilden had to put up with in his learning. It was plain and to the point, and sure left no doubt in his mind as to how he should do a thing. It was the same kind of talking-to the Kid used to get whenever he didn't do a thing right, and as a teacher he was only passing it on to his pupil in the best way he knowed.

Like one morning, long before Tilden had come to the outfit, the Kid had got on a pony that was a little too much for him. The little horse had bogged his head and made the Kid lose both stirrups. Every jump had sent the Kid higher and higher, and not wanting to kiss Mother Earth, he'd grabbed the horn and tried to get back in the saddle. About then, Skip had rode alongside of him, took holt of the Kid's belt and straightening him up in his saddle, he'd slapped his hands with his bridle reins till the Kid let go of the saddle horn.

"Now, set up there and *ride*," Skip had said, "and keep your hands off that horn or I'll whip 'em off of you."

The Kid had set up, and rode, and kept his hands off the horn.

Tilden was going under near the same teaching, but as much as that feller had grabbed the horn, the Kid

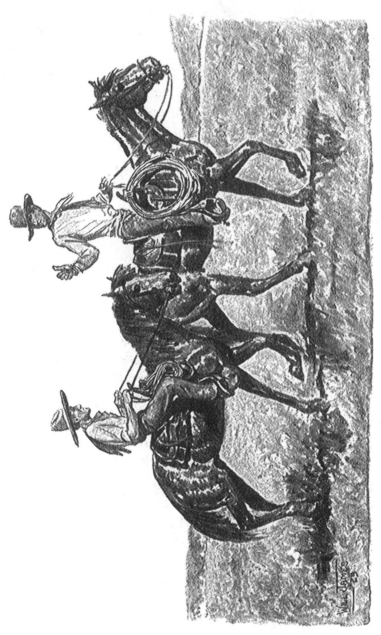

"And besides," the Kid went on, "you ought to set up in your saddle;
the way you ride now you're setting on half of your backbone and you'll be getting kidney sores.
Why don't you straighten up and get your knees down from under your chin?"

hadn't somehow been able to slap them hands of his. This was different, he figgered, and even tho Tilden grabbed the horn, on a horse that never bucked, the Kid couldn't do no more than talk to him about it. Sometime tho, he thought, he sure would rap them hands of his and make him let go of the "nubbin."*

"You'll never be a rider as long as you do that," says the Kid as he seen Tilden reach for the horn once again.

"No?" says Tilden, surprised, ". . . well, how am I going to learn to stay on then?"

"By doing plenty of riding, I told you already."

Tilden thought on that for quite a spell, then he asked:

"Do you think I would ever be a good rider, I mean a rider like Moran, or Skip, or any of the boys?"

The Kid shook his head, and Tilden's heart went up his throat as he spoke.

"No, I don't think you got it in you. . . . But still," went on the Kid, squinting at him, "you might surprise a feller, once you get onto things."

"How long do you think it would take before I got onto things, before I could be a good rider?" asks Tilden, all stirred up.

"That's all up to you and what you're made of," says the Kid. "If you ain't worried about your neck much, and go to it hard enough, you might be a pretty fair rider in a year or so."

* Saddle horn.

Being a good rider, according to the Kid, was in being able to set a good bucking horse. Any other kind was not talked of as good riders.

A year or so, or as the Kid hinted, maybe never, seemed sort of uncertain and a mighty long time to Tilden. Here he'd thought anybody could learn to ride in a couple of months, and realizing the length of time it would take before he might be able to qualify, a fear took hold of him, the fear that somebody else might get the black stallion before he could. He knowed that it'd take a man who could really ride to catch that horse, a man who was onto things.

The thought that somebody else might get the black horse more than worried Tilden. Such a happening would spoil all he was trying to work up to, and realizing what such a happening would mean he went to work all the harder. He asked the Kid questions, sometimes he'd hint about wild horses and how to catch 'em, but he was very careful on that subject for fear that him and the boys would know of his intentions. He didn't want anybody to know about that, for he wanted to surprise them, along with surprising himself.

As he asked questions, Tilden learned for one thing that a man don't have to be a bucking horse rider to be able to catch a wild horse, not unless he figgered on riding that wild horse. That helped some, but he was set back some more by also learning that to be able to catch a wild horse a man has to know a lot about horses and their ways, and that would take a heap longer than learning how to ride a bucking horse.

It seemed like there was a setback to every question he asked. Not a thing came up which in anyway encouraged him. "Well," he'd reasoned to himself one night after going thru one hard day a learning that seemed to get him nowheres, "I wanted to tackle the impossible, and I guess I've sure found it."

But with all the disappointments, and without Tilden realizing it, the little grain of sand within him was taking good root, and growing. He was getting more gumption to face them disappointments with and he kept a hitting at the new lead, which spread on the trail of the black horse, for all there was in him.

In a roundabout way, he learned from the wrangler that to be able to catch such a horse as the black stallion a man would have to know horses as well as he knowed himself. He'd have to be able to ride well and know how to save the horse he's riding. He'd have to be a sure hand with the rope, for with such as the black horse a man is very lucky if he can make one throw, that one would have to do. Then again there's tracking to be done, being able to pick one hoofprint out of the many others that's on the trail, following that one and being able to tell by it how long ago it was made.

Adding on to that was the country the black horse was running into. A feller would have to know that country mighty well, and for many, many miles around, so that if a chance showed up the man could give his horse the advantage. Along with the chase there'd come times when man and horse would have to rest and eat. Jerky and rice makes a good meal if a man knows how to fix it, but the horse he's riding has to have the best care, and he has to be tended to in a way so he'll get plenty to eat and be fresh when he'd be needed. A hobble or picket rope that's not tied right might cripple a horse or he might get away.

With all of that to contend with and supposing the wild horse is caught, the ticklish and knowing part is not over with, for the wild horse, if a man don't know how to handle him, might kill himself in fighting or he might kill the man that's caught him.

There'd been many other things which a man would have to know, but Tilden would have to go thru the whole of it to find out, for the rest couldn't be described by words. But anyway, before the wrangler got thru telling of some of what he'd have to know, Tilden realized that to go thru all of that and come out astraddle the black stallion, a man would sure enough have to be an all around cowboy, and know every detail of the game.

"It'd take many years to know all that," the Kid told him, and even tho the Kid was only fifteen summers old, he'd already spent a good ten of the fifteen summers in the saddle, and knowed pretty well what he was talking about.

Yep! Tilden had sure enough picked himself one impossible thing to do. Here he was fresh from all that's man-made into the thick of God's undisturbed creations, and he was figgering on going it all one better by hitting for the high spots in that land, hitting for something that none of the men born and raised in the country had, so far, been able to do.

It finally all got so deep for Tilden, as him and the Kid talked on the subject, that he quit trying to figger it all out. He'd wanted to do the impossible, and now that it faced him there was nothing for him to do but quit or take a holt. . . . He took a holt.

First, he quit thinking about the fact that some rider might catch the black horse before he could. He'd have to take a chance on that, the same as he'd have to take a chance on winning thru any part of the game. He went on with his riding lessons, fell off his horse and got on again. He felt sore and stiff and received many bruises, but he gritted his teeth, went at it all the harder, and kept his eyes and mind to working on all that could be learned.

Him and the Kid was together the whole day long. Tilden helped, or done his best to help, in corralling, herding, and moving the remuda, and in handling loose horses that way, along with the Kid's steady coaching, he sure received what's called first hand information. But the learning, with all the chance he had, seemed awful slow to Tilden, and the Kid, watching him, often wondered how anybody could be so dumb, for neither realized what a big jump there was between what Tilden had been used to doing and what he was now trying to do.

One day, while things was sort of quiet around the remuda, Tilden thought of riding over to the herd and watch the boys work, or help some if the chance came up, but the Kid headed him off, telling him in his frank style that he'd only be in the way there.

"Better wait a while till you know something," he said.

Tilden waited, and while he watched the big herd acrost the creek on a wide bench he sort of wondered if he'd ever be able to cross the gap into fitting with such as them who worked around that herd. He of a sudden begin to feel a little discouraged, for it looked like he had a mighty long way to go.

"Here's a knot you want to learn how to tie."

The Kid was speaking, and Tilden sort of perked up at the sound of his voice. Anything new or which kept him busy was always welcome. It all kept him from wondering if he could make a go of what he'd undertook to do.

The knot which the Kid wanted to show him was the Bolen, a knot that can be easy untied regardless how much pull there is on it. That one knot kept Tilden busy a trying to figger out, but he finally managed it. Then more knots, for all purposes, from the hondoo knot to them complicated ones that go on the hackamore, was worked at, and from then on, when Tilden had nothing else to do, he'd practice up on them and learning about their use. They all had to do with the handling of stock, specially horses.

But what made Tilden perk up his ears most outside of riding, was the handling of a rope. The Kid showed him the high points on that. He showed him how to make a loop, the different throws afoot and on horse-back, how to tie it to the saddle horn and how to handle the slack to the best advantage after the rope is throwed. He told him of the danger of that slack if not handled right, and in all he got the real chance to learn how to manipulate the hemp well.

But that took a lot of practice too, and as the Kid told him, the real practice comes in catching something alive, something that dodges and fights after it's caught. Tilden thought of the black horse at that, for as wild as that pony was supposed to be, there'd sure be some dodging if a rope ever headed his way, and a heap of fighting afterwards if that rope ever got around his neck.

But how was he ever going to be up to such? Here he'd been practicing for days and throwing his rope, and the wildest or fightingest thing he'd caught had been *a stick* which the wrangler had stuck in the ground for his benefit. Tilden had got so he could catch the stick pretty well and then the idea came that he could rope most anything. He was aching to try his hand at something more lively than that stick.

"All right," says the Kid, as Tilden told him of his hankering one afternoon. The Kid got on his horse, and knowing that the foreman had rode away with the boys, told Tilden to come along. They rode down the "sag"* to where a bunch of cattle was grazing.

"You better not try to rope anything bigger than a yearling for a starter, because not knowing how to handle your rope you might get your horse jerked down."

"Try that one over there on the edge," says the Kid as they got closer to the bunch.

The Kid had no more than pointed out when Tilden put the spurs to his horse. That pony come near going out from under him in starting, but Tilden stuck, and in a hand that'd been skilled only to handle a can or a cigarette case was a rope, a hard twist rope with a loop at the end.

His horse, wise to the game, took him on at full speed and towards the critter which he'd been headed to. The chase was on and Tilden wondered if he would be able to keep in the saddle at the speed his horse was going. Then he seen the yearling ahead of him, a slick little critter as fast as a deer. He leaned ahead and started whirling his rope, but the first thing he knowed the rope had got tangled up over his pony's head and around his own neck.

He pulled his horse to a stop and untangled the rope, and made another start. The same thing happened a sec-

* Slope.

ond time, but the third try he had better luck. That is, he at least didn't get tangled up, even if in throwing his rope he missed the calf by a good ten feet. Tilden hadn't as yet reckoned that at the speed he was going he'd have to throw his rope harder so it would split the breeze that was stirred.

The Kid told him about that, and also told him to try a fresh yearling, the first one was getting tired. Tilden started on again, and the second yearling was took around and around. Two more loops was spilled, and then a third yearling was picked on. Then true to the saying of the third time being a charm, Tilden caught that last yearling with the first throw. It was a lucky throw for it seemed that the yearling dived right into the loop a purpose, but that sure didn't make no difference to Tilden. He'd caught him anyway.

He was so tickled that it never came to him about what he was going to do with the yearling now that he caught him, and the performance had thrilled him so that he didn't care. His blood was up and a racing, and he wished somebody outside the Kid was around to see him, see him there with his rope on a critter he'd caught himself. If Miss Spencer would only ride up now. . . .

A sudden jerk which come near making him lose his seat jarred him out of them thoughts for a second. The yearling had took a run on the rope, and bellering, circled around and bucked at the end of it.

"Keep your horse's head to him," hollered the Kid, "or you'll get tangled up."

Tilden was laughing, laughing like a kid over a long hankered for toy. The Kid sort of wondered at that laugh, and fearing that Tilden would get tangled up in the rope he rode up, flipped his own rope on the yearling's hind feet, and stretching him, got off his horse and took Tilden's rope off, leaving the yearling free.

"Not so bad for a starter," says the Kid as the two rode back to the remuda.

But Tilden hardly heard him, he was in wonders at what he'd just done. For he'd really done something, something he didn't think he could do, and it didn't matter how little that amounted to, it was a start anyway, and the first encouragement he'd had in all he'd tackled which seemed so impossible.

# Chapter VI

The setting sun had took away its colors and disappeared behind a tall peaked badland ridge. Baldy Otters, after seeing the herd to the bed ground, was returning to camp and, with a loose rein, let his horse pick the way while with a pleased look he took in the growth and thickness of the spring grass. It would be a good year for stock, the calf crop had, so far, come above the average, and . . .

Baldy's thoughts was interrupted. There was a long drawed out holler came from camp.

"Y-e-e-p! . . . Stay a long time, cowboy."

Baldly recognized Skip's voice. That good feeling cowboy was always hollering, seemed like, and more than made up for the other riders' quietness. But, what could he be hollering at in that tone of voice, Baldy wondered. It sounded like some more of Skip's mischief. Maybe he'd bet one of the riders that such a bronk couldn't be rode backwards, or something like that. Anyway, Baldy was sure that some riding was being done and that somebody else was getting a heap of fun out of it. He could tell that by Skip's voice.

And sure enough. Baldy rode around a clump of willows, and a sight met him that made him hold his breath. But it was only for a second, for it was all so comical that he had to laugh, the same as the boys who'd gathered around was doing.

In a circle, between the rope corral and the chuck wagon, and formed by the cowboys, was a little buck-skin-paint horse. He was a crowhopping around in that circle and bellering his helplessness not to be able to buck any harder. On top of him, and working hard to stay there, was Tilden.

And a funny sight he made there. He was being bounced around from one side of the horse to the other, and from ears to the tail of him. At one time he'd have a hold of the saddle horn, the next time the cantle, or saddle strings, horse mane, or everything that furnished a holt. He was all over the little horse and never twice at the same place, and what tickled the cowboys most was that when Tilden would be about bucked off, the crowhopping buckskin would bounce him up once more and buck back under him.

The buckskin played ball for quite a spell with him that way, and then, like as if he was tired of playing, he bounced him up once more and dodged to one side as Tilden came down.

*The buckskin played ball for quite a spell with him that way,
and then, like as if he was tired of playing, he bounced him
up once more and dodged to one side as Tilden came down.*

Tilden was pretty well mussed and out of breath as
Skip came to where he'd landed so hard and straightened him up to a sitting position. His hair hung down
over his eyes and he looked thru the tangled strands in
the same way a cornered wild horse might look thru his
foretop.

"By golly, that little buck-paint is sure a tough horse
to set," says Skip sort of encouraging, "and you sure put
up a ride on him too."

"Yep," Moran joins in, "I don't reckon any of us could of rode him exactly the way *you* did. Fact is, you done so well, I think you ought to try him again."

Skip looked at Moran and winked, then he helped Tilden to his feet and slapped the dust off of him a little. "Yeh, I'd sure show that horse who's boss if I was you," he says, "and you can do it too. Only thing you got to remember is keep your feet down on both sides of him, and, maybe a pair of shaps' would help you. Here, take mine." Skip unsnapped his batwing shaps' and put 'em on Tilden, *backwards*. Tilden never noticed the difference and that all helped make things more comical, if that was possible, and the shaps' being backwards that way wouldn't hinder Tilden in his riding none at all.

"Now, get up on that pony and romp on him," says Skip, and then, grinning, he added, "and don't forget to keep your feet down on both sides of him. I'd fan him a little too if I was you."

Everything was all set for the second try. Skip eared down the buckskin like he was sure enough a bad one, and Tilden, not seeming to have anything to say about it and going by what all the boys would tell him, was getting ready to climb on.

"Now, boys, I wouldn't carry this too far."

Baldy had rode up. He wasn't laughing no more, and being foreman and feeling sort of responsible for what all might happen on his range he wasn't agreeable to rough play with strangers.

"This ain't none of our doing," says Skip, still hanging on to the buckskin's ears. "This is his horse, and we're only seeing that he gets a fair break with him. I warned him against him a trying to ride him too," Skip winked at Baldy, "and told him this was the worse bucking horse on this layout, but that didn't do no good and he said that's what he wanted. So, when he turns around and buys him from me I have no more to say."

"Well, all right," says Baldy. Then he spoke to Tilden, "But if you ride that horse you're doing it at your own risk. And another thing, this camp is no riding academy, nor senatorium. This is a cow camp and for cowboys, and if you feel strong enough to try and ride that horse you ought to feel strong enough to hit back to where you belong."

Baldy thought them words over as he rode away and he hated every one of 'em, but as a responsible foreman, he didn't want the company to be implicated in anything. There's plenty of responsibility on a cow outfit without taking on any extra worries. . . . Baldy had helped Tilden when that feller needed it, and as busy as he was, he'd even held up the works to get him to town if it had been necessary, but now that he was up and seemed strong, Baldy felt that he'd done his part and the stranger should know that he was overstaying. This was a busy cow camp and not a resort where guests are took in.

Besides, and now that Tilden had two horses of his own he was free to go anywhere he wished. He could be easy directed to the railroad and there was no strings on him no way, but he'd stayed on and often been in the way, and Baldy felt that his hospitality had been taken advantage of. He had no use for grub-line riders.

But Tilden had no way of knowing the unspoken laws of the range country. He'd got the feeling that everything was free, that all of it was sport and play, that nobody worried or had to make a living. Everybody laughed and joked, and it didn't seem to matter if the night-guard shift was stood in stinging sleet or under a starry sky. These cowboys laughed and joked just the same, like all of it was a game. It was a game sure enough, but underneath the rough happy-go-lucky surface was a discipline to live up to which would make an army general wonder.

Nobody was told anything, but every man knowed that at a certain time of a certain day or night he had to be on "day-herd," "cocktail," "night-guard" or "circle." There was certain horses for each one of them jobs, and each man took pride to make a hand of himself by being on the dot at all that work. Even the Kid, with his "growing appetite," was always right up to snuff and on time, often saddling his horse with a biscuit still in his mouth. It was the same way with moving camp, every man had his special work to do and none lagged. Some would

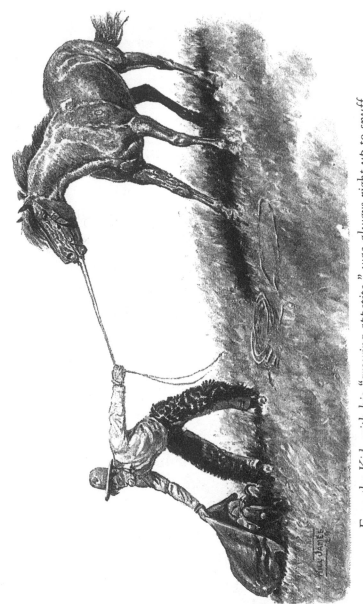

Even the Kid, with his "growing appetite," was always right up to snuff and on time, often saddling his horse with a biscuit still in his mouth.

catch and hook up the cook's team, others would coil up the rope corral and put it in its place in one of the wagons, and the rest would do the general tearing down of the camp. It was the same way in putting it up, and either job was done in less than twenty minutes, after which each cowboy went on to do his day's riding.

Everything went so smooth that Tilden didn't get no idea of the set rules that was with the well run outfit, and only one time did he get a hint of them. It was as two of the riders was rolling the dice on a saddle blanket one evening, both was having a great time taking away each other's earnings when one of 'em spotted Baldy riding in to camp. At the sight of him, the loser was just as ready to call it quits as the winner. The dice disappeared in a shap' pocket and all traces that any crap shooting had been done was blotched up. Gambling and booze is not allowed on a well run cow outfit. That all would interfere with the work, cause enemies, and sometimes bring on shooting scrapes.

There's also a set rule against grub-line riders which everybody knows and nobody speaks of. A grub-line rider is a feller who takes advantage of the country's hospitality and stays as along as he dares wherever there's no work for him to do and the meals are free and regular. He's a plain range bum, and not a cowboy, for a cowboy, to be classed as such, will always make a hand of himself and he'll always be where there's plenty for him to do.

No cowboy has any use for the grub-line rider, and it's a mighty good thing there's a big scarcity of 'em.

Tilden was fast getting to where he'd soon be classed with that breed. First he was just a stranded stranger who needed help. That was fine and everybody done their best to help him get on his feet. He was also mighty welcome to the hospitality he was getting while recuperating and the riders overlooked his mistakes. Baldy even tolerated his riding with the horse wrangler, and he was sure no good there only to disturb the ponies from their needed rest while he done his practicing. But the minute he begin to act up as such as trying to ride a bucking horse was when Baldy decided that feller should get a hint as to range ettiquette. By then Tilden wasn't far from being classed as a grub-line rider. He should of been on the move long before or as soon as he could travel.

And if Tilden had knowed he *would* have been on the move, for he wasn't the kind of a feller who'd take advantage of anybody's good nature and hospitality. He'd always respected that, but he'd been so interested here and, lately, the boys was getting to have so much fun with him that his last thought had been of moving. He'd enjoyed everything so much.

Every day he'd rode with the wrangler and learned something new, and one night, having the craving of wanting to stand guard around the big herd, he'd kept his horse picketed and rode out about the time of the "grave-yard shift." . . . There was a stampede that night and many cattle got away, and when the next morning Baldy asked the riders what had caused it, nobody seemed to know, but Tilden packed a guilty look all the next day for he knowed he'd been the cause of it.

He'd been riding around the bedded herd as the other boys was doing, and once, when he'd got down off his horse for some reason or other, he'd got off too close, and the sight of a human *afoot* against the skyline and so close was plenty enough excuse for some wall-eyed leader to start something. That leader jumped up and bellered and it seemed that the whole herd had evaporated like a band of antelope, and nothing was left to show they'd ever been there but the sound their running hoofs made.

Tilden had stood by his horse, sort of petrified by the suddenness of the happening, and finally, when he did come to, he'd thought it best to hit back for camp and hide in his bed as quick as he could.

He'd felt mighty bad about causing that stampede, and it was only by the fact that the cowboys on that guard seemed to enjoy it, for a change, that he kept from confessing to Baldy about it.

As day after day he'd go on riding, either by himself or with the wrangler, the guilty feeling had wore off, and with his bumping into other happenings and experiences it got to be just another event, a part of his eddication.

He'd been getting plenty of that eddication and many spills and knocks along with it. He'd tried his hand again and again at roping calves and wondered, as he went on practicing at that and other things, why it seemed to take so long to learn. But he'd stayed with it and come a time when the little horse he'd bought from the wrangler couldn't stand up under all the riding. That pony was getting poor and leg-weary, but Tilden, not knowing horses, didn't notice that, and if it hadn't been for the Kid he'd rode that horse to his finish.

Tilden had been surprised when the Kid remarked on that one day, and very sorry too. He was grateful to the Kid for telling him, and that's how come he begin looking around for another horse so he could give this one a rest.

A couple of the boys had horses which they would sell. One was a gentle old pack-horse, and the other was Skip's little buckskin pinto.

Tilden had picked on the buckskin because, as Skip had warned him, that horse would buck. That's just what he'd wanted, something that would buck. He'd been craving to get on one of them kind of horses and now was his chance, and anxious as he was to see if "he had it in him," he'd grabbed that chance like as if his life depended on it. He'd wanted to get at it, the roughest part of it, and to find out thru hard jolts if it would really take him a year, or two years, or maybe ten before he'd turn out to be a hand.

It was all up to him and what he was made of, the Kid had said, and how hard he went at it. Maybe he didn't have it in him at all, and if so, he'd never be up to such as catching or handling the black stallion. But the sooner he'd find out how much ability he had that way the better. In the meantime he was going to try hard and go to it at its roughest, and forget that he might not be fitted for the hard game.

He had one big natural advantage in his start to make a go at riding, and that was his ignorance about horses. He'd seen the cowboys handle any of the meanest ones, and the reckless way they saddled 'em and rode 'em off all seemed so easy. He didn't realize the danger in riding them horses and of what might happen if a man ain't at the right place at the right time. He didn't know that one of them mean ponies could easy hit a man with a hind hoof even while that man is slipping the bridle over his head. He didn't know them ponies could strike as well with their front hoofs or that they also used their teeth once in a while. There was lots of things he didn't know of what a horse can do to a man, wether that man was on the ground or in the saddle. And not knowing that was some risky for him, but that ignorance was a great advantage to him, by the fact that not knowing of the dangers, he had no fear.

There's a saying on the range that the Lord protects that kind. Tilden could have rubbed up against the mean-

*One of them mean ponies could easy hit a man with a hind hoof
even while that man is slipping the bridle over his head.*

est horse on that outfit, if the horse would let him get
that near, and most likely never get a bump, while a cowboy doing that same thing would get kicked to pieces.
There's no explaining the reason of that, only that the
cowboy would be taking them risks while he knows better, and the other would take them same risks because he
don't know of 'em, and the Lord, or some kind of power,
sure has to do a heap of protecting in the last case.

Like with Tilden and the little buckskin for instance,
the boys had lied to him and told him he was the worst
horse in the outfit. Tilden believed it. He didn't know
the difference, and if the boys had really brought him

the worst horse there he'd been just as ready to tackle him. The only difference would of been, with a bad horse, he might of got killed before he got started, because sometimes the Lord, being so busy watching other dumb ones, might overlook one.

As it was, the little buckskin was just right for Tilden, the most he could do to him would be to buck him off. Skip knowed there was no danger in the horse when he sold him, only a lot of fun, for the horse wouldn't kick or strike or take advantage of a man in any way, and he couldn't buck hard enough to make a cowboy proud of himself for riding him.

But for Tilden, that horse done just as well as if he'd been the worst outlaw in Montana. He believed if he could ride him he could ride any horse. The boys had told him so, and that's why, while the boys laughed and joked while he tried, that he kept serious, for in the little buckskin he seen the black stallion. If he could ride one he could ride the other, and his heart and soul was in doing just that.

But it seemed like, with the buying and trying of the horse, that he was due for disappointment and grief. The horse hadn't been his over an hour when Baldy had rode up and spoiled the greatest thrill he'd got since he'd struck the Ox Yoke camp, or since he could remember, for that matter.

Tilden was set back considerable at Baldy's words which as much as told him to "get out of camp," and he sudden-like lost heart in trying to set the buckskin a second time. He just wanted to find a hole and crawl in it and pull the hole in after him.

Skip laughed after Baldy rode away. "Don't mind him, Spats," he says, "that's just his way of talking. He's only sort of fatherly-like and he don't want to see you get hurt."

But Tilden, or Spats, as the boys nicknamed him, wasn't in no mood for any more bucking horse riding just then, and the boys' words more than failed to cheer him. He forgot the horse, which Skip was still holding for him, and he didn't see any of the cowboys that was around. Head down, he walked thru the circle they made, and went on out of sight to where the point of a ridge run against the willows of the creek.

There, amongst the thickest willow patch, Tilden stopped as if he was in a daze, like he'd been hard hit, and hard hit he *was*. He leaned against a tree, the clear creek was running at his feet, and staring at it he went on to think of what had just happened.

He wondered what he'd done to bring on such a blow as Baldy had handed him, and it hurt him deep, more so because he liked that man so much. He owed him a lot, and it hurt him to think that he done anything that would go against that man's feelings and cause him to say what he said.

He liked the boys too, all of 'em, and even when they played jokes on him and laughed at his expense. All them jokes had been mighty full of education for him and he'd welcomed 'em. But now it was all over, seemed like, and he'd have to hit out on the trail of the black stallion before he could ride or rope or do anything.

But that last, as important as it was, didn't worry him near as much as what had come over the foreman of a sudden. He began to think over all the things he done which might of been the cause of aggravating him to speak that way, and he was at his deepest with them thoughts when he heard twigs crack and the jingling of spur rowels. One of the boys was coming.

"Eh, Spats, where are you?" It was the Kid, the horse wrangler.

"What's the matter with you and Baldy?" the Kid went on, after Tilden answered him and the two got together.

"I don't know," says Tilden, in a half-hearted voice.

"I think *I* know," says the Kid, hitting right to the point. . . . "For one thing you been here quite a spell, about a month and a half, according the wages I figger I got coming. Maybe you could of stayed on a while longer and Baldy wouldn't of said anything, not if you hadn't tried to ride that buckskin of Skip's. He just didn't want to take any chances of seeing you get hurt at his camp. A cowboy can get busted up here and that's all right, he's a hired hand and belongs here, but a stranger straying into camp and getting hurt for no reason is another story, and it wouldn't go well with the superintendent."

"I see," says Tilden.

"And besides," the Kid went on, "I expect Baldy figgered you'd been here a good long spell anyway."

"But I wouldn't mind him too much if I was you, Spats. He's a kind of a rough talker anyhow. . . . You ought to heard him tell me to get out of the corral when he caught me in there a trying to rope my horse this morning. He called me a 'Button' too, but I jest laugh and I go in there and rope anyway, when he's not around."

That little talk from the Kid came just right to throw light on the subject which had stumped Tilden, and somehow when the Kid left he didn't feel so bad. He knowed what to do now. He knowed what wrong he'd done, and there was hopes that he could set things to rights.

He woke up early the next morning and started planning. When the cook hollered "grub pile" he stayed in his bed till all the cowboys got thru eating their breakfast. He sort of felt ashamed to face them all gathered there. But he was dressed in time so that when Baldy headed for the corral to catch his horse, Tilden sort of natural like found him there alone.

"I'm sorry if I've imposed on you," he begins as Baldy was saddling his horse. "I had no idea that I was putting you to so much trouble or that I was over-staying and taking advantage of your hospitality. I was so interested with everything else. I want to apologize and thank you for all you've done for me. . . . I will be leaving to-day."

Baldy acted busy cinching up his saddle while Tilden was talking, but his acting that way was only to hide how he felt for what he'd said the evening before. He got on his horse and looked at the country and towards the big herd, like as if he hadn't as yet noticed Tilden or heard him speak. He looked down at his rope and begin fooling with the coils and then, finally, he looked square at Tilden and the hard squint was gone out of his eyes when he spoke.

"I expect I been a little strong with my talk last night," he says, "and maybe for no reason, but it does rile me for strangers to come to my camp and get familiar with horses they don't know nothing about. It ain't good medicine."

"I realize that now," says Tilden, "and you're perfectly right. And as I'm leaving I'd like you to know that I appreciate your telling me, I . . . "

"You don't need to be in a hurry about leaving," interrupted Baldy, "and I don't see how you can leave for a few days yet, you only got one horse you can ride and that one sure needs a rest. So don't be in a hurry."

He reined his horse to a start and rode a ways. Then he turned in his saddle and hollered back. "Yeh, don't be in no hurry." He grinned. "I mean that, and I wish you'd take me up on it."

That was the only way Baldy could say he was sorry.

To please Baldy more than himself Tilden figgered it wise to take him up on his offer to stay. By doing that he'd be letting the foreman know that he was holding no hard feelings against him, that he, himself, had been in the wrong. Tilden was learning. That last had been kind of rough on him, but it'd done him a heap of good. It'd made him consider others, and it was an experience that was valuable to him.

So, after realizing that, Tilden, instead of holding it against the foreman for his rough words, felt mighty grateful to him, and in the few days he'd be staying on at the camp he'd do his best to show his feelings that way.

He got to watching the boys more than ever, how they acted, and how they done things, and he tried his best to copy them, tried to make a hand at what little he could do, and most of all, keep from being in the way, and not cause any trouble thru his ignorance, like that night, for instance, when he started the stampede.

He got to thinking things over a considerable, and, once, to looking back to the time when he'd first come to the cow camp, and thought of the strange happenings that'd come his way in that time. It all seemed to him like he'd been learning to live all over again. What all he'd growed up amongst and got to know had been not only of no use to him here but it'd shaped things so that that knowledge had been nothing but a big handicap. He'd been as helpless as a new born babe, and what he did know had only went to put him in worse fixes.

He'd been better off if he hadn't knowed anything, and hadn't tried to use his judgment, and the only advantage he'd had over a new born babe was that his brain, which even tho mighty hazy at first, was developed. He'd been able to learn quicker, and there'd been enough strength in his bony frame to navigate some, in or out of trouble.

It'd been a sort of second life to Tilden, like as if he'd been picked up out of one, and all at once throwed into another that was all strange, and where he'd had to begin all over again. But that had been easy enough, for there hadn't been much left of him from that first life. The second start was most of all from fresh material. And, in that country, amongst all that's natural, it all piled on and thrived mighty well.

His bony frame had begin to cover up some, not with fat but with stringy muscles. There was more flesh on his cheeks too, and it didn't take long for that tender hide of 'em to tan and peel and tan some more till they was near the color of the saddle he rode. His run of thoughts had also went under the same transformation and he'd got so interested in the new life that he'd near forgot the old one. He'd had no more hankering for any-thing that'd went with that old one, and trying to learn this new one as he had, a fresh run of thoughts had developed according, and to fit in.

He'd got to consider a lot of things which he'd never before given a thought to. He learned thru watching the boys that he done many things which he shouldn't of done, also many things he should of done which he didn't do, like rolling up his own bed when the wagon moved camp, or helping the cook or turning a hand whenever he could, and trying in some way to always make himself useful. . . . That had been something new to him.

Then again at eating time, for instance, he'd got to know that there was ettiquette at the round-up camp fire, as much as there was around any dinner table he'd ever set at. Only, this was an altogether different kind of an ettiquette. Tilden noticed that every rider begin to eat as soon as he reached the chuck-wagon, and without waiting for the others. The reason of that was so he wouldn't be in the way of them others as he went from pot to pan and filled his plate and cup of the victuals that was around the fire. Another reason, was that the sooner a man was thru eating, caught and saddled a fresh horse, and was ready to go, the better hand he was. These boys et because they was hungry, and didn't gather there to sip or hold any social meetings.

Tilden noticed there was manners too, and how each thought of the other. If the wind was blowing, every cowboy in walking around to help himself was careful to

*If a man got up to refill his cup of the black coffee and one
of the others setting around hollered "man at the pot," the feller
that was up was supposed to go around with the pot and
fill all the cups that was held out to him.*

walk behind the other so that no sand would be stirred
which might blow in that other's plate. If a man got up to
refill his cup of the black coffee and one of the others
setting around hollered "man at the pot," the feller that
was up was supposed to go around with the pot and fill
all the cups that was held out to him.

No man took the last piece of meat, or the last of anything, unless he was sure that the others was thru.

As Tilden got to noticing these things and trying to live up to 'em, he got to wondering how come the outfit stood him for so long as they did. He remembered how he'd even used to leave food in his plate instead of throwing it out to where the chipmunks and birds would get it, and also leave the plate out there on the ground instead of putting it in the round-up pan as the boys was doing.

He'd been so well attended to in his old life and so much without responsibility that he'd never thought of these things, and now, in the last few days he was to stay at the camp, he got to wondering how come the cook never called him on that. He wished he had.

But he was mighty glad that in his too short a stay there that he'd at least realized a few things. That wasn't much, he felt, compared to the many other things there was which he still didn't realize. But that was a start, a mighty fine start, for he'd never realized *anything* before.

And now, even tho he still felt he was helpless and of no use, there was one thing more which he was mighty glad to've learned along with his realizing. That was how he learned to keep out of the way of the men who had work to do, and not to cause 'em any extra trouble on his account. He didn't start no more stampedes, no more mad cows got to chasing him and no more riders had to come to his rescue. He'd even quit going out with the horse wrangler for fear he'd do something there that wasn't right, and he didn't try to rope no more calves, for one day he'd overheard Baldy telling a cowboy that "these cattle are raised for beef, and not to practice roping with." . . . It seemed like this cowboy, hankering to unlimber his rope-arm and wanting to give it a little exercise, had stretched his rope on a few critters during the monotonous dayherd shift, and somehow or other Baldy had caught him at it.

Unnecessary roping wasn't allowed, as Tilden had found out, and from that day on he didn't go out to try his hand on any more calves or yearlings. Instead, as he'd ride along by himself, he'd flip his rope at twigs and bushes. That wasn't so thrilling but it was easier to take the rope off of them when he did happen to catch one.

It was a hard time for Tilden, a time when he'd realized his helplessness and couldn't help much only by keeping out of the way, a time when he was at a standstill and where he seen he'd have to know a heap more before he could begin to be of any use. . . . This was time for him to go. This was a place for experienced riders, but some day, he thought, after he caught the black stallion, he'd maybe come back to the Ox Yoke spread and try to get on as a hand.

## Chapter VII

"Where d'you think you'll hit to, Spats? . . . Expect you'll be hitting back for home, eh?"

It was the Kid talking. He'd come up on Tilden one evening as that feller was busy gathering up what things he'd accumulated while he'd been at the camp. Tilden was getting ready to leave.

The Kid sat at one end of the tarpaulin covered bed, and Tilden looked at him and smiled.

"No, I'm not going back," he says. . . . He waved a hand at the country around. "This is the only home I want to claim, now. . . . But," he went on after a spell, "it's awful big and I don't know just where I'll go in it."

"Gee," says the Kid, "if I had a home like you told me you got back in the city, and where you don't have to do nothing, I'd sure go there. It sure beats punching cows, and standing guard, and riding bronks, and I don't see why you want to fool around here for when you don't have to."

Tilden smiled some more. He knowed the Kid and he knowed how long he would last back there, maybe about a week, and then he'd soon hanker for his saddle and his horse, with room to come and go, a big sky above, and good sod underneath.

That all had took holt on Tilden, and he knowed that one born and raised to it as the Kid had been would never be happy nowhere else.

"No," says Tilden, "I'm going to stay here, and if I can't find no place to live in I'll make one."

The Kid looked at Tilden for a spell, like as if to make sure he meant that, and then stared at his spur rowels and begin fingering 'em. He was thinking, or trying to think of some place where Tilden might be able to stay. . . . After a while he looked up again.

"I think I know of a place where you can put up for as long as you want," he says. . . . "It's Old Joe Deschamps' place over at the foot of them mountains." He pointed to his left. "You can't see 'em from here, but I'll show 'em to you in the morning."

Tilden looked up mighty interested, and pleased. Far as he could guess, the mountains the Kid was going to show him was them Skip had pointed out one day as the country where the black stallion was ranging, and it would sure be great luck to find some place, any place, in the black stallion's country where he could stay.

"Only trouble, tho, with Old Joe," the Kid went on, "he don't get much company, and where anybody comes around he daggone near talks 'em to death. You'd have to put up with that."

"That would be easy, I think," smiled Tilden. "I'm a good listener."

"That's fine, then; because listening is all you get to do when you bump up against that old boy."

The Kid went on to tell the good and queer points of Old Joe Deschamps, and according to the outline he give of him, Tilden hoped that he could "hole up" with the old bachelor. He wanted somebody who would talk, because by that talk he would learn a lot, especially from one who, as the Kid said, was sure enough an old timer.

"Nobody knows how old he is," says the Kid. "There's some here that's knowed him for forty years, and they say he looks just the same now as he did when they first seen him. Some say he's close to a hundred years old, and how he used to live with the Injuns before there was any other white men in the country. He used to trade with 'em, and trap, and kill buffalo for their hides. He was a scout for the soldiers too, and when the cattle begin to come into the country, they say Old Joe 'took on' a few of 'em, and some horses too. He had quite a herd up till a few years ago, but on account of not being able to ride no more like he used to he had to sell out most of 'em."

"When the cattle begin to come into the country,
they say Old Joe 'took on' a few of 'em."

There was a question Tilden wanted to ask, and as the Kid talked, he kept a wondering of a way to ask it without giving away any hint of his intentions.

"I suppose he's a great horseman, too?" he begins.

"I'll say so," comes back the Kid, not at all hesitating. "Why, that old feller can break a horse to ride without getting on him, and he'll take the buck out of him and learn him to rein without setting a foot in the stirrup."

"Wonderful, and I suppose he's caught many wild horses. . . ."

"Yess, Ssir. . . . They say he can go out afoot, or he used to anyway, and bring a wild horse into a trap without having that horse break out of a walk. He's got a way with 'em, and he sure knows how to set traps, wether it's for a wolf or a horse."

"But you don't trap a horse like you do a wolf, do you?"

"Oh no-o. A horse trap is just a blind corral, a corral that's hid so a wild horse'll go into it natural like and without his knowing it. You sure got to know how and where to set 'em too."

"That certainly must be interesting."

It certainly was, and the Kid, seeing that Tilden was aching to hear more about wild horses and how to trap 'em, was glad to oblige with first hand information. He told of how he'd helped on a good many runs, and how

Old Joe had caught a few off and on and the way he'd set his traps, how some riders tried to imitate Old Joe in setting traps for the black stallion, and without luck.

"That black horse is sure wise," says the Kid. "But I think Old Joe could of caught him if he'd had a mind to. I figger the riders didn't have enough patience, and they was always too much in a hurry to be going and getting him to stop and make sure everything was set and set right."

Tilden was all ears, and everything the Kid said sure went into one and not at all out of the other. But he was careful not to show too much interest, just enough to keep the Kid going and no more. Once in a while he'd ask a question on the subject, but it was always sort of general and never about the black stallion.

To kind of hide his interest, he kept on sorting out the stuff which he wanted to take with him. He'd lay some aside and pick it up again, and it seemed like, in the short time he was at the camp, he'd accumulated a lot of stuff to do that with. There was rawhide hobbles, a marlin spike, a few strips of whang leather which, as Skip had told him, was handy to mend things with. Then, amongst other odds and ends, was a hackamore, a rope full of the knots which the Kid had started teaching him to tie, and a hair "mecate."*

Some of these things he'd bought from the boys, others had been given to him, and more which he'd picked

* Rope.

up after they'd been throwed away. They'd all be mighty necessary, he thought, when he got on the trail of the black stallion, and as he stuffed 'em in the flour sack the whole of 'em tallied up pretty well with what all goes into a cowboy's warbag.

The same with the bench-made boots that was on his feet. They was the regular range rider's boot, and he'd got 'em from Cliff Moran. They'd been a little too big for Moran but happened to fit Tilden like as if they'd been made to his order, and he'd bought 'em.

Tilden was all thru putting his stuff to order so he could be ready to go in the morning. Him and the Kid talked on about wild horses, and traps, and Old Joe Deschamps, for a while longer, and, as some of the riders was heard to ride out for first guard, the Kid stood up.

"Well, I guess it's time for me to hit the soogans," he says. "I'll see you in the morning before you go, and I'll steer you to Old Joe's place so's you won't miss it."

But, when the next morning come, there was no steering nobody to no place much, specially a stranger like Tilden still was. Low-hanging dark clouds had covered the land, and a steady drizzle was coming down which made it impossible to point to any land-mark that was over half a mile from camp.

There was no use for Tilden to start out in such a day. He'd only get lost and wander around, and even tho the boys had saddled and rode away as early as usual, he knowed better than try and do the same, and expect to find any certain place in such weather.

Tilden was disappointed. Now that he knowed of a place where he might be able to stay, and right where he wanted it, he was anxious to be on his way there and start in to map out a way of catching the black horse, and before anybody else could have a chance to put a rope on him.

But there was nothing he could do now, only wait for this storm to let up. He rolled his bed so the rain wouldn't be so apt to soak thru the tarp', and, at the Kid's suggestion, moved it up on high ground where the running water wouldn't get into it. It was a kind of a dreary day for Tilden. Everything was wet and he was surprised to find that his boots leaked. He didn't know that cowboys' riding boots was made only to fit a stirrup and ride with, and not so good when it come to waller around in soaked grass or mud.

The canvas "fly" which extended over the chuck-wagon and back of it a ways was the only shelter in camp, all excepting a couple of one-pole tepees which belonged to some of the riders. One of 'em was shared by the Kid who used it at night, and the "nighthawk" who used it in daytime. Tilden could of went in there, but he didn't want to disturb the "nighthawk," and besides it wouldn't be so cheerful inside that cold and damp tent.

So Tilden, a big yellow slicker over his shoulders, stuck around under the "fly" by the chuck box, and he didn't like that either because he was afraid of being in the way of the busy cook. There was only one thing to do and that was to offer to help for the privilege of that shelter. He went out in the rain and chopped big armfuls of wood and stacked it all under the wagon where it'd keep dry. Then he went under the "fly" again, more sure of himself. A while after that, and looking around for something more to do, he spotted a big bucketful of potatoes, and asked the cook if he could peel 'em. The cook was more than agreeable to that, and after telling Tilden that'd he'd like to have some of them potatoes left after he got thru peeling 'em, that job was took on like it was sure enough a pleasure.

By noon time Tilden felt he had a right to stay under that "fly." Even when the cowboys rode in and crowded under it he stuck to his ground, but he didn't take much of it, and to save room, he waited till they all got thru eating and was out to the corral again before he begin filling his plate.

Squatted there, with the plate on his lap, he looked toward the muddy rope corral as he et. The cowboys was gathered there and two at the time went in to rope their horses. The already spooky ponies shied at the long yellow slickers, and the slippery mud made it hard for the men to get around. Everything was wet and stiff and sticky, and the hunks of mud that hung on the boots made it hard to tell if spurs was spurs or just another hunk of the stuff.

To live out in such weather and work thru it as these cowboys was doing was a part of the life that didn't as yet appeal to Tilden, and it was during such dreary spells that he wondered if Mother Nature wasn't a little too rough on a man. It was at such times also that he'd remember the dry carpets and steam heat of the places he'd left behind. He remembered the cozy little library back there at home, the gas-heated fireplace, and the other comforts that was. He wouldn't mind being there now and set in the big overstuffed chair, just for a spell. Queer, he thought, how he'd never stuck around that library much.

Thru a hazy picture of the dry corners and comforts of that library and other cozy places he knowed of back home, he watched the cowboys get on their horses and ride away. Some of the horses bucked and stampeded thru the rain-soaked country. What a difference this was as compared to what his mind pictured of his home surroundings.

He remembered back there how, in a cold rain like this, folks would bundle up, put on their rubbers, and call a taxi, only to go a short distance to another as dry and warm place as the one they'd just left. And even then they'd shivered and remarked about the miserable weather *outside*.

These boys *was* outside and in the thick of it all day along and a lot of the night. Sometimes it was snow instead of rain, or cold sleet, and plenty of raw winds in between, the kind of weather that made town folks run from one doorway to another. The cowboys worked thru all of that, and cussed and grinned the same as they did in fair weather. The work was more dangerous in bad weather too, the horses are cold and touchy, and it's at such times that even what's called a gentle horse will act a considerable against cold and stiff saddle leather being slipped on his back. Even twenty-year-old ponies will do a fair job of bucking in such weather and that's not saying how a big four-year-old bronk will act at them times.

The long yellow slicker the cowboy wears is a mighty fine excuse for an ornery horse to spook up at, and, as he's always ready to tear things up even when the sun is shining and all is hunkydory, there's no telling of his acting when he's cold and touchy and that long slicker swishes around him. Ropes are muddy and stiff, so are the latigoes and everything else a cowboy touches. Then again he's hindered by the yellow slicker, boots heavy with mud, and a slippery footing. A wet slippery stirrup to step up on such a horse with sure don't go with "safety first" rules either.

But that ain't all, the fun begins when the cowboy misses a flying hoof and gets up in the saddle and gives the bronk his head. That bronk will buck out a ways and

A wet slippery stirrup to step up on such a horse with
sure don't go with "safety first" rules either.

maybe slip and fall, sometimes on the rider, but whatever he does the rider will hang on to him, and if the horse does manage to stay on his feet thru that performance, he'll go to bucking again and most always on the side of a slippery hill and where even a centipede, with all its legs, would have a hard time to find a footing.

But the cowboy will ride him on thru somehow, stay on top, and bring the cattle he's out to circle after. It's all in the day's work.

With Tilden, a setting there under the shelter of the "fly" and comparing the life of the cowboy along with that which he'd left, he didn't see only the surface of what went with the work of the cowboy in bad weather that way. To him it all struck him as only sort of disagreeable and dreary, things being wet and so on. He couldn't get the meaning of why a cowboy cussed when he missed a throw and his rope dropped in the mud, and why that same cowboy should laugh when a few minutes later his horse bucked and fell in the mud with him. The first happening had only been sort of aggravating, while the second, even the more serious, had a twist to it that proved his being a hand. That was it, being a hand. Laughing when there's danger and hardships, laughing when there's danger of getting a leg, or neck, broke, the same as laughing when stinging sleet stiffens the muscles and makes laughing hard to do. That's all in the making of a hand, a principle which every cowboy does his best to live up to.

That bronk will buck out a ways and maybe slip and fall, sometimes on the rider, but whatever he does the rider will hang on to him.

It's the cowboy's religion, and living up to it makes him of a breed that's all his own. With that it already takes a certain breed of man to make a cowboy. That breed might be found anywhere so long as it's stirred and the start is early enough, but as a rule that breed grows up right in the heart of the cow country, and the true cowboy, even tho he knows of many other ways of living that are soft, will always be a cowboy. He won't care if his wages are low so long as the ponies are rough and the country is big.

Tilden was fast getting a hint of that, and it'd get him to do a heap of wondering and trying to understand. He watched the boys ride out, rain streaming down their faces, and none was lagging behind. All was always ready to make a hand of themselves at anything that might come up, and the way they joked and laughed as they rode on showed how they lived up to the spirit of their breed. It seemed all the same if it poured rain or sunbeams.

The riders hadn't gone over half an hour when a low fog bank, seeming like to be on their trail, came down from the bad-land ridges and made things impossible to see for more than ten yards. Tilden couldn't see beyond the fire which was right there at the edge of the "fly," and he wondered how the riders could go anywhere in such thick weather, or could find their way back if they'd decided to return.

But it wasn't long after the fog appeared, and Tilden was just starting to peel another bucketful of potatoes, when there was a sound of running hoofs and he heard the voices of the riders. Tilden couldn't see as far as the rope corral but he heard 'em ride on to it and knowed they was unsaddling. After a spell, Baldy and a few of the boys came up to the fire, and rubbing their hands at the flames passed remarks on how many cattle they hadn't seen that afternoon.

It soon was pretty crowded under the "fly," but it wasn't crowded for long because under that shelter was the cook's territory, and it was respected as such. Soon as the numbness was out of their fingers and the water quit dripping from their hat brims the cowboys begin to file out. Tilden had no idea as to where they could be headed in this weather and no shelter near, but after a while he heard the crackling of a fire and thru the fog he could see the light of it.

How could they start a fire in the rain like that when the wood was all wet? He wondered, but they had started one sure enough, and it was of some size too.

He heard Skip's high voice and the boys' laugh after it, and he begin to peel the potatoes faster. He wished he was thru so he could join them by the fire they'd made, . . . and after the last potato had lost its last piece of peeling he wasn't long in heading toward it.

But he was sort of surprised as he neared the riders and their fire, because, by the sound of their voices and all he'd figgered that they'd built some kind of shelter to keep out of the rain. Instead, the cowboys, slickers over their shoulders, was all standing around the big open fire, with no sign of shelter nowheres.

Tilden edged in amongst the riders and stared at the big limbs that'd been made to burn. They looked wet, steam was coming out of 'em, and it was sure a mystery to him how the cowboys ever got 'em to burning and making such a hot fire. The flames reached up ten feet in the air, and he was surprised that it wasn't so bad to stand there in the rain so long as he was close to the heat of 'em.

There was something about that big fire too which made him contented to just stand there and watch. Every flame and burning limb held the eye, sort of soothed the mind and stirred the imagination.

The fact that it did stir the imagination was proved by "the big ones" Skip was telling on and on. But maybe that didn't prove anything either, because that cowboy was always telling big ones wether he was looking at a fire or saddling a bronk.

Another big one came to his mind as Tilden was spotted standing there. It was an old one to the boys, but it'd sure be new to Tilden, and would most likely take effect.

"Did you ever see a side-hill-winder, Spats?" . . . Skip was mighty serious as he asked that, and acted like he was only wanting to give some interesting information. Then again, Tilden noticed before answering, that all the boys also seemed serious and anxious to hear.

"No," he says, after feeling his ground to make sure that this wouldn't be another one of Skip's jokes, "I don't think I ever did, I wouldn't know what one was if I saw it."

"Well, they're sure worth seeing," says Skip shaking his head, "because they're mighty scarce. . . . A side-hill-winder," he went on, "is a wild horse that used to run in the rough country to the south a ways, and as the professor sayd, the specie is about extinct. They only run on side hills and can't navigate on the flats at all, because running on them side hills for so many generations has made 'em freaks of nature, and their legs on one side are about a foot shorter than they are on the other. . . ."

Tilden glanced all around at the boys. They all seemed mighty interested in watching the fire, and none of 'em was caught grinning. But he'd been fast getting wise to their tricks, and as interesting as it would be to hear more about such an animal he didn't dare take a chance on having them put one over on him.

"Did you ever see any of them yourself?" he asked.

"Oh yes, I even caught one of 'em one time, but I had to turn him loose."

"Why?"

"Well, you see, his being short legged on one side that way he fell over soon as I got him on the flat, and being I couldn't get him to the ranch, why there was nothing else I could do. Too bad too, 'cause he was sure pretty and I figgered on selling him to some circus."

Skip went on to tell some more about the side-hill-winder, and being so serious in the telling, Tilden wasn't sure if he should believe him or not, but he was wise enough to keep neutral and he didn't bite so good no more at the traps that was set for him. And, when the subject begin to die down, Tilden was pleased with himself that he didn't bite because it had turned out to be a joke after all, only Skip was the one that was laughed at this time, for not being able to put it over. And the boys didn't spare him no more than they'd spared Tilden when he'd been the victim.

But that all didn't faze Skip much. He'd have another one some other time and with better bait. In the meantime he'd wait till he caught somebody off their guard, and to square himself, that somebody would have to be Tilden.

Tilden didn't know he was an intended victim that way, and he wouldn't of been worried any if he had knowed. He was busy listening to other subjects that'd sprung up, and being there was some joke at the bottom of most all of 'em, he kept busy a trying to pan 'em out as quick as the others did. The only thing that kept him wondering at times was that some of them stories turned out to be serious facts, and that sure kept him guessing.

He hated to be caught laughing when he should of been serious, and serious when he should of been laughing.

As he listened, Tilden wondered where all them stories, so many of 'em, came from. They was all so well told too, and he wondered at the humor or tragedy that was in all of 'em. There was sure plenty of that, but not at all of the kind he'd ever heard before. These boys seemed to dote on the telling of them stories, and developed an art at that that compared well with the way they rode or throwed a rope, all in their own style and with the same skill.

Their stories, like with their songs, was these men's "earmarks," and identified 'em as to their strange breed. They all had developed from the life they lived and the spirit they put in that life.

Like for instance, Tilden noticed while these men was telling their stories that . . . even tho they stood in the rain, feet wet, and water oozing out all the way from their hat brims to their boots, a cold heavy fog bearing down on 'em, . . . they talked and joked the same as if they'd been dry and warm and under a roof. He noticed a heap more cheer there at such a time, than he'd ever found by any fireplace or any expensive club he'd ever walked into.

It seemed like, with these men, that the tougher the break was the more they joked and laughed. He remembered how, during a snow storm, a few weeks past, most of the boys had maneuvered around under their snow-covered tarps' and put on frozen socks. Some of 'em, who had leaky tarps' stuck their head out from under in the gray morning and joked about having their morning baths, saying they had a little lake in their bed and slept in it all night. None of 'em had seemed to worry that they couldn't get to dry or thaw out any of their clothes before they went out on the day's ride. Instead there was jokes about getting an axe to chop a way thru so a sleeve or pants' leg could be slipped on.

A cold wet snow was falling as them jokes was passed and others was brought up, and on account of the stiff wind blowing, the words could hardly be heard. Tilden had thought all of that joking to be mighty strange. He sure didn't feel that way himself, and once in a while, when he'd hear a cowboy pass a cuss word that fitted the time, he'd been sort of disappointed to see that the strength of that cuss word had been spoiled by a good sized grin.

It'd been impossible for him to figger it all out at the time, and it was only thru steady thinking on the subject and watching that he got a hint of the spirit which went with "cowboy religion."

He'd got a better hint of that with this last storm, and it all struck him as sort of unbelievable. . . . Where did this spirit sprout from, he wondered, and how did it get to grow to such strength?

The answer to that goes away back to the days when the first Injun fighter decided to dab a long rope on the long-horns of the wild cattle that run by thousands in the range country at that time. The days of the first cowboy.

The dangers a man faced then, . . . with the Injuns, riding wild horses, amongst everything that was wild and aching for a fight, not mentioning many things he faced every day which, even tho considered as trifles has cost many a man's life, . . . all went into the shaping of the first cowboy, from head to toe and from heart to brain. He'd turned out to be a breed of the kind who learned that to keep on living in the wild and open territories a man sure had to keep an eye open, even while asleep, and make a hand of himself. He'd learned it was best to laugh when things went wrong, to keep on a fighting and never to hoist the white flag.

These cowboys, which Tilden had lost himself amongst, had sprung from the same breed as that early day Injun fighting first cowboy. And outside of the Injuns, which now done no worse than bum for tobacco or some such like, their life was pretty well the same, and there was still plenty of room for that early day spirit to keep on living.

All these things Tilden noticed, and which hinted to that spirit, was only trifles as compared to what really was at the bottom of it. But what he did notice, little as it was, had surprised him and kept him wondering, and he was anxious to know more.

He had a chance to know more that evening. One of the boys had been heard to grumble. He'd been cussing the weather, the horses, and the cook's wet biscuits, and when all had gathered around the fire again before first guard, he was heard to cuss the luck for having to stand guard in a night like this, and Cliff Moran took him up on it, for that all was kind of tiresome to listen to for very long.

"Why, this is just a summer night, feller," Cliff says to him, "and if you've never stood guard thru worst nights than this you've sure had it pretty soft."

"Yeh!" Skip chips in and speaking to Cliff, "pretty soft is right. Maybe he's used to tending bar in a soft drink parlor, or some such place where it rains *outside* and the breeze is from an electric fan inside."

Other remarks was passed back and forth amongst the circle of riders for a spell and all against the grumbler, till that feller begin to wish he was somewhere else. He wasn't very popular there, as he soon found out, and he seen where it was best for him to keep quiet.

Before the talk was thru on that subject, Tilden found out that grumblers and agitators don't do well in a cow camp, and that the general feeling for such simmers down to just a few plain words which is "If you don't like it, shut up, or get out."

These men wasn't laborers who just put in their time in the easiest way they could and dropped everything when that time was up. There was no union amongst 'em or strikes. It was a work that every man took great pride in doing, and a trying to do it better than the other. All was contesting to be recognized top-hands, and only for their own satisfaction. For to be a top cowhand, roper and rider, to be fearless and reckless and have the guts to go thru a day's work without a whimper regardless of what comes up, is every true cowboy's high ambition.

That all stacks up to *"making a hand,"* and them who make the top at that are as highly thought of and admired as any king on any throne, for a cowboy's throne is a hard one to set and do credit to. There's always plenty of room for improvement, and every man, even the top hand, will do his level best to do still better. There's jealousy too amongst some of the best ones, but each man is careful to keep that in his chest, and that jealousy, instead of being a fault, turns to be a quality, because the only relief for it is to try and do better, and there's no limit there.

Having a hint of that, Tilden wasn't surprised to learn that night that the grumbling rider was "no cowboy." Such was the words the Kid used. Of course, it was understood that he had a job as a cowboy at the "wagon" and drawed regular wages and was just as regular as mealtime, and so on, but he was no cowboy, "no hand."

"We call the likes of him 'freaks,'" says the Kid, "or 'pumpkin rollers.'"

"Well, why does Mr. Otters keep him?" asks Tilden.

"I guess it's because he's a little short-handed. He does all right holding a herd or something like that, but he ain't worried to try and make a hand of hisself. . . . I wish Baldy would give him my job and let me have his, because I know I can beat him to a frazzle at anything he tries to do, even if I am just a kid."

As the two talked on about the "freak," Tilden finally got to understand that to be "a hand" a feller also had to live up to the principles that went with the life. The argument at the fire that evening proved that, for the cowboys had showed, mighty plain, their dislike of peace-jarring grumblings. That hadn't at all been in accord with cowboy religion.

"You run acrost fellers like that once in a while," says the Kid, "but they don't last long anywheres, and I figger the reason for their acting that way is because they been weaned too young. Their ambitions is sort of stunted, like a 'leppy'* calf."

As Tilden crawled in his bed that night, and the rain kept a pattering on his tarp', it struck him that there was sure a whole lot to this being a hand. He'd no more than learn one thing when ten more would sprout up which was brand new, and it'd get him to worrying a heap if he'd ever make the grade. . . . In his interest to

* Orphan.

151

catch up on that he'd near forgot about the black stallion. Of course he was still as serious in doing that as
ever, but being he realized what a hand he'd have to be to
succeed, he'd went at the start and to trying to be such a
hand. The catching of the horse would come afterwards.

The rainy day, with all the boys around, had learned
him many things which was just as necessary to know as
how to ride and rope. There was one strong point which
had been brought up that would be a great help to him if
he could live up to it, and that was the spirit to take
things as they come, and as these boys done. Face 'em all
with a grin, and turn the hard parts into jokes. To take
all bumps and hardships as tryouts so a man can show
what he's made of, and that way add 'em as another notch
to the top instead of a setback.

Tackling the impossible as he had, Tilden knowed
that he'd sure have need for such spirit to carry him
thru. He felt mighty thankful to the cowboys for making him see things in that light, when they went wrong
that way. But, he wondered if such spirit could be in
him, if, when things really did go wrong and he failed on
all sides, he would have the gumption to grin and try
again. . . .

Well, there was nothing to do but give it a test, and
he was beginning to ache for that test to hit him.

## Chapter VIII

"Ain't you glad you ain't a cowboy, Spats?"

It was Skip speaking. Tilden, after shivering thru the gray dawn, had jumped up, took in a lot of black coffee, and then made a bee-line for the big fire which the cowboys had brought to life again. He'd no more than got there when Skip greeted him with the question. He looked at the wet wood, which seemed to burn fine, then at Skip's grinning face, and grinning back at him he answered:

"I don't know. . . ." He was just being neutral. He'd learned it was best to be that way when Skip took the lead.

"I wouldn't be at all doubtful about that if I was you," says Skip. "You ought to know when you're well off." Then the cowboy begin to act serious and squinted at Tilden under his dripping hat brim. "But it seems to me like," he went on, "that you'll *have* to be some powerful all-around cowboy before long."

"I don't understand," says Tilden.

"I don't, either," Skip comes back at him, "but if all I hear about you setting out to catch that black stud is true, I'm thinking you'll have to develop your rope-arm and riding ability a considerable."

Tilden missed a few heartbeats at them words and his breath came short. Could it be that Skip was speaking of the black stallion, the horse he'd planned to catch? . . . But how could Skip know of that? He'd kept it all a secret and hadn't spoke one word about the black horse to no one, not even to the Kid.

Tilden didn't know that these boys were past masters at reading signs, that a dim track on a trail, an action of any kind from man or animal, told 'em more than if all the goings on had been printed down in big letters. They lived a life where words was only to tell stories by, or pass an opinion, and signs was their main lead. It was thru signs that they done their work, in hunting horses, cattle, or camps. If the "wagon boss" caught his best circle horse that was a sign that a big "circle" would be made and the cowboys caught their own horses according. If that same wagon boss took your top horse out of your string and turned him over to another rider that was a sign he wanted you to quit, or else you'd get fired. A restless herd at night was a sign of not enough grass or water. A skinny leg-weary horse was a sign that the man riding him is no cowboy, and so on till that life could be lived thru with nary a word needed to be said.

That sense of sign reading being the cowboys' main lead that way, it was easy to figger what Tilden was up to. Many had watched his listening and sudden interest when anyone spoke of the black horse, and many knew, after Tilden was up and around, that something was up soon as it was seen that instead of wanting to go back to where he came, as was expected, he'd stayed on and tried to learn the game.

The boys had grinned at one another when one day he bought a saddle from one of the boys, and later on a bed-roll from another, then shaps', and everything that went to make up a regular outfit. Of course that could of been layed to that of his just wanting to be a cowboy, but Cliff Moran got to wondering. He'd seen Tilden's admiring glances set on Rita Spencer, how that feller had listened so close when she spoke of the black horse and how she wanted him. Then again, Rita had asked Moran a lot of questions about this feller Tilden, who he was, where he came from, and so on, and she'd seemed pretty interested.

So, maybe it was no more than natural that Moran should of wondered and maybe got a little suspicious. And seeing Tilden stick around and gather up an outfit instead of going back, all sort of pointed towards the fact that that feller might be fool enough to try and catch that horse for her, and get on the good side of her that way.

*Rita had asked Moran a lot of questions about this feller Tilden, who he was, where he came from, and so on, and she'd seemed pretty interested.*

He'd laughed at the idea of such as Tilden ever being able to even get a glimpse of the black horse, and as Tilden stayed on and seemed to be serious in carrying out his intentions, he'd told Skip about it, like for a good joke, and the two'd had a good laugh over it.

There was more laughs as the subject scattered around the fire that drizzly and foggy morning, and them laughs was just of plain good nature, with no sarcasm in 'em, for, even tho near every one of the riders wanted to be first in catching that black horse and leading him to Miss Rita, there was always room for another to try. And what fear could there be from such a feller as Tilden?

"You want to be sure and take a bag of salt with you when you go after that horse," says Moran. "They say the only way he can be caught is by putting a grain of it on his tail. But you better take a whole bag along because one grain might not do the work."

Tilden was so set back in learning that his secret was out, and so busy wondering how that happened, that he didn't hear many of the things that was said. When Moran spoke he just grinned at him a little, sort of sickly like, but he didn't hardly hear, and he didn't ask him to repeat what he'd said. It wouldn't matter anyway, because he knowed that they all was just having a lot of fun, and the less he'd say the easier it'd be for him.

For Tilden's benefit, there was many ways suggested on how that horse might be caught, and every one of them ways was so out of reason and the boys was so busy a thinking 'em up and laughing about 'em that they'd got to forget asking Tilden's opinion on 'em, and Tilden was glad. He was thinking hard, for the way these boys was laughing at his plans sure upset him in more ways than one. They made it all so much of a joke that he got to fearing of it really being such. If there was some chance that he *might* be able to catch that horse, he thought, they'd realize it, and they wouldn't make so much fun of his plans then. But the way they kept it up and seemed to get so much pleasure out of it all, like it was the best they'd ever heard, sure left no room for any serious hopes.

Wondering hard on that, Tilden forgot about his secret plans and how they come to get out. He'd forgot to think that the boys, being wise to them now, might try to catch the horse before he'd have a chance at him. All he thought about was how foolish he might of been to ever want to even try to get the horse. The boys' steady laughs sort of proved that. He'd been laughed at many times and he'd laughed with 'em afterwards when he'd realized his mistake. Now they were laughing at him again, and more than they'd ever laughed before. But if *this* was all a mistake, a foolish thing for him to try to do, he wouldn't be laughing afterwards, not this time.

Not knowing of what all he would be bucking up against in trying to catch the black stallion, he got to feeling mighty doubtful. Maybe that was so impossible, for him, that it was a good joke. It sure seemed so the way the boys was carrying on.

He felt mighty bad, disappointed and hurt, not from the jokes the boys was getting out of his plans, but from the fact that them plans, as serious as he'd been in making them, and as much as he'd meant them, could furnish so much to joke at. There must be something to it.

Tilden being so wrapped up in his plans, and so set in carrying 'em thru, had forgot for the time being, that carrying on jokes was only a good way of entertaining around a fire, specially in a dark gloomy day. He wasn't used to them as yet and took 'em too much to heart, but even tho they hurt, they was good for him. Being joked at would make him ashamed at first, then to realizing, to trying to get above 'em, and then to do things so well that there would be no cause for such jokes. After a man had proved himself so perfect as all that he can laugh at the things others do, but even then he's not safe, not around a cow camp, for that perfect man will be joked at for being perfect, and if ever he makes a little misslip there's never no let up on him.

A good joke, in words or action, is the cowboy's staff of life. That's what they keep one another primed up with, and there's been many a cow outfit what'd hired some feller just for the "laughing stock," some green-horn who'd want to be a cowboy. That would be just to keep the cowboys happy and to matching wits

*A good joke, in words or action, is the cowboy's staff of life.*

with one another on remarks about what that feller done or would do.

Every kid horse wrangler gets it in the neck that way for a while, but them, being sons of cowmen themselves, don't take long to get onto the ropes, and soon comes a time when they're eddicated so as they're beyond reach of them jokes. But them jokes is what has helped a heap in making them the real cowboys.

Tilden had been spared many of them jokes, because, for one thing, he didn't belong with the outfit, and another had been his condition. He'd needed help and care. Then again, when he got better, it was hard to pin any joke onto him because there'd always been a smile on his face. There'd been no chance to get at him much, not till the news of his trying to catch the black stallion leaked out, and that's why, when the chance come, the boys made so much of it.

That's how come Tilden didn't know how to take it all. It had been a ticklish subject with him too, and not knowing how foolish his plans might of really been he didn't know wether to get peeved at the jokes or shrink away to where he couldn't hear. To laugh was the least thing he felt like doing, and as the boys went on to make the most of the subject he kept his head down, and with the toe of his boot seemed busy a trying to dig a root out of the muddy ground. If he did look up once in a while it was with a vacant stare and the forced grin on his face matched that well.

After a while he begin to listen to Skip's voice, for that cowboy, even tho having a failing for joking, did now and again get serious and tell things that was more than worth while listening to.

"I know of a better way than that," he was saying, as the laughs from the last suggestion died down. "I seen it done in a moving picture show one time at Miles, and," he said, grinning, "you all know that must be correct.

"The way that bold hero done it, on the screen, was easy as falling off a log, remarkable easy. He finds this wild horse he wants, bogged down, and after he gets him out of there by some simple twist, the horse, feeling so grateful and appreciating, of a sudden forgets that he's a wild horse, and sticks around him like a sugar-eating pet. It ain't no more than two hours later when that wild horse begins to carry messages to this hero's sweetheart. He seemed to know where she lived too, and everything.

"The picture and goings on was so interesting that I had to get out before it was half over, it stirred me so, and besides I'd happened to think that I had to get a tooth pulled, and that would be interesting too.

"But anyway, there would be a mighty easy way to get that black horse, Spats. Just trail along after him till he bogs down. It might be a good idea to pour a lot of glue in all the bog holes you can find too so you'll be sure he'd stay once he got into one of 'em."

Tilden wasn't listening towards the last, and he never even looked up when his name was mentioned. . . . One suggestion kept a following another that way for a spell, and then, finally, when none seemed to bring satisfactory results from Tilden, the boys branched off on other subjects, and new victims took Tilden's place. Even Skip, himself, was drawed in as one, for butchering a yearling too close to camp the night before. That critter had tore things up a considerable before going down for the last count.

"It's a wonder," says Baldy, "that you didn't put 'er in the cook's vest pocket and do your butchering there. I'm glad your turn don't come often."

"Well," says Skip, grinning, "it was cold, and you wouldn't blame a feller for doing his work close to the fire when he can, would you?"

There was no use a trying to get anything over on Skip much, but none of the boys overlooked the chance when one showed up.

It was going to be a long day for Tilden. The heavy fog hung down and penetrated to the bone, even when close to the big fire. His feet was soaking wet, and water kept a dripping steady from his hat brim.

"Oh, for the life of a cowb-o-y. . . ."

One of the riders had started singing, a song that was old, but which must of been made up by one who's never rode the range, for that song was only of blooming

wild flowers and sunshine, of riding that was all roman-
tic and play, and no work. It was all such a contrast to the
life, espccially on that day, that it went well, and many
voices carried it on.

Tilden found himself grinning as he listened. Even
he knowed better, with as little as he'd tasted of the life,
but the song had its qualities sure enough, for it at least
was a song and as long as it was sung it done as much as
any song would do. No gloomy fog has any effect on
harmony, any kind.

The song even done its work on Tilden that way, as
downhearted as he felt. He got to looking up more and
more, and with less fear that the wild horse subject would
be stirred up again. He sort of felt now that the boys had
already forgot about his plans and how foolish he might
of seemed to them, and he gradually got to feeling at ease
amongst 'em once more.

Only the big doubt of ever being able to carry out
his plans bothered him, and that was a plenty, for them
plans had been everything, seemed like. They'd been the
makings of him in trying to fit himself to be up to such
and now it looked as if the bottom had dropped out of
'em and all was a big joke, a dream that such as he could
never make come true.

The long dreary day sure didn't help him out of them
thoughts. It seemed in cahoots with the heavy fog to
make them darker and seem more hopeless, and when

night come and he hit for his soogans, a very miserable feeling tagged along with him there, and aggravated him till, tired and wore out, he finally found rest in sleep.

It was while he slept that the heavy fog lifted, and evaporated away to leave a skyful of bright stars' shine on the rain-soaked earth. Tilden woke up once, and for no reason only of the feeling of sudden relief, and not hearing no rain pattering on his tarp' he'd pushed it back to stare at the great sky above.

Away to the south he seen what was left of the fast disappearing fog, and it seemed like his dark and hopeless thoughts of the day before had gone with the remains of it. The bright sky and fresh smelling earth, like as if against all that's discouraging, held promises of all that's fair, and the stars above twinkled as if in faith that hopes would come true.

Tilden stared up at 'em, for a long time, and it seemed like as he kept on staring, and thinking, that the grief and misery he'd went thru the day before was just like a nightmare, something that was scary for a while but which wasn't at all to worry about. If he'd remembered the one point which the cowboys had stirred to within his reach and which he'd wanted to keep to mind always, that wouldn't of likely happened. But he'd been too worried then to think of it, and as it was he'd let his spirits dwindle away according. But he'd remember it now, and he went to running the lay of it thru his mind.

It was: "To face all disappointment with a grin, and turn the hard parts into jokes. To take all bumps and hardships as tryouts so a man can show what he's made of, and that way add 'em as another notch to the top instead of a setback."

That was a part of cowboy religion which he'd adopted, and which he'd been aching to put to test, but when the chance come he'd forgot about it. Now he took it on for all it was worth, and he was in better shape to appreciate the full value of it than he'd been the day before. He turned the belief over in his mind and worked it at all angles, and he seen how well it fitted against all that'd stumped him and made him wonder the day before. And not only that, but he seen that living up to that belief would encourage him to go on all the harder, thru every bump and disappointment, "so he could show what he was made of, and add on another notch."

If a man had the gumption to back that belief there wouldn't be anything impossible. . . . Tilden went back to sleep on that, and when he woke up at the cook's holler a couple of hours later there was no sign of the expression he'd packed on his face the day before. Instead he looked as if he might try to hire out to ride the "rough string," in Cliff Moran's place.

# Chapter IX

The Tilden who rode up to Old Joe Deschamps' corrals one evening was a mighty different looking Tilden from the one who'd stumbled and fell in at the Ox Yoke cow camp near two months past. This new Tilden was on horseback and leading a pack horse, and at a distance, he looked like a sure enough cowboy.

There was no scary look on his face, nor puny cheeks. No shirt sleeves was a flapping, no bony elbows or knees was in sight, and a glance at his wrists and neck showed that he'd took on considerable tallow and muscle and tan. The look in his eyes had also went under a big change. It was the look of one who knows where he's at, where he's going, and with confidence of his getting there.

Old Joe took that all in as he came out to meet Tilden, but he was sort of puzzled, for he seen as he come near that here was a stranger in the country, and he wondered what was that stranger's idea of rigging up like a cowboy and going thru the country by his lonesome that way. Most of them he'd ever seen had a guide with 'em.

It would of been a real surprise to Tilden to know that the old timer seen thru him that way, for he thought he'd pass for a cowboy sure enough. He had the clothes on and everything, but he'd overlooked the fact that them was cowboy clothes and that somehow they don't seem to fit so good on a man that's growed up with a collar around his neck and creased clothes from there down. He might of put on a plain laborer's bib-overalls and get by as such, but with a cowboy's clothes it was different. It takes a cowboy to wear 'em, one raised in the saddle, and Tilden wasn't that.

His shaps' didn't hang right on him, his hat had the wrong slant, he didn't set up in his saddle, he didn't handle his reins right, and when he got off his horse he showed that he wasn't used to spurs and that low cut shoes had been on his feet a heap more than riding boots.

He done many other things which was a dead give away, but, being he didn't know of 'em, he went on a trying to act the part as much as he could. He had the spirit with him anyway, right inside of his chest, and that chest expanded so that that spirit wasn't all cramped.

And Old Joe made him feel at ease from the start. There was just a plain "howdy, Stranger," and a welcome smile, and if that old timer wondered it didn't show on his face, not any.

"Take your pack horse up to the house and leave your bed there," he says. "Then turn your horses out in the pasture over yonder. While you're doing that I'll scrape up something to put inside your belt."

Tilden was sort of set back at all the hospitality. He'd figgered on riding up to Old Joe and get to the point about his being able to stay with him first off, and tell him that he wanted to pay for his board, and for whatever trouble he might be, the price was no object and so on. But that old timer hadn't given him time to even get started on the subject. He hadn't asked him one question, where he was from, where he was going, or anything. And Tilden found himself doing nothing only what Old Joe had told him to do, that was to unpack, turn his horses to feed, and make himself to home.

Tilden wondered, as he went to unpacking and unsaddling, if everybody was took in the way he'd been, if all the folks in this big country kept the same open door as Old Joe or as was at the Ox Yoke camp. He'd offered to pay Baldy before leaving that camp, and he'd been surprised how Baldy had been took back by the offer. Queer country, he thought, and mighty fine, if all the folks in it are like that.

It was dark when Tilden headed for the two-roomed log house, and as he came nearer he heard Old Joe a humming on some old tune like to keep in harmony with the clatter of the dishes and pans. A lone candle was on the table and throwing the only light, and when Tilden stepped on the big stone slab by the door there was another greeting for him to "come right in and set right up."

"If you want to wash and comb your ha'r there's a basin and everything right there on the bench."

Tilden said "thank you" again. That's all he'd ever got to say since he come. And when, after he washed, he sat up at the table there was no more chance for him to say much then, only maybe "yes?" or "yes, sir." There was no room for comments of any kind, for Old Joe had took the floor as usual and started on to tell what all had accumulated and which needed airing since the last visitor come. That must of been quite a spell back.

As Old Joe went on a talking, first about the weather, then on what all he'd read in the papers and so on, Tilden remembered the Kid's words, how "Old Joe didn't get much company, and when anybody comes around he daggone near talks 'em to death." It was beginning to prove pretty true, but as Tilden listened he figgered if he was to be talked to death it wouldn't be such a hard death, for Old Joe was mighty interesting to listen to. He'd lived a long time and covered a heap of territory and had many experiences, all which Tilden would want to hear about, and his voice and talk didn't only sound good but there was a feeling about it that told of how welcome he was and how that welcome was mighty apt to last.

Tilden went on listening and eating. He went on listening some more as he helped Old Joe clear away the table, and on till his eyelids begin to droop for the want of sleep. Old Joe noticed that, and at the first hint he showed Tilden where he could spread his bed. Tilden remarked a little about his being tired and then crawled in. The candle burned for quite a spell after that, for Old Joe was reading, his second best to talking. But Tilden didn't know he'd stayed up, for, being wore out by the long ride of that day, it hadn't took him long to go to sleep.

But his sleep wasn't very sound. He woke up after a couple of hours, like for the want of air, and he wondered why, for the windows was open and even the door. He figgered maybe the reason of that was on account of his being in a strange place. That had a little to do with it, for the main reason was he'd been used to sleeping under the stars and have the night breeze blow by his ears, and coming into a house, no matter how big and airy it might be, would feel mighty stuffy after that.

Tilden didn't think that would be the cause of his restlessness because he wouldn't of believed that just a couple of months of outdoor sleeping would change him so quick. But there's where the trouble layed just the same, for a man, any man, gets used to sleeping out in the open mighty quick, a heap quicker than he can get used to sleeping indoors.

Tilden had a hint of that as he walked in the house the night before. It had struck him queer to have a floor under his feet, walls around him, and a roof over his head. He'd felt sort of strange in setting at a table, and cramped, like as if there wasn't room for him to crook his elbow on. He couldn't figger out the feeling none at all, and he just layed it to his being in a strange "camp." He would never thought that him, who'd spent all his life on sidewalks, between walls, and under roofs, could be made to feel strange in being inside again by just a couple of months of outdoor life.

He woke up many times during the night, and felt like he'd have to take his bed outside and sleep there, but he was afraid to disturb Old Joe, who was sleeping in the same room, and when the sun topped the eastern ridge it wasn't any too soon for him.

It was after a short restless snooze that his eyes opened again to stare at the rough board ceiling of the cabin. After a while he turned his head to look at Old Joe's bed. It was empty, and not hearing any sound that the old feller had started fixing up breakfast, he thought of just laying there a spell and sort of go over his plans.

But them plans of his didn't seem to want to come to the top right then. Instead he found his thoughts trailing along on the events of the past two months and from the time he first lost himself in the big country. Coming to Old Joe's place had stirred that up, and it seemed like, with all of that which he'd went thru, it was years instead of months, or long enough that he felt he always belonged here. Maybe that was on account of the strange life he'd bumped into and the way it all impressed him. Anyway, he hardly ever thought of his home territory or the folks back there, like as if that was now all strange to him, a life which he'd read of in some book.

He wondered at that. He wondered how come he thought oftener of the Kid, or Baldy, or Skip, who he'd just left and knowed only a short spell, than he did of any of the crowd he'd run with for so many years in and around his home city. He wondered how come he remembered the sayings of the cowboys and hardly any which he'd been brought up with. Was it that his interest for this was strongest, or was it because it was here he'd come to life again and made a stand to take a long new lease on it?

All them thoughts sort of stumped him, but there was one thing he did know, he knowed that it was here he begin to realize his uselessness. It was here he took heart and caught holt, and it was here he found a lead, not such a worth while lead in itself maybe, but a lead that would sure build him up in trying to accomplish, a lead that'd prove he'd be able to succeed in any other he'd set his mind to.

Tilden remembered the day when he sat on the knoll and first seen himself as he really was. He'd wondered then if there was enough left of him to build up on, and now it struck him queer how, in his interest to carry out his new made plans, he'd sudden forgot about that, and he was sort of surprised to realize, in comparing the way he felt then and now, that he'd built up so. His mind was clear, his confidence was up, and his body didn't seem to tire no more. A considerable change, he thought, from a month or so past.

A month or so ago, he'd never dared hit out by his lonesome, with two horses, and only the description of a mountain peak to go by. But he'd started out on this move with as much ease as if he'd just ordered a taxi to take him somewhere, and he'd guided his horse to Old Joe's corrals in pretty fair style.

From his bed on the floor, he begin looking around the room. What a change this was to his own room back home. This was all out of big logs and unplaned lumber. The ridge logs up above was a foot thru, some of the boards had sagged from many winters' heavy snows, the floor was warped, and there was no carpets, just plain unpainted boards. But there was a cleanliness about the room that he noticed, and even tho furnishings wasn't of the kind he'd been used to there was everything that was needed and all a setting to order.

Tilden wasn't comparing this with his own room. He never even thought of that room of his, and that was on account of his interest for this one. He just took it in for what it was, the same as he took in the country and the men, and he didn't compare, because there was so much here that drawed his interest that he'd sort of forgot all he'd been brought up amongst.

Tilden had come to life in a new world, seemed like, and he was beginning to live all over again, and he didn't wonder what there was about this new life that drawed him. He didn't wonder how come he liked this life that was rough in preference to the one he'd left, where all could be got by crooking a finger and pressing a button. He just went to living it for all he was worth and all with the one idea in mind. That was, to some day catch the black stallion. And this, what all he was seeing and experiencing, was on the trail that led to him.

The jingling of spur rowels stirred him out of them thoughts, and he was up and dressing as Old Joe came in the other room.

"Well, how's the young feller this morning?" says Old Joe, when he heard Tilden moving around.

The day started pretty well as the evening before had ended, with Old Joe still a talking. "I expect," he was saying, after the breakfast dishes was washed up, "that I'll have to go run in some horses this morning, but I'll be back about noon. So, you better rest up till I get back. You ain't in no hurry to go, are you?"

"No," says Tilden. He was anxious to tell him about his wanting to stay instead, but he had a hard time to bring himself to speak of that, somehow. Maybe the lesson he'd learned from Baldy about staying or overstaying made him hesitate. He didn't know that this was different than a busy cow camp. Anyway, Tilden put off speaking on the subject. What was worrying him most right then was if he'd be welcome to go with Old Joe to run them horses in.

"Sure," says Old Joe as Tilden finally asked him, "I'd be glad to have you. I always like company, and I'll loan you a good horse too."

Tilden was pleased, and he wished he'd give him some horse that'd buck, but he didn't know what a lot of territory he was taking in that wish or he most likely wouldn't be so strong for it. Old Joe took care of that tho. He knowed the minute Tilden rode up the evening before that that feller wasn't up to riding, and he gave him a horse according, a fat and gentle little buckskin which he used only to wrangle on and could be caught anywheres with a pan of grain.

Tilden was disappointed when he was told the horse was "plum gentle," but he cheered up at some more that was told him, which was that the horse was "sure a running fool, and a plum good horse."

"T'ain't often you find a right good horse that's gentle," says Old Joe as the two rode away, "but you're sure setting on one of them few now."

The horse did sure enough prove to be a good one, and a bunch of horses was no more than located when

Tilden of a sudden realized that he was *too* good. That is, he knowed his business of running horses too well, and Tilden had a mighty hard time to stay in the middle of him as that pony dodged around timber on the trail of Old Joe and the half wild horses. The horse done the work and Tilden was busy doing nothing but trying to stick to the saddle. He was just a sort of a decoy setting up there and he bobbed around like he might fall off any minute.

Somehow or other he managed to stay on till he was out of the timber, but he'd held the horse back a considerable, and when he got down to more level country and where he could see for a ways there was no sign of the horses or Old Joe, only a dust away off to the right.

But that dust told him enough, for he'd been in the country long enough now to know that it was raised by running hoofs and not by a whirlwind, and that if he was to make sure of finding Old Joe's place again he'd better keep tab of that dust. He gave the little buckskin his head on the trail of it, and the ride he made from then on was wilder than any he'd ever made at the Ox Yoke. Over rocky and brushy knolls he sailed, down acrost washes and dog towns, all at the same speed, and as it kept up, he got to gradually enjoy it, like if he was on the trail of the black stallion.

He was thinking of that as he put his horse up a knoll, but on reaching the top them thoughts soon went from his mind, for the dust he'd tried to catch up to had disappeared, and all at once. He let his horse lope down the other side while he wondered what to do. Then he noticed that the little buckskin wanted to run some more, like as if *he* knowed for sure where to go, and Tilden let him have his head again. There was chances that the horse did know. And sure enough, Tilden rode on over a couple of ridges and there, right below him, was Old Joe holding the bunch of milling horses.

"I kind of figgered I was going a little too fast for you," says Old Joe soon as Tilden got to within hearing distance. "This is a pretty rough country to run horses in, but I'll be going slower now, and if you'll just keep the ponies coming I'll take the lead on in."

Old Joe took the lead, and Tilden learned to his surprise that these spooky horses followed a man on horseback mighty well, if the man could stay in the lead of 'em. Of course, Tilden had to ride from one side to the other once in a while just to sort of keep reminding the horses there was a rider behind 'em, but as Old Joe had warned him, he didn't crowd 'em.

The corrals was reached in good time, and there Tilden seen some mighty skilful work in corralling range horses. These was most all unbroke and was nowheres as easy to corral as the remuda at the Ox Yoke had been, and if a rider wasn't at the right place at just the right time there wouldn't be no corralling 'em. There was too many snorty leaders that was ready to break away.

*Old Joe took the lead.*

Tilden just took the place of a fence post there. He'd learned at the round-up camp that he'd only be in the way and queer things at such a job. So he'd edged out to one side, and put all his attention on how Old Joe maneuvered around to get the bunch thru the corral gate. He was at last where he could watch a top hand work and right close.

There was some more learning for Tilden that afternoon, and he was all eyes, for Old Joe was branding some colts, strong little fellers and full of life and fight. Tilden wanted to help but he found himself just a staring at the ease and sureness that was in every move Old Joe made, wether it was roping, tying, or branding. He wondered at a man of his age still doing a work that needed so much skill and action. It seemed to be of no effort to him, but Tilden realized what there was to it, and he feared it would be many a day before he could rope a horse by the front feet, and get him down, and brand him in half the time and ease it took Old Joe.

But he would learn, he'd have to. And now, if he could stay with the old timer, he'd have the chance he was looking for.

It was after supper that night that he finally seen his way clear to speak on the subject of his staying. Old Joe hadn't said a word for five straight minutes and that way left an opening for Tilden.

"I guess you get pretty lonesome once in a while, in being here all by yourself," he says for a starter.

"Me?" Old Joe looked at Tilden sort of surprised. Then he smiled and shook his head. "No," he went on, "I never get lonesome. If I did I'd go where I wouldn't be."

"But you do like company, don't you?"

"Oh, yes, but that don't prove I'm lonesome without it."

"The reason I asked," says Tilden, sort of fidgeting around some, "is that I thought, I hoped, you wouldn't mind my staying here with you for a while. I . . . ."

"Why, sure," Old Joe cuts in, "you can stay here as long as you want and you're mighty welcome. I never get lonesome but I always like company and that's kind of scarce around here. So, if you're willing to batch with me I'll be durn glad to have you."

"But I want to pay for the trouble," Tilden grinned, "because there's lots of things I don't know and I expect I will be of trouble to you, and then there's the food and quarters. . . ."

"Yeh, such as they are, but don't talk about the pay even if you do burn the beans once in a while. I'll put up with that if you'll put up with my talking."

Tilden had liked Old Joe from the time he first set eyes on him, and before he was thru with this little talk he liked him a heap more. Only he wished he'd let him pay for his staying, it'd made him feel more like he had a right to, but he'd make up for that somehow by trying to be useful, like washing dishes and cutting the wood and such, and maybe there would be some other way come up which would give him the chance to even things to his liking.

Anyway, and as Old Joe told him to, Tilden went to making himself at home, and started on to making a hand of himself, around the kitchen at first, and then down to the corrals afterwards. He went out and helped Old Joe bring in a bunch of cattle one day. He helped him cut out a few, and then tried to help at branding, but he was pretty well lost at that last and he stuck close to the branding fire, where he could at least hand out the branding irons every time Old Joe called for one.

"Try your hand at wrassling this one," says Old Joe as he roped one of the smallest calves and brought him close to the fire. Old Joe had seen the look in Tilden's face and he thought of cheering him up some by letting him chip in on the work, and it seemed that he'd understood that look, for Tilden's face sure lit up, and he came towards the calf like a kid goes to a Santa Claus. The calf bellered and bucked at the end of the rope, and he bellered and bucked all the more as Tilden came near. Tilden slid his hand down the rope as he seen Old Joe do and went to reach over the calf for a flank holt, also exactly as Old Joe had done. But somehow, when he reached over, the calf wasn't there no more. Then, just that quick, the rope jerked his feet from under him. He was kicked in the stommack at the same time, and in the next half second that little calf, in running around him to get away, had him all wound up with the rope till, when the calf had no more rope to play on he was right on top of Tilden, and there he bucked and bellered some more.

Old Joe couldn't help but laugh at the sight, but Tilden didn't hear him, for all had happened so sudden that Tilden was still confused a lot. The calf stopped his bellering and bucking and stood plum still, he was taking another breath to start in again.

That was Tilden's chance. Somehow or other he seen it and he wasn't slow in taking it. He scrambled up, rope and all with him and he fell on the calf as if to squash him down with his weight. But his weight wasn't so very much as yet, and the calf, being of range stock, didn't squash worth a doggone. He took Tilden around and around, stepped on him often, and it looked for a while like the calf was going to win. But Tilden hung on to the rope, and once, when the calf had him down again, he grabbed the leg that was closest to his nose, his head was under the calf's belly, and when he straightened was when he finally upset Mr. Calf to lay.

"Pretty good for a starter," grinned Old Joe. And Tilden, looking thru his tangled foretop, grinned back at him.

Old Joe caught and wrassled the next calf. It was a good sized one, and he done it so easy that Tilden was

When the calf had no more rope to play on he was right on top of Tilden, and there he bucked and bellered some more.

again reminded of his own helplessness, but he wasn't going to let the thoughts of that down him, not no more. He watched Old Joe wrassle three more, and then asked for the next one.

That next one didn't get to make quite so much of a clown out of him, but when he finally got him down he was pretty well out of breath. Old Joe caught and wrassled another calf while Tilden rested up, and after that every second one was his, if it wasn't too big, till the branding was over for that day.

It was that way, day after day, that Tilden started breaking into the game. He rode out with Old Joe every chance he had and that was often. One day he'd help him round up a little bunch of cattle and try to hold 'em while the older man cut out what wasn't wanted. The next day it'd be horses, and once he was tickled pink when, finding one big unbranded calf, Old Joe told him to go ahead and rope him.

Tilden missed four throws, and Old Joe, fearing that the calf would get overheated in running, seen where he'd better rope him himself. He done that in quick time, and explained to Tilden, afterwards, why he butted in.

But Tilden had got that much practice anyway, even if he did miss, and maybe there'd come a time when he wouldn't miss, quite so much. He had a good chance to learn things with Old Joe, a heap better chance than he would ever had at the Ox Yoke "wagon," because there, with the big outfit, was no place for beginners. The big herds that was handled and the horses that was rode, all made it a mighty serious business, a work where there was room for none but experienced men.

With Old Joe it was different. He was used to handling his little herds by his lonesome anyway, and what wasn't done to-day could be done to-morrow. He was never pressed for time, and even tho Tilden was often more trouble to him than help, he liked his company, and he was getting so, as he noticed how he was so anxious to learn, that he began shoving little jobs his way. They was jobs that he could of done better himself and been a saving on his stock if he had, but he wanted to help the boy, and he took near as much interest in seeing him learn as the boy did in that learning.

Old Joe handled Tilden like he might of handled a promising colt, and, according to that, there was a great chance for him to be as good a cowboy as there'd been for the promising colt, which Old Joe broke many of, to turn out to be top cow horses. . . . Old Joe savvied.

Many a time he sent Tilden out to do some little job which he wondered at the boy being able to do, and no time was he disappointed, for he always kept on a trying. And if he did fail he never seemed to realize that he did. He never quit, and often Old Joe would have to ride up

186

*The big herds that was handled and the horses that was rode, all made it a mighty serious business, a work where there was room for none but experienced men.*

to him and smooth things over, but he'd never let him know that he'd tackled too much.

That way Tilden was learning, and fast developing a skill at what all he done that more than pleased Old Joe. But Tilden, himself, wasn't noticing any improvement much. He still felt mighty ignorant and helpless and he worked steady and mighty hard to overcome that. Every day he was down by the corrals, with a rope in his hands, or out with Old Joe after some horses or cattle, and always, wherever he went or whatever he done, it was with the idea in mind to master that "simple twist of the wrist" by which he could do the things Old Joe and the cowboys done, things he couldn't begin to do no matter how hard he tried.

He felt like he could ride pretty well now of course, and the last time he'd went to help run in a bunch of horses he hadn't been so far behind in none of that ride. But he didn't think that was so much to crow about. It hadn't been such a hard run as the others, and anyway he should of been right up and coming and kept alongside of Old Joe all the way in. What chance would he have following the black stallion, he kept a asking himself. Not much.

With such thoughts, there was times when he felt mighty disappointed in himself, and sometimes he wore such a disgusted look that Old Joe, noticing it, would have to grin. He understood that look.

"I'm thinking the young feller is too anxious," says Old Joe to himself one day as he watched Tilden practicing getting on and off a horse. The old timer shook his head, "But he's sure got grit, and that's what I like about him."

One morning Old Joe started to do a little fence fixing, and thinking that that wouldn't be of any interest to Tilden he asked him if, while he was gone, he wouldn't watch a pot of prunes which he'd just put on the stove.

"Keep 'em boiling for a couple of hours," he says as he started off, "and don't let 'em get too dry."

Old Joe was no more than gone when Tilden looked at the prunes to make sure they had plenty of water and then hit out for the pasture where his two horses was grazing with them of Old Joe's. He circled around 'em afoot and maneuvered till he got 'em all in the corral, and as these horses was used to being corralled every day he had no trouble there much. He closed the big gate, and then, mighty business like, he went to the log stable. A few seconds later he appeared at the door again and there was a rope in his hands.

He was going to rope a horse, or try to, but which one he was trying for was hard to tell, for his rope sailed towards one horse one time and another horse the next, and the loop would twist so every time that it'd been a puzzle for a horse to get his head inside of it if it had come his way. He throwed his rope twice and the loop didn't even catch air, for it closed every time. Queer, he thought, that his rope should do that. Why he was even a worse roper now than he'd been when he first started.

He studied his rope for a spell, carefully got the kinks out of it, and made a perfect loop flat on the ground. Then he picked it up as carefully, located the horse he wanted, and let it sail. It sailed on in fine style, so fine that he caught two horses at once, but as luck would have it, he didn't want neither of the horses he'd caught. They was two gentle, old work horses. His loop had went their way, and the horse he'd wanted had dodged and went another.

Tilden laughed. He should always laugh when things like this happened, and right away he set to building another loop, and that loop caught something too. It was a corral post this time, and the loop had sailed over the horses' heads to get to it. It was about then that he thought of something that made him drop his rope and started him a running for the house. He'd just thought of the prunes, and not any too soon, for when he lifted the lid the juice at the bottom of the pot was near as thick as molasses.

He put some more water on the prunes, stirred the fire and put in more wood, like he'd done things like that all his life, but he never gave no thought as to his learning there. In a short while he was back to the corral again and making another loop. This is what he was after to know.

And this time, when his rope sailed, it sailed true and over the head of the horse he wanted. It was the little "paint" buckskin he'd bought from Skip and which had brought him so much misery when he'd tried to ride him at the "wagon."

Yes, Tilden was going to try to ride that little horse some more. He'd never tried to ride him since that time at the outfit, and he'd been aching for another chance, and now that Old Joe was gone would be as good a time as he could find to try him again. There'd be nobody around to laugh at him if he got throwed, nobody to see how helpless he was or to coach him as to what to do. He'd do this all by himself, as a sort of practice for when he caught the black horse, and he wasn't going to get throwed either, he'd made up his mind to that.

He acted sort of reckless, as he often seen the cowboys do, while the little buckskin fought the rope that held him. And he even whistled a cowboy tune to show how little he cared how bad the horse was, like as if he was just another horse and to be rode the same as all the others was rode. He thought of Moran as he done this and that and he tried his best to imitate him.

But, somehow or other he couldn't handle this little horse near as easy as Moran handled even the biggest and most powerful outlaw in his string. He never seen Moran getting drug all around as this little buckskin was now doing with him. Tilden wanted to get peeved, but

191

he couldn't remember of Moran getting peeved at a bad horse, and so he tried to keep on whistling, as his boot heels missed holt after holt, and when the little horse finally stopped and faced him, he went on to whistling all the more. He'd need a lot of courage to compete against the wild look that was in that pony's eyes.

But this was a test he'd been looking for and wanting, and if he couldn't get to handle and ride this little pony he'd better hike back to where he came and trust to luck for his keeping. So he thought as he gritted his teeth and went to put the saddle blanket on the slick back of the buckskin.

The first attempt wasn't so good, even as determined as Tilden was, for he missed that slick back by over six feet. So then he went more easy, and after a considerable lot of maneuvering around, he finally got the blanket to where it belonged.

Next was the saddle, that would be more complicated, and according to that it would take more time and care, but Tilden kept a trying to act as reckless as the circumstances would allow him, and he whistled some more as he drug the riggin near the horse and prepared to swing it on top of the blanket that covered the quivering back.

The horse stood spraddle legged like as if ready to quit the earth, for he knowed what was coming, and he wasn't expecting to be there when it did come. And sure enough, when Tilden lifted the saddle and marked the distance to the buckskin's back he seemed to all at once miscalculate by a whole lot, and instead of finding a back to lay the saddle on, he found a rump. The little pony had gone "south."

Tilden had to go look at the prunes and put more wood in the stove a couple of times more before he finally managed to get the saddle on the little buckskin's back to stay. By then he wasn't whistling no more. But he'd learned many things about saddling a horse that's a little spooky, and he couldn't found a better teacher than that little buckskin was, for even tho he was spooky and *acted* bad there really wasn't a mean hair in him. And that was a good thing too.

Next on the program was to get up in the middle of the saddle, but, being the little horse was good to get on to, he didn't worry so much about that as he did about staying in the saddle after he got in it. The saddle looked awful slick too. But what did that matter? Tilden begin a whistling again and looked the direction Old Joe had gone to make sure he wasn't coming back as yet, and then he pulled his hat down tight, and pulled up his shaps' a little, just like he'd seen the cowboys do before getting on a bad horse. In the next second he'd gathered his reins, stuck his foot in the stirrup, and still whistling away like his life depended on it, he climbed on.

The little buckskin stood plum still while all of that went on, and he cocked his ears back at Tilden, like as if waiting for the signal to start in. Finally, after Tilden was well set, the signal came. It was just a timid little jab of one spur, but that was enough and a plenty. The little buckskin let out a squeal, and of a sudden his head disappeared from Tilden's sight.

With the disappearance of the pony's head there came a hump in his back which took the saddle up quite a ways and tipped it near on end, and then a jolt, like as if the earth raised up too sudden. Tilden was loosened at the first one of them jolts. He was still looser at the second one, and when the horse went up the third time and the cantle hit him, he didn't feel that third jolt. He'd come down all by himself, and when he hit the ground he faced East and the horse faced West.

Tilden got up, looked for his hat, and then looked at the horse. There was a sort of puzzled expression on his face, but that's all it was, no doubt showed there yet. He followed the horse around the corral till he got him cornered and then he caught him by one of the dragging reins.

He got on him a second time, and that performance was pretty well the same as the first one only it was still shorter, for Tilden lasted just two jumps. The little buckskin was getting warmed up on the subject.

And so was Tilden. He wasn't whistling no more as he got on him the third time. There was a scowl on his face as he climbed him again the fourth time, and when he tried him the fifth time the scowl had vanished and a determined look took its place. The determined look was still there at the sixth performance, and a grin also begin to appear.

"Better call that off for a spell now. It's about noon and I reckon we better gather up a bait."

Old Joe had come up on Tilden as that feller was picking himself up for the sixth time, and at the sound of the voice he straightened up pretty quick. He hadn't wanted to have Old Joe catch him at this, for he well remembered what had happened at the Ox Yoke, with Baldy.

He didn't know that it would be different with Old Joe, that this old timer didn't have the same kind of responsibility that Baldy had, and he didn't know what to expect. He looked at him like he did expect something sure enough, but that look soon disappeared for a heap pleasanter one when the old feller spoke some more.

"I'll show you how you might be able to ride that horse after we eat," he says.

"That will sure be fine," says Tilden as the two started for the house, "and . . ." but he didn't go on with whatever he'd wanted to say. He'd just thought of something else and started on a high run towards the house. When he got there the fire was out and lifting the lid of the pot he seen what was left of the prunes. They'd burned down to what looked like a speck of hard tar.

## Chapter X

Out on a stretch of many miles of broken and rough range land was a tall peak, a peak that shot up like a lookout for the big country that was around, and it was near as tall as the range of mountains that could be seen away to the north. On the highest point of that peak was a man. He'd been there since the sun come up, and now, as the sun was close to setting, he still kept his place like as if he'd took root up there.

In his hands was strong field glasses, and the way he kept a looking thru them, along with the worried expressions that appeared on his face once in a while, showed that he wasn't up there just to admire the scenery. And sure not, there was a dust out there which he seemed awful interested in keeping track of. Under that dust was little bobbing objects, and he'd kept a watching them bobbing objects till it seemed like he couldn't see no more. Them bobbing objects had went around the peak twice during the day, in a big twenty mile circle each time, and now they was going at it a third time, always one a trying to catch up with the other, and at last it looked like that might happen. The object in the lead seemed to be lagging, and that's what brought the worried expressions to the man who watched, for that man was Tilden, and the moving object in the lead was the black stallion, the horse he'd set his heart to catching himself and which now was threatened to be caught by somebody else.

"Why didn't that black horse leave the country instead of going around in a big circle," he wondered, "and staying in the path of the fresh relay horses the rider had stationed every few miles." He'd heard how that horse could never be relayed on that way on account he was always leaving the country, but now it seemed like there was no getting him out of it. And Tilden was mighty fretful, because now it looked like the rider was catching up to him and it wouldn't be long when a rope would stop him in his run for freedom.

Tilden was up on his feet, and he could hardly stand still by the fear of that happening. What if the rider did catch that horse? . . . That was a question that held a powerful lot, and the answer held a heap more than he dared think of.

The black horse went to lagging more and more and the rider kept a gaining, and as Tilden watched he near stopped breathing, for the rider was only a rope's length behind. He seen the rider uncoil his rope and make a loop, seen him whirl it a couple of times and then . . . Tilden couldn't look no more. He sat down and the glasses hung heavy in his hand. He stared not seeing, and he couldn't think.

He sat that way for quite a spell, sort of vacant like, and then feeling the weight of the glasses he raised 'em up for a last look, like as if he'd just as well know the worst and have it over with. He stared thru the glasses for a minute, then he stood up, not believing his eyes. Out a mile or so away and running along a narrow trail on the side of a steep badland ridge was the black stallion. Tilden had raised his glasses just in time to see the horse make a wonder of a flying leap acrost a wide and deep cut in the trail. The rider would never try to make that, he thought, but the rider did try to make it and never even hesitated, and that jump came near being the last one for him and his horse, because his horse, being tired, hadn't been able to clear the gap as he should. His hind feet had struck only crumbling dirt, and it looked for a spell like both would tumble over backwards into mighty deep space.

Tilden wasn't watching the stallion no more about then, he was watching the rider's horse struggling to get a footing on the trail, and not a natural breath did he take till, after what seemed a powerful long time, the horse clawing at the earth finally got a solid footing. . . . When he did look for the black stallion again that horse

And that jump came near being the last one for him and his horse, because his horse, being tired, hadn't been able to clear the gap as he should. His hind feet had struck only crumbling dirt, and it looked for a spell like both would tumble over backwards into mighty deep space.

was half a mile in the lead and hitting straight out of the country.

Tilden jumped up and down like a kid. "Great horse, great horse," he laughed and hollered. "He'll never get him now."

And Tilden was right. The black horse seemed to find new speed and hit straight out and away from where the rider had his other relay horses stationed. One more fresh horse might of done the work, but as it was now the black stallion still had too much speed for the rider's tired horse, and all that rider could do was to pull up and go back.

Tilden seen the rider stop and turn. Then he went on watching the black horse again and a mighty pleased grin was on his face as he did. It was a pleasant sight to see that black horse lope on free that way. And not only that, what was most pleasant was that hopes came to Tilden as he watched. He'd been on the top of that peak four different times when that horse was being chased. They'd been long and hard runs, and after each run, when the black seemed to tire some, he'd just lined out away from the relay strings. Twice he'd went different directions, and now this made it twice that he went the *same* direction.

That's what Tilden had been anxious to find out, if that horse would ever go twice in the same direction. If he did, that would prove that he'd do that a third time and off and on every time he was run. It'd also give a hint of some regular territory he'd hit for whenever he was hard pressed, and that territory is what Tilden wanted to find.

The sun had set when he picked his way down the side of the peak to where his horse was tied. He got in the saddle and turned him towards camp, hardly realizing he was doing so, for his mind was all on perfecting the plans which he'd made, and now that there was hopes of them plans working out he went into the thick of 'em and for all he was worth.

He was still in the thick of 'em when, topping a rise, he met up with a rider. It was the rider who had been after the black horse, and Tilden, recognizing him on sight, was mighty surprised to see that it was Cliff Moran. But if Tilden was surprised Moran was more than puzzled, for even tho he recognized him after a spell he couldn't account for the transformation none at all. He'd never seen anybody change so in his life, and from a weak excuse of a human to a well set up rider.

"Yes," he says, after the howdys was over, "I've heard about you staying with Old Joe, but I didn't know if it was true or not. I didn't think you'd stay this long."

"I like it here," says Tilden.

"You sure *must* like it, and it looks like the country is more than agreeing to that. But you're kind of far from home just now ain't you? . . . better come over and camp with me."

"Thanks, but my camp is up at a spring not far from here."

Moran squinted at him. "Still got your mind set on catching the black stud, I see."

"Yes, but I'm not going to try for a while yet."

"I wouldn't try at all if I was you, not according to the way he slipped away from me to-day."

"Maybe you should have had some salt with you," says Tilden, grinning. "I hear the only way he can be caught is by putting a little grain of it on his tail."

The two riders rode on each toward their own camp. "He's snapping out of it pretty good," thought Moran, "and in another year or so I wouldn't be too surprised if he did catch that black stud." Then he laughed, a little.

Tilden reached his camp, picketed his horse, seen that his other horses had new picket grounds, and then went on to cook himself a bait of bacon, rice, and flapjacks in near as good a style as anyone used to it. And he really was getting used to it, for he'd been in the country and right amongst the thick of that life for a year now, and over a year, by two months. He'd passed the summer with Old Joe Deschamps, also that fall and winter. When spring come he was still in the country with him, and now he was going on his second summer, and right in the same country.

Right now, at his camp, he wasn't over forty miles from Old Joe's place, and that's about the furthest he'd ever been from it. He'd come here and camped by this spring often tho, ever since one time, the fall before, when him and Old Joe came to it and camped while hunting some stock horses which, was suspicioned, had been appropriated by the black stallion.

It'd been two days later when, climbing on top of the tall peak, Old Joe showed Tilden a little bunch of horses on a knoll below.

"That's him now," Old Joe had said. By "him" he'd meant the black stallion. "And doggone his hide, I wish I had time, I'd sure give him a merry chase."

Tilden camped by the spring and came to the peak many times that fall, alone, and always with hopes of getting a close look at the black horse, but in all the times he came he'd only got two far away glimpses of him, and once, when spotting a bunch of horses from that peak, and taking near a whole day to sneak up on 'em, he'd been pretty disappointed to learn that he'd been trailing the wrong bunch. The black horse wasn't in that one. What's more, in maneuvering around thru the junipers to get close to the bunch, he'd forgot to spot any landmarks, and he'd got lost, so badly lost that it was many days before he found his way back, long days when he got pretty hungry and thirsty. In that time he'd learned to shoot a little for his living, and the bit of teaching Old Joe had given him in manipulating the shooting iron had a chance to develop some more by necessity.

He'd lived on sage-hen and jack rabbit which he'd cooked over roaring fires. They was more scorched than cooked, but he hadn't knowed as yet how cooking could be done without pots and out on an open fire that way. Anyway, it sure had all tasted good, and he'd got a heap of satisfaction to find that he was making a go of it in the wild country, even tho he did go mighty hungry at times.

That experience wouldn't of been so bad, only, on his second day of aimless ramblings, he'd lost his horse. He hadn't picketed him right and one of the knots come loose. It was then he'd appreciated a horse for the first time in his life, and not only because the horse was useful to ride either. He'd found that a horse was a lot of company and kept a feller from feeling so all alone, specially when bedding down for the night.

He'd tried to track him the next day and only got lost some more. He'd realized that when, finally giving the horse up as gone, he tried to get back to where he'd left his saddle. There'd been some cooked rabbit in the pockets of that saddle too, but he hadn't been able to find his way back to it, not as much as he'd circled and hunted.

It'd been pretty lonesome rambling from then on, and sort of aimless, but not near as scary, nor was he near as helpless and weak as he'd been that first time over a year past when the train had first left him in the big country. He'd been more cool headed, and when he seen an object he'd most always knowed what it was. Then again, the cowboy religion he'd picked up at the Ox Yoke camp had seemed to hold him up a considerable. He'd already found good use for that many times before and he'd got to be a mighty firm believer. He'd grinned often at the fix he was in, and kept a saying to himself that this was a good lesson, how he'd ought to knowed better and so on, and he'd kept a clear head and learned instead of getting excited.

But it'd been a mighty tired looking feller who'd stumbled up to the steps of a ranch house one day. A grizzled old cowman had greeted him at the door and told him to come in, and to Tilden's surprise, he learned that he'd drifted right in Rita Spencer's home. She'd fixed him up something to eat, all with her own hands. And then as she and her dad kept him company he'd told 'em how he got lost and so on, and he'd grinned about it, like to sort of apologize for being such a greenhorn.

The girl had smiled a little too, but, as pretty a smile as it had been, he hadn't liked the meaning back of it. There'd been too much sympathy, like as if he'd been a child who'd burned his finger.

But he'd liked the way she'd listened to what little he'd felt like saying. He'd wanted to say a whole lot and get her to say more too, but feeling as insignificant as he did then he'd been more for going on and not so much for talking. It'd seemed like this girl always seen him when he was the least proud of himself, like the first time when she run her horse between him and the mad cow.

He'd been made to stay there that night, for the reason, as her dad had said, that it was a long day's ride back to Old Joe's place, and when morning came, and he was staked to a horse and saddle, along with directions on how to get to the other end, all from the girl, he'd sort of lost a lot of his uneasiness. He'd got acquainted some, and on his way back to Old Joe's he'd never once thought of the black stallion.

He'd seen the girl twice more that year, once when her and her dad camped at Old Joe's place for a night, and once again by her lonesome on the range where she'd been hunting horses. The last time he'd seen her had stuck in Tilden's memory pretty well all that winter. She'd invited him to come over to the ranch whenever he happened to be near. Of course that'd been just a custom of the country, but she didn't have to invite him at all, did she?

Tilden didn't get to happen to be near the ranch none at all, and he'd often wished some of Old Joe's stock would of strayed that way so he could get there without making it a plain visit. He hadn't liked the idea of making a plain visit because he couldn't see where he had a license to, him amounting to so little.

So, he'd let the visit ride till a chance come along. None had come, and as it was he'd kept pretty close to the place and put all his energy to making the most of

He'd seen the girl twice more that year, once when her and her dad camped at Old Joe's place for a night, and once again by her lonesome on the range where she'd been hunting horses.

every bit of learning the old bachelor could hand him. He'd been very good at that learning, and he couldn't of found a better teacher than Old Joe was. Consequences is, when Tilden got lost again that winter, he'd wandered around just one day and a night, he didn't lose his horse either this time. And he'd finally found his way back without straying to another ranch nor having anybody steer him. He wouldn't of minded tho if he had strayed towards Rita Spencer's home once more.

He'd finally got so he could set that little buckskin too that winter. That is, nine times out of ten, for that little horse kept a bucking every time Tilden got on him, and that young feller was sure of practice whenever he caught him, which was often enough.

He'd also got steady practice on other things that mixed in steady, such as roping or wrassling husky calves and such like, not mentioning hundreds of other things which all went into the makings of him. Old Joe had always been right there to help and coach him and with such a teacher, and a pupil so willing and anxious to learn, there would be but one result.

"I think you've got it in you," Old Joe had told him one day. "That is," he'd went on, "if you stay with it."

Tilden had been mighty pleased at that, and not at all slow in assuring him that he sure would stay with it. Then was when he'd told Old Joe why he was so strong on learning the game. He'd told him of his plans in catching the black horse. Old Joe had grinned, but he didn't make fun of him because, somehow, he'd had a hunch of what all that might mean to him. The boy had talked of his past and made a few slips off and on, and Old Joe wasn't at all of the kind who took a long time to understand. He'd understood more when Tilden had refused his offer to help in catching the stallion.

"No," Tilden had said, "I want to catch him all by myself, and my main reason for that is to see if I can."

Old Joe had been for the boy more than ever from then on and he'd done his best to teach him the game. But in his teaching the boy that game, he'd been careful not to let him think that he was doing anything that would lead to catching the black horse. Tilden had been sensitive about anything like that. So, Old Joe had to be sort of underhanded in his teachings. He'd showed Tilden how to trail stock, and as the two rode together, he'd kept a telling of their ways. He'd showed him how a feller can keep from getting lost in any country. "Just keep a looking back over your shoulder every once in a while," he'd said, "and get acquainted with the country behind you. Then spot a few land-marks now and again and keep a spotting 'em."

Tilden had been out every day of that winter, most of the time with Old Joe, feeding what stock needed it and riding out to keep an eye on this outside stock, sometimes bringing in more to be fed. Once in a while he'd ride out alone to look for weak stock that way, and he'd learned many things while handling 'em.

When spring came, Old Joe had took a four-horse team and wagon and gone to town for a supply of grub. He'd done the same thing the fall before, and each time, on asking Tilden if he wanted to come along, the old timer had been surprised how the boy hadn't been at all interested. Only thing was he'd need a few things, such as clothes and so on, and if Old Joe would get them for him, he'd rather stay and take care of the place.

So Old Joe had gone on alone as usual, and Tilden had used up that time to perfect a throw with a rope, or see if he could ride the little buckskin without touching the saddle horn. He'd had a failing to do that.

With Tilden so anxious to learn that way the winter had gone by pretty fast. Spring come before he'd knowed it, and summer, with all its riding and promises of new experiences, was going by pretty good too. Too good, for he wanted to have the black stallion as his before fall come, and it wasn't so far away now.

As he set by the fire of his camp that night, after he'd met Moran, he stared at the flames and went to figgering on the different ways on how that black horse might be caught. He didn't know of many ways as yet, for even tho he'd found out a considerable about catching wild horses by watching the other fellers run 'em, he'd never really started out to catch one himself, not any. But with his figgering, the main thing was the saving time, how to catch the horse as soon as possible and before somebody else did catch him. Moran hadn't been far from doing that to-day.

He had one way mapped out but that would take time, maybe two months, and the only other way he knowed of was to relay on him as Moran did. But he couldn't do that, for one thing he didn't have the good horses necessary to relay with. Then again, that seemed useless, for that horse, when a rope threatened to slip up on him, always seemed to hit for new territory, all excepting the last time, which was when he took the same direction twice.

That came back to Tilden once again as he'd tried to think of other and quicker plans, and this time it stuck, even if catching him that way would take two months, and even tho he wasn't at all sure of catching him after that. He'd have to take that chance for it was the only way he could think of.

He was up at daybreak the next morning, and his outfit all packed and all ready to ramble by sunup. He was riding one horse and leading two, and the horse he was riding was none less than the little buckskin which had bucked him off so often.

But the ride put up on him this early morning showed that he'd won out at last and quite some time back, for he didn't seem worried much if the horse did buck, and not once did he touch the saddle horn.

*He was riding one horse and leading two, and the horse he was riding was none less than the little buckskin which had bucked him off so often.*

After the little buckskin had his fun, Tilden lined him out in pretty fair shape, and picking up the lead rope of his other two horses he went to cutting for tracks. Luck was with him too, for there'd been a shower the afternoon before and the fresh track of the black horse would show pretty well on the half bare soil. His intentions was to find that black horse's tracks, and follow 'em till they led him to his hiding place, if he had one.

He run acrost the tracks a half a mile or so from his camp, and the sight of 'em meant a heap more to Tilden than anything he'd ever glimpsed at for a long time. It was the first he'd ever glimpsed of that black horse's tracks when he could be sure of 'em being his. He got off his horse and studied one after another of the hoof prints. They looked like they'd been make by iron hoofs, for not a nick showed in them prints, only that of a smooth hard hoof, and he'd never seen one so round and perfect.

No prospector ever studied a gold ledge any closer than Tilden studied them hoof prints, and no gold ledge ever meant as much to any prospector as them hoof prints did to Tilden. It'd been over a year now since he'd first heard of the black stallion, a whole year of steady hoping and doubting and working. And to no end, only to some day be able to put his hand on the slick hide of that black horse. Now he seen one of his hoof prints at last, and he didn't remember of anything ever bringing him so much of a thrill.

Leading his horses, he followed the trail of the black on foot, like if he was afraid he might lose sight of 'em if he was mounted. He didn't think that he'd never catch up to him on foot that way, but he wouldn't of cared if he had thought. He just wanted to glimpse them tracks good and close and on and on, and he had no eyes for anything else as he wound around the junipers and pinons and followed the tracks up and up.

Finally he mounted again, spotted a few landmarks and took in the lay of the land around him. He held his horse still while doing that. After a spell he reined the little buckskin on the trail of the black horse, and there was a happy look on his face as he rode.

He followed up on the trail of him for three days, and without ever getting a glimpse of the black. But that was all right, he didn't expect to, and all he wanted to learn was if the black had a hiding place or what country he'd got thru in his running away from his usual range.

Them three days took Tilden thru quite a scope of country. He crossed mountains, badlands, and brakes, and always, when he made camp for the night at some spring, the tracks of the black showed he'd been there and Tilden would take it up again early the next morning.

The horse fed as he went and he'd hardly seemed to ever stop only to drink. It was towards evening of the third day when Tilden, still on the trail of the black and topping a high mountain pass, stopped his horse to try and spot some of the back-trail's landmarks. There was one away to his left which he recognized. It was the sharp peak of a mountain that bordered the range where the black had been running that summer. Then, as he looked back at the country thru which he'd come he seen that he'd made a half circle in following the black horse's trail. He recognized one long juniper covered ridge which he'd rode along onto, and then to the left of it a few miles was a high flat topped butte which he wondered at. He'd seen that butte before, before these last few days. And then, as he kept a wondering, it all came to him. Right at the foot of that butte was where Rita Spencer lived. It was the butte he'd headed for that time he was lost.

Tilden grinned at the memory of that. It had seemed quite awhile ago. And then he thought of Rita. He hadn't seen her since the fall before. Maybe he'd drop by and see her on the way back. He'd sure like to, but, right now the black horse stood first, for many reasons.

He stayed on the trail of him another day. It'd been hard trailing that day too, for the horse, feeling safer, had stopped to feed more, and his trail wound around considerable, sometimes mixing in with that of other horses. But Old Joe had given him a few pointers on what to do when tracks mixed in that way. That was to know the general direction the animal would be taking, and then ride right on thru the mixed tracks and cut for the others afterwards.

Tilden had got to be quite a hand at that, the same as he'd got to be quite a hand at many other things. Seldom would he have to circle much if he did happen to lose the tracks he was following, and at the end of the fourth day he'd got so he'd see tracks in his sleep, round smooth tracks made by a hoof that didn't have a nick.

It was on the morning of the fifth day that Tilden left off following the black horse's trail and started back towards home, and he felt some disappointed to learn that the black horse didn't seem to have no certain territory to hide in. He was sure of that, because the night before he seen by that horse's tracks that he was heading back to the range where he'd been run out of. By them tracks he also seen that the horse was taking his time and feeding and resting. Maybe it would be quite a few days yet before he could be seen in "The Big Basin," and a few days more before he found the bunch of mares which he'd appropriated from Old Joe's stock horses, but he was coming back sure enough. Then somebody would run him some more and he'd fool that somebody by quitting the country again.

Tilden sure hoped for that last to happen, and he also hoped that the horse would never quit coming back even if rider after rider did make it hard for him to stay in the country. But he worried, because that horse had the reputation of ranging pretty well where he happened to be, and it hadn't mattered where much, so long as no riders bothered him. The last year or so had been the only time he'd stayed in one country so long, and as Old Joe had guessed, the reason for that was the mares, Old Joe's mares which had been raised close to home, and they was hard to drive away.

But even as it was, with the horse always coming back to the country, a feller could never tell when he'd get tired of being chased and go to leaving it for good. And what's more, a feller could never guess how that horse was going to run one day from the next, and for that reason he couldn't be caught by relay strings and no trap could be set for him to run into because he couldn't be made to turn. He was too fast, and he never went in the same direction twice. Not till that day when Tilden took up his trail.

There was chances that he would come the same way again, but anybody knowing that horse would never bank on it. There was more chances of him leaving the country than to ever make the mistake of going over the same place too often when being chased. Tilden knowed the horse pretty well by now and he thought of that. If the horse had a hiding place that would of given him the confidence that he'd more or less take the same trail to it while getting away, but that pony was too wise to have a hiding place, for he knowed there wasn't such a place nowheres, and that it'd be found out if he went there more than once.

His freedom had lasted because he'd never ranged or run in any perticular place, not till the last year. Tilden got to fearing that he might be easier caught on that account, maybe too easy. But as he thought on that it wasn't long when he begin to grin.

If Tilden ever used his head before in his life it had been just easy as compared to the way he was using it now. He'd made camp on top of the long juniper covered ridge which he'd rode along on top of a couple of days before while tracking the black horse. There was no water up there, but he'd watered his horses at the spring below and filled his canteen, and being there was better feed on top for his horses he'd decided to make a "dry camp." He could study the country better from up there too.

But Tilden was mighty careful as he made camp on top of the tall ridge not to be anywheres near the tracks the black horse had made, because he sure wanted that horse to come by there again and often, and as Old Joe had told him in an off hand way one day, a wild horse will turn and never come back at the sight or smell of a camp fire. Even a lightning-burnt tree will make him suspicious and turn him. Tracks don't matter so much because the rain or wind blots 'em out pretty quick, but a feller shouldn't leave any rubbish where he's camped and should bury all the leavings.

The safest thing to do was to camp away from where a feller would want wild horses to come, and that's what

Tilden did. He could do that and still stay on the ridge for it was near a quarter of a mile in width. He'd cooked his evening meal, made away with it, and then went up on a high rock formation which he'd camped close to. From that rock sticking up quite a ways above the tallest juniper, Tilden could see for many miles around, and not only that, but he could see every edge of the ridge he was on.

The ridge was about a mile long, and Tilden sizing it up, seen that the junipers was awful thick on both sides of it. There was a lot of dry ones too, and on top of the ridge there was very few of the cedars. The top of that ridge was just the kind of a place a suspicious wild horse would want to run along on, he thought. It was no wonder the black horse had took it.

He kept on a sizing up the ridge, and using his head as he was, it wasn't so very long when some sort of idea begin to take shape up there. The new idea sort of originated from the first plans he'd made, and that had been to find the black horse's hiding territory, then build a big tall fence around it, leaving a big opening for the horse to come into without his knowing, then close it before the horse could come out. He'd figgered on having that fence take in at least two miles of land both ways, and after the horse got in he was going to run him around in there till he could haze him in a corral he'd build in a corner.

That idea might of worked out all right but it would of been mighty expensive if carried out so it'd be successful, for the fence would of had to been made of heavy double weight woven wire, barb wire that would of cut such as the black stallion to shreds. Then, that fence would had to be at least eight feet high, posts every few feet and deep in the ground, all well hid. Tilden had sort of figgered on all of that, and even tho he thought the idea seemed to be sort of wild, he wasn't going to let that stop him. He wanted that black horse, and all that kept him from carrying that plan thru was that the black horse had no such hiding place which he could fence up that way.

He kind of laughed at that idea now, for he'd got to know better. But just the same, being that idea could stand such heaps of improvements, he'd kept on working from it till, now, something better was beginning to crop out. He stared at the dry junipers that was all along both edges of the ridge, they looked like they wanted to tell something. After a while, nothing definite coming to his mind, he got down off the tall rock and started walking thru the trees, and then it all came to him in a flash. As he was walking along, thinking, he'd come up against a few dead junipers all leaning and one holding up the other. There was no going thru them, and there's where the idea struck him, what a fence they'd make.

He felt of their dry branches which stuck out at all angles. They was sharp and stiff, like so many bayonets, and then Tilden remembered how, when he was running horses with Old Joe, his horse hadn't wanted to go near any of them dead trees. The loose horses also had given them lots of room.

He walked along the edge of the knoll to take in an estimate of how many of them dead junipers there was. There seemed to be a plenty of 'em, more than he would ever need, and all within easy reach. He yanked at one of 'em and he was surprised how easy it was to pull up. The rotted roots had no holt much in the gravelly dirt. The trees was light, and just to sort of see what could be done he lined a few up into the kind of a fence he'd want. That turned out a heap more than satisfactory, for the stiff dry limbs, like the prongs of elk horns, seemed to've growed to grab a holt with one another and lock.

In half an hour, Tilden had over a rod of fence up. It wasn't a fence that would stand the weight of a wild horse if such would hit it, but no wild horse would ever hit that, they're too wise to the sharpness of them limbs. And as it was, it was a better fence than any woven wire could of made. It averaged eight feet all along, and as Tilden went on top of the ridge to look down at it, he seen how well it blended in with the other trees. The dead junipers didn't at all look as if they'd been set there for any purpose, and mixing in with the live trees and other dead ones that was on the ground or standing up, no horse would ever suspicion that a fence was there till he come alongside of it.

It was long after dark when he hit back to his camp and crawled into his blankets, and it was quite a spell later before he could get to sleep. When he did it was with a vision of a long ridge flanked on both sides with a well hid juniper fence, and right between, on top of that ridge, was a long-maned black horse a loping along and making the vision complete.

# *Chapter XI*

"You sure ain't much company for this old man any-more, Bert," says Old Joe, as Tilden was making ready to leave again the very next day after he'd come to the place. "Here you been gone about ten days now, you keep me company a few hours, and then you're rarin' to go again."

Old Joe acted like he'd been neglected something awful, but there was a grin back of his words, and Tilden, or Bert, as Old Joe called him, didn't know for a spell wether to take him serious or not. He thought maybe the old feller really was missing him a whole lot. And he thought right, for Old Joe did miss him. He'd took a mighty strong liking for the boy, and staying away like Tilden had, had made the old timer sort of keep looking for him. But he knowed what the boy was after, and he was more than with him in hoping and coaching him along so's he'd win out.

"Now, don't forget," he says, changing the subject, while he stuffed some "huckydummy" and a jar of home-made tomato preserves in the "aparejo." "Don't forget to put the stockade corral posts in plenty deep, and you better take them two cow hides that's in the shed to wrap around and draw 'em together at the top. Just soak 'em up over night and cut 'em around and around in one long strip. They make a corral strong, and you'll sure need it that way when you get your black horse in there. As far as the wings to the corral is concerned them dead junipers, stood up, will make a good fence and they'll hold him, unless he's crowded too much."

It was late that night when Tilden reached the spring at the upper end of the long ridge. He watered his horses, filled his canteen and rode back to make camp a few hundred yards away from the spring.

From early the next morning Tilden started mapping out as to where he should build his trap, for that's what it would be, a wild horse trap. Not of the kind with long wings on the sides which horses are run into, but more of the kind where a horse would go in of his own accord, without his knowing, and while he's trying to make a get a way. Old Joe had drawed him a few plans once on how he built his traps. But Tilden, wanting to feel free of any coaching, had mapped out different plans, his own, and the way he went to laying this one showed that he'd improved a considerable in his knowledge of wild horses. This one he had in mind, when built, would trap a wild horse sure enough. The only thing was, would the wild horse he wanted ever come this way again?

Tilden didn't want to think about that as he set to building the trap. He knowed that no man was ever sure of catching any wild horse till he had his rope on him. Even then the rope might break, and many other things can happen which all has to be chanced on. With him, he'd have to take the chance of the horse ever coming up on the long ridge again after a chase, and going into the trap if he did come. He'd given all of this a lot of thought, a powerful lot more thought than any cowboy would have the time to put on any wild horse. For, with Tilden, he'd be catching a heap more than just a wild horse.

The proof of that was in the way he went to work building the trap. To watch him, a feller would of thought that he'd fell in the neighborhood of a snake den and started in to kill a few hundred of 'em. Big dry cedars was uprooted and drug to be stood up and entangled with the others in the making of the fence. And the way he kept the weathered side on the inside of the trap showed that his work was also being done with a lot of care. He knowed that a rotted limb sticking up would be suspicioned by the wild horse. It'd show that something had been disturbed or built, and that would be a plenty to turn the wild one before he got well into the trap.

He was working along one day, at his usual gait, when, stopping a minute to take a breath, he heard

*No man was ever sure of catching any wild horse till he had his rope on him. Even then the rope might break, and many other things can happen which all has to be chanced on.*

the sound of running hoofs. They sounded like they was coming along the ridge, and he wondered if his saddle horses hadn't broke their hobbles and got stampeded some way. Only the sound came from the wrong way for them. For some reason or other which couldn't be accounted for, unless it was just a plain hunch, he run up on the ridge, ducked behind a big live juniper, and squinted thru the branches at the long open stretch.

He could see a dust amongst the scattered junipers on the ridge. The sound of running hoofs was plainer and plainer. Sage brush was crackling, pebbles was a scattering. He heard a heavy breathing, and then in a cloud of dust, came an apparition that just about took Tilden's breath away from him.

It was the black stallion, hide covered with sweat and acting a little tired. But, with long flowing mane and tail, rippling muscles under a smooth hide, and fire in his eyes, he was a picture that made Tilden feel mighty privileged to just be able to stand there and gawk at.

And that's all he done, just gawk. He stood petrified and watched the horse go by, watched him disappear over the brow of the long ridge, and it wasn't till the dust and the sight of him was no more that he took a first long breath. No thought had come to him that he could of roped the horse if he was good with the hemp and was well mounted. He didn't realize what all it meant to him to have the horse come along that ridge a third time. All he'd done was stare and take in the sight of him.

The horse he'd set his heart to getting had passed by, not over thirty yards away. It was the first time he'd seen him at a close distance, and right then was when a new feeling which he'd never experienced before had took a hold of him. It was a sudden hankering to own that horse, a craving to put a hand on the silky hide of him and run his fingers thru the long mane. He wanted that horse for the horse himself now, and for the time being, he'd forgot the reasons why he'd set out to get him. He'd forgot that the horse had been just a lead, something to try and get a hold of just because that'd seemed impossible, something that'd give him confidence to tackling other impossible things, if he succeeded.

All he thought of now was the picture of him, and that had stirred a new feeling that left him unthinking. He couldn't account for it. He just wanted to run out after the horse and calling him. And that new feeling being so strong, he'd thought it reasonable right then for the horse to turn back at his call and come to him. How he'd loved to put a hand along his neck, felt the thump of his heart quieting down, and have the horse recognize him as a real friend.

But Tilden realized there could be no such a happening, not for a while anyway. It was too bad, he thought, that he had to build a trap for such a horse, but there was no other way, for the horse was just like a hunted outlaw, always on the dodge, and scheming ways to never be caught.

He sighted the horse again, still going strong, and up a slope above the point of the ridge. He'd gone on his long circle once more, and near on the same trail that Tilden had trailed him on a couple of weeks before. In another week or more he'd be back in The Basin again and with Old Joe's mares, then somebody would run him another time. There was no rest for such a horse. He was always feeding and drinking on the run, and, as Tilden figgered, he'd be doing him a great favor to catch him, make himself his friend, and after he was tamed, to give him as much freedom as he could, and in some big pasture where nobody would bother him, at peace under the shade of the junipers in the summer, in the shelter of a warm stable in the winter, that all would be a heap better than the wild freedom which he was now trying so hard to keep.

Tilden more than hoped that the horse would try and make another get-away on this long ridge. He felt sure that he would now. Hadn't he come up this way three times already?

If Tilden worked hard and fast before, that had little to do with the way he worked now, for he had no more doubt of the horse coming by again, and he'd have the trap done so when the horse did come again he'd be ready to close it up on him. Daybreak found him wrassling with junipers and setting 'em up in place. Darkness found him doing the same, and before another week went by he had a trap built that'd fool even the human eye.

The entrance into it was on top of the ridge and about fifty yards wide. Green junipers hid the fence plum up to both sides of the entrance, and dry ones was stacked out of sight and ready for use to close that entrance with soon as the horse came in. From that entrance the trap took in the shape of a heart, the fence falling on both sides of the ridge to run alongside of it and to a point around the upper end. At the point of the heart-shaped trap was a little stockade corral where the horse could be run into to be caught.

The distance from the big entrance to the corral was near half a mile. By the time the horse would get in the big trap and find out he was caught Tilden could have a rope, which he'd already fixed with hanging rags, stretched from one side of the entrance to the other. Then he would go ahead and close it up with the dead junipers which he had ready for that purpose.

Satisfied that the trap was now ready, Tilden had no more to do but wait, and he wondered how long the waiting would last. He hated that. It made him restless, and it was after a couple of days of it, and as he tried to account for the restlessness, that he found out the something which all was the cause of it. It wasn't the waiting.

It was that he'd planned to catch the horse after some-body else had chased him, tried to catch him, and more or less run him his way. He felt he would be benefiting from somebody else's work, and there he realized sud-den that, if he caught the horse that way, he really wouldn't be the one who done the catching.

That's what had disturbed him, not the waiting, and when the straight of it came to his mind, he felt mighty pleased that it all had come in time. He'd get ready right away and try his luck at trailing the black horse and maybe get him to come up on the long ridge into the trap. He had three pretty fair horses. They was in good shape to run, and if he used two to relay on, the best one for the last lap towards the trap, he didn't see why he couldn't do all by his own self. He'd *have to* if he wanted to feel that *he'd* really caught the horse.

He'd waited at the entrance of the trap them two days, and now, as he rushed back to his camp on the second afternoon to make ready to go, he felt sort of shaky. An awful fear took a holt of him that somebody was already relaying on the black horse and would cause him to leave The Basin and come into his trap most any time. He didn't want to catch him that way, and the thoughts of that happening more than worried him. For no matter how much he wanted the horse now, if that happened it would spoil everything for him. All the principles of what he'd set out to do would fall in the mud, and it would be a heap better if he didn't catch him in that way.

He straightened up his camp outfit so as to have it all ready to put away first thing in the morning. Bedding and all was going to be hoisted up a cedar tree till he come back, for he was to take nothing with him but a few strips of jerky. He'd be traveling light and fast.

It was evening when he went up to the entrance of the trap again. He wanted to make sure that everything was set and that not a chip or anything was in sight which would make a wild horse suspicious. He walked out away from the trap and looked towards the entrance from a distance. Nothing showed that didn't look natural, and nobody could tell a trap was ever there.

He was starting to walk back, all mighty pleased with himself, when the sound of running hoofs coming along the ridge made him turn. He seen a dust and he dodged behind a juniper. His heart was beating fit to bust as he squatted there, for an awful fear had took a holt of him that here was the black horse and coming into his trap.

And sure enough, here he come, as big as life and making a picture that of a sudden made Tilden forget everything else but the want of him. It didn't seem to matter how he got him now, so long as he did, and he didn't think or care if anybody else had helped him by starting the horse his way.

*And sure enough, here he come, as big as life and making a picture that of a sudden made Tilden forget everything else but the want of him.*

Not a breath was took in as he watched the horse go by, and even tho he felt like letting out a war whoop for joy as the horse sailed straight into the entrance of the trap, he stayed tense and only his eyes showed what all was going on in his mind. He'd wait a second and till the horse was out of sight, and then he'd run and close the entrance with the rope and cedars. He was just about to spring up and make that run when the sound of more running hoofs made him squat back to where he was. And he wasn't any too soon, for it seemed like not more than a wink later when another horse went by him on a tight run. This one was a long bodied sorrel, and there was a rider on him.

Tilden could do nothing but stare at the sudden appearance of that horse and rider. Somebody had followed the black horse on up, maybe figgering to take him on the whole circle, but there was the trap, the black horse was in it, . . . and he'd helped that somebody catch him.

Tilden stared as in a trance. One minute the horse was his, and the next he was somebody else's, just like that, and before he could make a move. That happening was a blow that left him numb, there was only one thing he realized and that was how the horse was lost to him, lost after he'd put in near a year and a half in fitting himself to catch him. He didn't think or care about the time and work he put in, he'd been glad to do it all over again for such a horse. If he'd only had a few more days he could of been his, but there was no more chance now, he couldn't claim the horse even if he *was* caught in the trap he'd built because, as he figgered, the rider couldn't of knowed the trap was there, it had just been that rider's luck.

But, Tilden wondered, as he stared at the rider who, now off his horse, was tying the rope with its spooky looking rags fastened to it across the entrance. The rider *did* know the trap was there. If not, how come he found that rope? It'd been well hid and how come he stopped at the entrance? No rider would of noticed it, specially when chasing a horse at the speed he was going, not unless he knowed the trap was there, and then again. . . .

Tilden stood up and started toward the rider who, by this time, was busy dragging up the dry cedars. The cedars which he, Tilden, had stacked there was for his own use and when he caught the black horse. The rider was placing them along the rope of the entrance.

"Why hullo there, Spats." The rider, hearing footsteps behind him, turned to greet Tilden. There was a grin on his face as he spoke, and he didn't show no surprise at seeing him. None at all.

The surprise was for Tilden. He'd recognized the rider as Moran.

"Sure a dandy trap you got here." Moran went on, not a bit disturbed by the look on Tilden's face, "I'd never caught the black stud without it. Sorry *you* didn't get him, in a way," he grinned again, "but there's some nice little fillies left that you can get. They'd make you good hobby horses, and there's a few old mares too, and . . .

"Did you know this trap was here?" Tilden interrupted. He didn't care to hear about fillies or old mares.

"Why sure I knowed it," says Moran, "that's why I followed the black stud on in."

"Been sneaking around, huh?"

"Not so's you'd notice it." Moran grinned. Being the winner he could afford to be good natured. He pointed up to the flat topped butte which wasn't more than a mile from the trap. "You can see good from up there," he went on, "and I spotted you working on this trap with my field glasses. I . . ."

Moran stopped talking, and the grin went from his face as he stared up a slope above the point of the trap. Tilden noticing the look stared at the same place, but not in the same way, for, going up the slope a half a mile away was a horse. The long flowing mane and tail identified him as the black stallion, and he was free as the hawk that soared above him.

No words was said as the two stared. Moran was the first one to make a move, and he wasn't at all slow or grinning when he did. In no time he'd unfastened the rope at the entrance, pushed a few junipers to one side, caught his horse, and rode on thru towards the upper end of the trap. A big surprise was waiting for him there, for the trap didn't seem to have no upper end, a big gap had been opened in the side of the dry juniper fence and all traces that one had ever been there was gone. Moran seen that, if he hadn't knowed the trap was there, he could of rode right thru without ever noticing it. That's what the black horse had done.

Tilden came up a panting a few minutes later, and stopped in his tracks as he seen the opening in his fence. He was just as surprised as Moran, but a heap more pleased at realizing what this opening had done for him. It had given him another chance, and not only that.

"Did you do this?" Moran asked, squinting at him and waving a hand at the opening.

It was Tilden's turn to grin, but he done better than grin, he laughed. "No," he says, between laughs, "but I'd be mighty proud of myself if I had."

Moran glanced around for bootheel tracks in the dirt, but realizing that they wouldn't tell him anything if he found some, and knowing that nothing could be done he started to ride away.

"Better take a little salt with you next time you go after that black horse," Tilden hollered at him, laughing. Then of a sudden he got serious, "and let me tell you," he went on, "that the next time you try to catch that horse in this trap there'll be something else than an opening waiting for you."

Moran stopped his horse and stared back at him. There was a mighty hard look on his face. "What, for instance?" he asks.

"A thirty-thirty slug," says Tilden without blinking.

Moran grunted. "Huh, you couldn't hit the side of a barn with a shotgun," he says, "not even if you was inside of it." He laughed and rode on.

Tilden watched him ride away, and he wondered, as he watched, how he come to speak to Moran that way. It wasn't like him to use such language, and he'd never threatened anybody before no matter how much wrong was done him. He couldn't account for this sudden standing up for his rights, and in such an unblinking way too. Then the words he used. A year before he wouldn't of knowed the meaning of such, and a year before he'd have apologized for the hole being in the fence. Now he was mighty thankful that there'd been a hole, and what's more, he'd been peeved at Moran for trying to use his trap, and he'd come right out and said so.

That all was mighty new to him, and he couldn't account for the feeling. It wasn't a hard feeling to take either, and even tho he wondered at himself he was sort of proud at the stand he'd took. Of course, Tilden wasn't the kind of feller who'd be apt to take a shot at anybody, and threatening Moran with a thirty-thirty slug, maybe it wasn't the right thing for him to do, but he felt sort of riled up at that feller deliberately using his trap for catching the black horse when he, Tilden, had built that trap for the same purpose. If Moran hadn't knowed about the trap it would of been different. But he did know, he'd tried to put something over on him, and that's what'd made him sore. He felt a whole lot like he would do something sure enough if that feller tried that trick again.

He turned to study the hole in the fence. It was queer, he thought, how come that opening to be there. It had all been up and solid just that morning when he'd went all around to look the trap over. He sized up the opening. Whoever had done it sure had been perticular in brushing out all the signs of the fence. None showed that it'd ever been there. Then again it was right in the natural way a wild horse would take.

It would be no job to close that opening again, not more than half a day's work, and that didn't bother Tilden any. It was worth a heap more than a thousand times that to have the horse get away at such a time. He looked at the tracks the black horse had made, just to see if he'd skirted around any while inside and maybe against the fence, but them tracks had led straight to the opening natural like, and he was sure that the horse hadn't suspicioned anything. He'd come again.

Tilden walked back to the opening, and it was while fooling around the edge of it a bit that he run acrost both heel marks and then a whole print. He stared at it, knowing at a glance that he hadn't made them tracks, they was

too small. And he seen that mighty quick when he compared the track with one of his own. He couldn't for the
time think of anybody who wore such a small boot. It
looked like a lady's. . . .

A lady. Could, could it be Rita? . . . Was it her who had
made the opening in his trap? It was possible, but. . . .
There was many other questions which Tilden wondered
at. If it was her, was she on Moran's side, or his? Did she
make the opening so that Moran couldn't catch the horse,
or did she plan that so he, Tilden, would be the loser if
he'd run the horse in the trap?

There was no answering them questions, and for the
time being he'd rather hope she'd done this for *his* benefit. He was thinking strong on the subject, and looking
for signs that'd tell him more, when he heard a twig snap
a ways behind him and the brushing of saddle leather
against juniper limbs. He turned, and riding out of a
thick patch of junipers, he seen a rider heading his way.
After a spell, and as the rider come closer, he recognized
Rita Spencer, herself. His heart seemed to turn over and
lay still at the sight of her.

He took his hat off, and seeing she was smiling, he
begin to do the same. That was about all he *could* do.

"I thought I'd come and tell you about this, this hole
in the fence," she says, waving at the opening. "I thought
you'd wonder about it, you have plenty of reasons to."

"Yes," says Tilden, having a hard time getting his

tongue to working. "I have been wondering about it this last half hour. Ever since I found it."

As the two looked at one another and spoke, there seemed to be a sort of something in the air which of a sudden took away all needs of questions and answers. Tilden understood now, and as she went on to explain her reasons he found it mighty easy to understand more.

"You see," she was saying, "I had an idea that Moran would try and use your trap to catch the black horse in. He just as good as told me so the other day, and I didn't think that was a fair thing for him to do. I tried to make him understand, but he'd just laughed and thought it a good joke if he did catch the horse in your trap. So when I heard he would try and carry it thru to-day, there was nothing for me to do but tear a hole in your fence and to give the horse a chance to slip away. I hated to go against Moran, but there was no other way, and as it is now I feel guilty, like I'd done something sneaky or small."

"Too bad you feel that way," says Tilden, who towards the last was getting anxious to speak. "For my part I think you did a great thing and I appreciate it more than I can ever tell you. I also want to compliment you on the neat way you made the opening. I don't think the black horse ever suspicioned that he passed thru a trap."

The two talked on for a spell and then the girl started as if to ride away. "It's getting dark," says Tilden, "and would you mind having me ride along with you and see you home?"

"I'd be glad to have your company, but I'm used to riding alone, and besides I'm afraid if Moran seen us together he'd know then it was me who made the hole in the fence. You see," she smiled, "I feel pretty guilty."

"I'll ride just a little ways then," Tilden had managed to make quite a stand, "and I'll leave you to go on alone as soon as we see the lights at your house."

"All right then, if you wish."

Tilden never had such a hard time getting ready to go any place before in his life. His horse, even tho hobbled, was hard to catch, and then when he put the saddle on him he got to fumbling with his latigoes. The more he hurried the more they seemed to twist and tangle, and everything was like against him to make time.

At last he rode up to the side of Miss Spencer, and the two started on acrost the juniper covered hills towards her home.

# Chapter XII

A bright moon was like skimming along on the edges of light fluffy clouds. Tilden, riding on, was looking up at it as he let his horse wind around the junipers, and, to him it seemed as tho he'd never seen a moon so bright. Everything else around him seemed bright, even the soft shadows of the junipers. But all this brightness was more in the rider's chest than anywhere else, and, if it'd been raining and dark clouds had hung low and no moon had been in sight, things would of been bright just the same.

Tilden was riding back to his camp after seeing Miss Spencer home, and that young lady was, in some way, responsible for his seeing things so bright that way when, after all, they was only averaging. Still, Miss Spencer hadn't said or done anything that'd cause a man to see things as Tilden was doing. She'd let him escort her home of course, but all the talk on the way over had been of horses, the black horse, and a little about Moran. That was about all, excepting, when they come to where she

243

decided to go on alone, she'd invited him to come over to dinner some day, any day.

Maybe *that* was it, the fact that she didn't mind his company, even after him making a clown of himself most every time she seen him. Like the last time, for instance. If it hadn't been for her Moran would still be laughing at him and thanking him for the use of his trap in catching the black horse. The girl had come at the right time there, the same as she'd come at the right time when the mad cow was after him, again when she loaned him a horse and saddle and directed him when he got lost. She struck him as a little guardian angel who always happened along to, natural like, save his neck. And while he felt mighty insignificant at his show of helplessness he was pleased a whole lot to see that she didn't hold that against him, that she even allowed his company.

Tilden had admired Rita the first time he'd set eyes on her. There was everything about her that called for that, and her grace and ability was to him as if she sat on a throne and away above. Any kindly glance from her would of sent him a soaring, but she hadn't glanced at him after that first meeting at the Ox Yoke camp, and maybe, she'd only been hospitable when he wandered in to her home that day he got lost. But, as he figgered, there was no reason for her to do what she did for him at the trap, none but plain interest. A show of that from a girl like her was a heap more than he could ever hope for.

That all gave him the confidence that maybe he wasn't so insignificant no more, and when she allowed him to ride to her home with her and then invited him to come over some day, any day, why that was enough proof that she more than allowed his company.

That's how come Tilden rode on wings and all was so bright on his way to camp that night. This girl, which he figgered had no equal in the world, had welcomed his company, and sure, no such girl as her would ever bother with the likes of him if he wasn't worth bothering with. His own worth was all he thought of. He didn't try to figger how he himself liked her company outside of what that company of hers would prove, and now he felt he was at least worth opening a gate for her if she happened to ride by.

Outside of such he wasn't considering his feelings towards her much. The fact that she allowed him around and talked to him was as much as he could hope for just now, and the thoughts of that, along with his worrying about the black horse and other things, more than kept his mind occupied.

The black horse wouldn't be back to The Basin for many days more. Tilden stayed at the spring by the trap, and he came and visited the Spencer ranch twice. The first time had been pretty well spent with Rita's father. Rita hadn't been present much, and he had to listen to her father who, for a starter, begin to complain some of the bullet in his right leg. "If the pain don't stop soon," he'd said, "I guess I'll have to go to some doctor and have it took out. But," he'd went on, "I wouldn't be much use any more nohow, and I'd be doing that only because Rita has kept after me to get tended to as she says I should. But you know, Mr. Tilden, the pain I feel in my leg ain't worrying me near as much as how my girl has to work to take care of things. Of course she keeps on a harping how she likes it, but you can't tell me that a right pretty and healthy girl like her don't hanker for other things besides tallying up on fool cows, riding all the time, and seeing that I'm never wanting for nothing. Me that's just an old decrepit and wouldn't make good cayote bait, and," here after looking around to make sure he was alone with Tilden, he lowered his voice, "I'm thinking strong of selling this place so I can move to town and give my girl the chance she ought to have. I got a buyer now, and if he bids right the place is his."

"But maybe Miss Rita does like it here," Tilden had got worried somehow, "and," he'd went on, "it wouldn't be fair to her to sell without she already knows about it."

"Maybe you're right, but . . ."

A door had opened and both stopped talking to see Rita walk into the big room. "Don't let me disturb you two," she'd said smiling. "I'm only after my gloves. I'm going out to run the horses in, and I'll be just a little while."

Tilden had started up to go with her but she'd stopped him, saying that he'd better keep company to her dad. "I'll be just a little while," she repeated.

"That's just the way it is with her all the time," her dad had said after she left, "just got to rustle around and make a hand of herself, and what makes it bad is me. I can't do anything any more, but it's a daggone good thing I can at least hire a cook and a man to do the rough work. Moran does the rough work. He's a good man too, and if it wasn't for him I don't know what I'd do. I kind of wish sometimes my girl would take a shine to him, and sometimes she seems to, but it's funny that when she does I get kind of riled up. I don't know why either, unless it's because, with my girl tied up to Moran, I get visions of her putting up with this all her life."

"What's wrong with this?" Tilden had asked, while trying to forget that Moran had been mentioned.

"Well, it's all right I guess, but I'm thinking it's a little raw and rough for a girl. She ought to have the company of other girls more often, and the things the other girls get."

"Yes, I agree with you on that, but I've never seen a girl anywhere look so happy and contented as Miss Rita."

Old Spencer had talked on, and Tilden had been glad of the chance to listen to him. The only thing that bothered him had been what he'd said about Moran, and that had bothered him considerable. But, as he rode back to his camp that evening and figgered things out some, Moran didn't seem to bother him so much no more. He didn't try to figger out why just then, but he kind of overlooked him, like he'd overlooked much that was away deep, too deep to crop out as yet.

The next time Tilden had come to visit Miss Spencer, a couple of days later, done a whole lot to stir up some of what all had been so deep in him. He seen her in a light silky dress, the kind the girls wore in the city. He wondered at the transformation of her in that dress, for she looked even better in it than she did in her riding skirt and boots, and that was going some.

He wondered some more when he told her how pretty the dress looked on her, for instead of taking it for granted she'd seemed pleased to hear, as if that was sure enough news to her.

That evening had been a mighty pleasant one for Tilden, and the girl had seemed to enjoy it some herself. Also her father who, once in a while, looked over the paper he was reading and chipped in on the conversation. That conversation had kept up well, sometimes touching on Tilden's coming into the country, and then drifting on the other subjects, like with life here and there, and when nine o'clock come and Tilden rode back to his camp, he went over what all had been said and wondered if he hadn't said a little more than he should. They'd made him feel so much at home.

Another two days went by and Tilden rode to the Spencer home once more. That would be his last visit for a while because the next day he was figgering on riding out to The Basin. The black horse would be back there most any time now and he wanted to be the first one there when he did come. He wanted to see Rita once more before leaving, and he hoped she wouldn't mind his coming so often.

He rode on in and towards the corrals to tie his horse, and as he spotted Moran a standing there, like as if he'd been waiting for him, Tilden had a hunch that he was due for a little disappointment, for there was a look on that feller's face which hinted that all was well for him and not so good for Tilden.

"Take your horse in the stable and tie him up to the manger," says Moran, and the way that feller grinned as he spoke made Tilden sort of suspicious from the start.

But being that to accept hospitality goes well with giving it, Tilden took his horse on into the stable and as Moran had invited him to. Moran followed him in and Tilden was glad to see that one of Rita's horses, her saddle on his back, was tied there. He'd see her anyway, and that's what he'd come there for.

Tilden tied his horse in the stall next to hers, and sort of unconcerned like, started to walk out of the stable. It was there that Moran stopped him. He was still grinning.

"If you've come to see Miss Spencer," he says, "you've wasted your time, because she ain't home."

"Her horse is here," smiled Tilden, "and she can't be very far away."

"But she ain't home," Moran repeated, "not to *you* anyway."

Tilden stopped, and his smile faded away as he looked at Moran. "If she's not home," he says, "or she doesn't care to see me I'll find that out without *you* telling me."

With that he went out of the stable and walked on towards the house. A mighty disturbing fear was fast catching up with him as he walked on, but as he neared the steps to the house he figgered that Moran being jealous, and he didn't blame him, was only trying to stir up a few snags.

He climbed the steps to the house, and, as he noticed that the door was closed, the fear came back to him that after all Moran might be right, that Miss Rita wasn't home. But he wasn't going to be put out by anything that feller had said. He knocked at the door twice, and three times, and waited. No answer, then he looked around hoping he could see her somewheres near. The only person he could see was Moran saddling a horse in the corral and that only made him peeved. Maybe she was at the back of the house. He went there and all around, and finally, not getting no sight of her he started back towards the corrals. He'd wait there, for most

*The only person he could see was Moran saddling a horse in the corral.*

likely she'd just gone to do some little chore and would soon be back.

"Some folks have sure got a lot of nerve," says Moran as he noticed that Tilden was going to wait.

"Who do you mean by some folks?" asks Tilden.

"You, for instance."

"Me?"

"Yes, *you*. Anybody that ain't got no more consideration as to come and pester a girl the way you pester Miss Spencer sure don't amount to much. You ought to see that she just tolerates you because she don't want to hurt your feelings. If you wasn't a pore half-wit that needs sympathy she'd asked you to hit the breeze a long time ago. But she feels sorry for you and invites you over once in a while, and you take advantage of that and work on her sympathy for all you're worth."

Tilden had stood up as Moran started speaking. His face had a color that'd never been there before, and his hands was in unfamiliar position too. They was clenched and the knuckles showed white. He looked mighty threatening, and he stood that way for a spell, till, by the time Moran was thru talking, the threatening look had disappeared. The color went out of his face and his hands hung limp.

What Moran had said was just what he'd already hinted to himself about. Moran seemed to know too, like someone, maybe Rita, had already told him. He thought of her help in letting the black horse escape. That had been his hole card, but she could of well done that thru feeling sorry for him, and Moran could then have other chances of catching the horse.

Tilden stared thru the corral poles up towards the house, like a hoping Rita was there to sort of explain. Then he went in to the stable and somehow he felt glad he didn't see her as he come out and started to get on his horse, for he sure didn't want to "pester" that girl. He felt now like he had, everything pointed that way. There was her saddled horse in the stable, the closed door at the house. It had always been open, and there was other things. But what could he expect? What was he that a girl, a girl like her, should at all be interested in or even tolerate?

He stood by his horse and looked at Moran. "Well," he says, his jaw set and lips hardly moving, "if it's your intentions that I shouldn't see Miss Spencer you've sure succeeded. But look out if this is a trap," he went on, "there might be a hole in it."

The ride back to camp was sort of hazy to Tilden, and when he got there he hardly realized it. What Moran had told him, along with what he noticed himself and what he figgered out, was more than a blow to him, and he was having a hard time coming out of it. The thought of being pitied and tolerated on account of his helplessness was where the hurt layed most. It wasn't so much that he'd miss Miss Rita's company, because he figgered he was still a poor excuse to deserve such, and as much as he liked her company he'd expected very little of it.

He put in a mighty restless night, wondering, and fighting to stand up for himself. He couldn't be so useless. He was at least trying not to be, and if they'd give him a chance he could prove he was as good and as much of a man as anybody. No, he didn't want anybody to give him a chance now, he'd prove it all by himself, and against what all everybody seemed to think.

By everybody, he was going pretty well by what Moran had said, and then again, maybe a ghost of his old self was still there to remind him. Anyway, when the sun lit up the hills the next morning he'd come out from under all of that a considerable. He'd spent all night thinking about it. It was a tired, but mighty determined looking Tilden moving around the camp that morning. Not at all the kind of feller that Moran had talked about the evening before.

He wouldn't "pester" anybody any more. And that wouldn't be all, he'd show 'em all how he wasn't so useless. . . . He spent the forenoon in mending the hole in the trap. He went all around it good after that, seen that the entrance to it was all straightened up and ready, and then he begin to hoist all of his camp outfit up a juniper tree, all of it but the "jerky" which Old Joe had stuffed in the pack bag for him. Great Old Joe, he thought, one real friend that he wasn't pestering. Besides the "jerky" he took a little salt too. That'd been Old Joe's advice that he should never leave that behind, even if he took nothing else.

The sun was straight up above him when Tilden topped off the little buckskin and, leading the other two horses, rode away towards the black horse's territory. He made a "dry camp" that night, changed horses twice the next day. The same on the day after, and on the evening of that day he made camp, with jerky and salt and a saddle blanket, by the spring just a few miles from the tall peak that overlooked The Big Basin.

He was on top of that peak the next morning and looking the country over thru his field glasses. He stayed there all that day, chewed on "jerky," and kept a looking for a dust, or the mares the black stallion always came back to, but no dust showed up, and the few horses he did see didn't at all tally up in size and number with the bunch he was looking for.

It was the same thing the next day, and towards evening, as Tilden rode back to the spring, he begin to feel restless, restless with the thought that Moran was also watching for the black horse somewheres. He'd sure hate to have Moran get the lead on him.

With that in mind, he was undecided wether he should go up on the peak again the next day or circle around in the low rough hills. The horse should be in the country now, and maybe hiding out some in such a place where he couldn't be spotted from the peak.

So, with the hopes that he'd be the first one to bump up against him, he started out on a long circle early the next morning. That was better than setting on top of the peak and waiting. That had struck him as waiting for something to come to him instead of going out and getting it. . . . Another feather in his cap.

He made a big circle that day and without any luck. He used his field glasses on every hill he rode up onto, and all he seen was little bunches of common wild horses, none that looked like the bunch the black stallion was used to running with. He made another big circle the next day, in another direction, and it was the same thing. No sign of the black horse nowheres. And as Tilden turned back towards camp he begin to thinking all kinds of things, that maybe the black horse would never come back, or that Moran had started on after him and might of already caught him, maybe used his trap.

He was kind of puzzled as to what to do now. He'd rode and watched and rode and watched some more, and that, he figgered, was about all a feller could do. He'd try watching from the peak again for one more day and then he'd ride some more after that.

The "jerky" was running low. To save that, and for a change, he'd shoot rabbits and sage hens and cook 'em over the coals with a stick. All he had to go with that was a little salt, and that was running low too. Tilden was getting so that while he watched for the black horse or rode to look for him he could see visions of bread and potatoes, and right then he wouldn't worried none about any amount on the cover charge if a platter of what all he was craving for had come before him.

But it'd took more than cravings for food to make him quit now. He'd long ago forgot there was such a word as "quitting," and if he'd went to tally back on himself, and thought of other days, he'd been mighty surprised how he'd developed such staying qualities. But he never thought of that, no more than he did of any other big changes that'd come over him, for that had all come so natural like and with his living up to what he'd lined out to do. With his interest all stirred up and towards that end he also never thought how he could do things now that a year or so ago would of been more than impossible. His body had filled out in mighty fair size to meet all which he kept a trying to accomplish, and muscles, long sinewy strings of 'em, had piled on layer after layer. There was no more flabby flesh on him and fat didn't have a chance to grab a holt. His mind tallied up well with that body of his too. There was no more haze around it. It was clear and not only that but many corners of it was aired out and used which before had only been pockets where soot had gathered.

Finally the "jerky" gave out one day. Tilden had petted it so it'd last, but his appetite couldn't stand him packing that in a pocket when the stommack was craving for it. The salt dwindled down too till not a pinch of it was left. Tilden then held out for one more day, and being already more than fed up on rabbit and sage hen, the taste of 'em without salt decided him to move.

There was plenty of grub up at his camp, and more salt, but he more than hated to take the chance of riding back up to get it. Moran might find the black horse while he was gone. But there was a thought, maybe Moran had already caught the black horse and run him up in the trap without being noticed. This was a big country he was in and it could be easy enough done. So, the time riding up to the camp wouldn't be wasted. He'd see if the horse had been caught, for if he had there'd sure be signs.

It was a great relief when Tilden rode up to the trap a day later and seen no signs there. That is, no signs of the black horse, but when he went to where he'd hoisted his camp outfit up the juniper, so pack rats and other varmints wouldn't bother the stuff, he was mighty surprised to come across boot tracks there. Rita Spencer's, they couldn't be nobody else's, that he could see by their small size.

He wondered as he stared at 'em, what could she be doing here? Maybe she'd felt sorry for him again, and come to apologize for what Moran had said. Well, she'd never need to feel sorry for him. But, as he kept a look-ing at the tracks he begin to wish he had been at the camp when she came. And still it was a good thing he wasn't, not with the feeling he had in his chest. He didn't want anybody to feel sorry for him. He didn't want to feel that he was helpless. As it was now he figgered Moran and a lot of others was still laughing at him for his trying to catch the black horse, and he wouldn't feel good in seeing any of them, much less the girl, till he did catch the horse, and that he *would* do.

There was another proof of Tilden's stay qualities. If he'd been at all weak or a quitter, it would of been easy for him to drop the whole idea and hit for other territo-ries. Most men would of gone back to where they left and forgot about it, but Tilden stayed on and lived on "jerky" and rode at all hours to accomplish what he'd started to do, and all when he was laughed at, being discouraged, and reminded of his helplessness.

It wasn't the girl that was holding him either, for, to him, she'd seemed too far out of reach and he hadn't as yet felt that he might be anywheres near her level. He was nothing, just a clown who was satisfied to just be in her company once in a while, and with no thought that he could ever ride the same trail with her, not for any distance.

A cold fall wind was blowing, and, as Tilden faced it the next morning while on his way back to The Basin, he got a strong hint right then that summer had slipped by. Before many weeks now there'd be snows, and then the black horse would quit The Basin for good and hit for his winter range. Wherever that was at nobody had ever seemed to find out.

Tilden looked back at the two horses he was leading, the same as to say, "Well, I've got my outfit with me anyway, and I can go a long ways and stay a long time." And sure enough, he wasn't traveling light no more. On one horse was his bed tied with a squaw hitch, and on the other was a pack saddle, aparajoes on both sides and filled with enough flour and bacon and things to last him for a couple of weeks. That is, if he chipped in a sage hen or rabbit once in a while. The whole pack was tied with the diamond hitch. Old Joe had learned him to tie it the winter before.

He camped at the same spring again, near the tall peak, and went up on it the next day so as to get a quick look at the whole country. It showed him nothing new. Not a bunch was in sight that he wasn't used to seeing, and not a glimpse did he get of the bunch the black horse always came back to. It was a windy gray day up there on the peak, a day when a feller's mind was more apt to cater at the wrong side of things than the right. And Tilden, being mighty human, wasn't spared any of the common thoughts, at such times, that things wasn't going so well. It struck him up there on the peak that all and everything was against him. Even the country seemed to be in cahoots with all else to make him a laughing stock.

It begin to rain, and before the day was over a steady drizzle had settled over the country. The kind that lasts a couple of weeks at a time, and that didn't help things any. Tilden stayed in his camp the next day and made a shelter. Then he gathered dry junipers and started a fire, and setting by it the whole day along, and feeling sort of dejected, there was many things came to his mind which he'd never thought of for quite a spell. Things that was away back and like a bad dream, things that made him say to himself, "It couldn't be me who done those things." But he'd finally laughed at that. It'd been him sure enough, and his laughing was half disgust at the past, and the other part gladness for what he'd shed clear of in that past. He felt sure now that he could go back there, walk thru what all had dragged him down, and come out without a blemish. But he'd never go "back there" any more, not unless his father had come home and waited for him. He'd often thought of him, and that spring, when Old Joe had gone to town for a supply of grub, he'd sent in a telegram saying, "All okay with me Dad and am coming back to life."

His dad hadn't answered, for he was the kind who wanted to be showed rather than told. If he'd knowed what his son was up to he'd maybe thought him foolish, but Tilden hadn't let him know. He had grinned. I'll show him, he thought. And then, as tho a thought wasn't strong enough, he'd stared in the fire and spoke out loud, "I'll show him and all. . . ."

A couple of days went by when Tilden could do nothing but stay under the shelter and keep the fire going. And then, not at all according to what could be expected, the skies lightened up and some clear blue showed in the big territory above. To-morrow Tilden would be riding again, and he was glad for that, because his thoughts, with the past, and then the present with the black stallion, Rita, and Moran had all left him in a tangle that'd take a heap more than thoughts to get him out of. He was called on for action, and that he figgered on furnishing.

But, as much action as he furnished in the next few days, that all hadn't brought him much results. Not any, far as locating the black horse was concerned. He'd gone up on the peak one day, made a big circle the next, and tried his best to locate him, but not a sign was there of him nor his bunch anywheres. Tilden begin to wonder a lot of things at that. He got to wondering if some rider hadn't already caught the horse, some other rider besides Moran. It was early yet for the horse to hit for his winter range, and he worried if he'd ever come back. The summer had been hard on him. He'd been relayed till it was a wonder how his hoofs held out, and most likely, being weary, he'd hit out to wherever he would find rest. Wherever that was.

Tilden, knowing the horse by now, wondered how he'd stayed in The Basin as long as he did. It was like as if he'd been sort of challenging any man to catch him and got pleasure in outwitting 'em. He'd done that mighty well, all excepting once. That was when he run into Tilden's trap. But that was nothing against his thinking ability, for Tilden had made that trap so it'd make any human wonder.

But as good as Tilden succeeded in making that trap, he was now the one who was doing the wondering, and more than that, for he felt a pinching feeling at his middle which, if he wasn't so young and full of ambition, would have started a few gray hairs to cropping out. . . . Here, he'd planned to get the horse before the first snow fell, and now, it seemed that that horse had just left the earth and hid amongst the clouds above. But that would of been better, if such he'd figgered, than have somebody else catch the horse. Not that he was selfish in that way, for the horse was to anyone who could catch him. It was a contest, and where the winner got the honors.

Tilden didn't care about the honors and such like. There was more than that for him, and he was contesting for all he was worth.

He was still at that when, fogging along on blind trail as usual, he spotted a rider. Tilden's first thoughts was of Moran, for that rider was sure doing some tall riding. He'd kept on riding that way till a knoll took him out of sight, and Tilden wondered.

He wondered if that rider had found and was fogging on the trail of the black horse. But, when night came on and he hit back for his camp, he seen where all his wondering had been wrong, for a standing there by a fresh-built fire was Old Joe busy mixing something. Tilden found out afterwards that the rider he seen had been Old Joe hisself, and doing nothing but looking for him.

"Well, how goes she, young feller?" he'd said when Tilden rode in. "Hope you ain't too surprised to see me." He'd went on, "Got the taters started, and I'll have a bait ready soon as you move your ponies on fresh feed."

Tilden was mighty pleased at the sight of Old Joe. There was none he'd rather see any time, specially at such a time as this, when all had him puzzled and up a tree.

Old Joe kept up a conversation all thru the meal, a mighty comforting conversation too, and when the tin plates had all been washed and stood on edge after the meal was when Old Joe sort of cleared his throat to say more.

"I'm sorry to have to inform you, Bert," he says, "but I'm thinking the black stud left the country for good."

Tilden jumped at them words and looked at him. "What makes you be so sure?" he asks.

*But, when night came on and he hit back for his camp, he seen where all his wondering had been wrong, for a standing there by a fresh-built fire was Old Joe busy mixing something.*

"Well," says Old Joe, staring at the fire, "I was riding along outside the lease the other day, and I seen my mares have come back. The bunch he stole from me last spring. He'd never let 'em get away before."

"Now," Old Joe went on, as he seen how Tilden was absorbing the news, "if a feller knowed where he's hit to, what I mean is, if a feller knowed where he ranges of winters, there'd be a good chance to get him, because there's where I think he's gone, on his winter range. And it must be *some* place, some place where it's low and rough, and where nothing but an eagle can look into."

Tilden was quiet for a long spell, and like Old Joe, he kept a staring at the fire. Finally, still staring, he passed this remark:

"I'm going to be that eagle, Joe."

# Chapter XIII

A November blizzard had been howling for three days, and sweeping the country with hard hitting, drifting snow. In them three days, Old Joe had been steady looking out a window of his cabin a trying to see and listening for sounds, sounds of a man shuffling in thru the snow. The wind whipping around made such sounds at times and Old Joe would jump up and imagine he seen the figure of a man wrassling with the storm and trying to get to the door. At that he'd throw more dry wood in the fireplace and rush to open the door, only to have a swirl of snow come in. No man had been out there.

For three days, Old Joe had waited that way, sometimes going out to the stable and waiting there too, for that's the first place a man on horseback would come. Too worried to set still he'd went from house to stable and back. That had been all he could do, for it wouldn't been any use of his going out hunting because in that storm a rider could pass another by just a few feet without either one knowing of it.

The cause for all this fretting was Tilden. That feller was out somewhere in the storm, and Old Joe wished he knowed where, for he sort of pictured him wandering around, lost and freezing, and maybe starving. It had been over a month since he'd seen him at the spring by the tall peak, and the country he'd hit for in hopes of finding the black horse's territory was mighty bleak in weather like this. No ranches was near that he could of drifted into, and his grub supply sure must be all gone many days ago.

The blizzard was going on its fourth day, and Old Joe was setting up and snoozing in his chair, when the door of the cabin opened and Tilden walked in. Old Joe never heard, but he felt the cold outside breeze, and he woke up sudden to find himself facing him.

"Well, by golly," he says, jumping up and rubbing his eyes, "here you are. How did you make it in this weather? Been kind of worried about you, and . . . "

Old Joe kept a raving that way for quite a spell, and Tilden could do nothing but stand there and grin. It was a pleased grin, pleased for the shelter that'd been reached and the welcome that went with it. But there was a mighty weary look back of that grin, a look that's seen on a man's face when the body quits and the spirit keeps egging on.

His face was brown and drawed, the frost had nipped one side of it, and his many weeks' beard was crusted

*The blizzard was going on its fourth day.*

with hard driven snow. His short mackinaw coat, from collar on down and in every crease of it, was also crusted with the snow, which had caught a holt there that only good fireplace heat could loosen. He made a queer looking picture there by the light of Old Joe's fireplace, like as if he was half snow man and mummy, something that'd layed and been preserved in a glacier for centuries and which had been bared to life by the winds of the storm.

It seemed as if that body of his was just a support for two eyes, and kept a going so as them two eyes could keep a searching. But another day in the storm and them eyes would of dimmed, for Tilden had gone as far as he could.

For over a month he'd wandered, day in and day out, with only half enough to eat, and in as wild and rough a country as a man could find. Determined to find the black horse's winter range, he'd given no thought of food or what a body could stand, no thought of anything excepting finding the black horse and hoping for some way to catch him there. Not once in that time did he ever see a sign of the horse to encourage him, not even a hoof print. But he'd kept on searching, in all kinds of weather and riding tired horses. His grub had run out many days before the big storm, but there was deer in the country and he shot a young buck. As long as the salt lasted he could get along on that alone, and he did, till the blizzard come.

"How in samhill did you make it back in this storm anyhow?" Old Joe asked for the third time, and while Tilden was doing his best to clear the table of all that Old Joe had put on it.

"That was easy. I got my bearings with the wind. It was on my left, and then that little horse you loaned me seemed to know where to come. I guess he was glad of the chance to get back."

Old Joe shook his head. "You was sure lucky," he says. "Supposing the wind had switched? And then again, supposing the horse took you to his range instead of here? He's more apt to do that specially when the snow hits him."

The storm held on for a couple more days, and then a cold stiff wind begin to rid the sky of clouds. In them two days, Tilden just rested and fed up, and when Old Joe caught him outside trying to chop wood once he done his best to send him back in the house. Tilden hadn't listened to him just then, but seeing how the axe seemed so heavy and hard to manipulate, he finally gave in and he didn't go out again in them two days.

"All you got to do," Old Joe had told him, "is set here by the fire and keep me company. Of course I don't mind you tending to the stove and such like. But doggone it, man, you need a rest."

But the skies no more than cleared when, regardless of what Old Joe said, Tilden was out again, and on one of

Old Joe's fresh horses, begin to help with the stock and bringing the ones that'd need feeding closer to home.

The good weather held on, and all indicated that it'd hold on for considerable more. It had turned warm too for that time of the year, and Tilden begin to get restless. He wanted to start out again and try and locate the black horse.

"Well," says Old Joe when Tilden told him of his intentions, "if you ain't got any better sense than to try anything like that so late in the year, why I won't stop you, but your horses are pretty leg weary yet, and they wouldn't be much use if you did find the black stud. Better give them a few more days' rest, anyway."

That being mighty true, Tilden waited. He waited one whole week, and then another storm came along, a steady snowfall. It lasted for four days and when the last cloud drifted away, there was a foot of snow covering the country. A cold snap followed on, and Tilden seen where he'd have to postpone his hitting out for some time.

And *some time* it was. More storms came on, one right after another, and with only very few days of clear weather between. The clear days was mighty snappy and more than made a human want the shelter of a warm house before night come. Tilden was satisfied to stay there and help Old Joe feed the cattle, and comes a time when, as the rough weather held on, that he decided to put off trying to hit out till spring break-up. It sure wasn't the

kind of winter a man could camp out in, but in his decid-
ing, he wasn't thinking only of himself, he was considering his horses. They'd have to have feed, and hobbling
'em in deep snow, like he'd have to while camping out,
would be a good way to starve 'em to death.

Tilden sure hated to give up the chase till spring
came. That seemed a mighty long time off for him to
worry along specially when there was so much at stake
for him, but there was nothing else he could do. This
was another one of these instances which he'd have to
take and grin about.

"This is going to be a hard winter," Old Joe would
say off and on during every storm and when Christmas
come, that had turned out to be a fact for sure. "Yep," he
says, as he was warming his hands by the stove on that
day, "so far, it's the worst winter I've seen for nigh on
forty-five years."

The winter held on that way all thru January. That
was a long month for Tilden, the longest he'd ever put
in. For there was so much he wanted to do, so much that
kept him on the trigger edge for fear that something had,
or would, happen which would queer him from complet-
ing the job. All depended on him getting that horse,
everything, seemed like. Then there was Rita. Maybe
she wouldn't pity him any more if he succeeded, and
Moran would have no more laughs a coming. But that
wasn't all, there was the horse himself. He wanted him

just for the flesh, hide and spirit of him, for with the first sight of the stallion, a sudden love had been stirred, a mighty new feeling which he'd never experienced before for any animal, and in all ways he wanted him, he'd have to have him.

That being so strong, he didn't no time stop to think of what use he'd have for the horse if he caught him. All he worried about now was getting him, and that worried him a plenty. It worried him that some rider might of already caught the horse, that he might never come back to The Big Basin, that he might never be found, or that he, Tilden, would never be able to catch him if he did see him again.

All them thoughts, along with many others, such as the hurt he still packed from the memory of his last visit to the Spencer ranch, all kept him a dodging the comfortable rawhide covered chair by the fireplace. The flames made too many pictures, and unless Old Joe was setting there too and talking to him he kept away from it.

This all which Tilden was going thru was mighty new to him, and he didn't know just how to meet up with it. He'd never worried much about anything before. Of course, that was because he'd never set out to get anything, all had been the same wether it rained or shined, but it was queer now, he often thought, how there was so much that was pleasing even while he worried. He felt so much alive now, he could appreciate things when they was good and enjoy the fighting when they was bad, and nothing could down him, not even when they was at their worst, for then he enjoyed the fighting all the more.

The only thing that stumped him was the hurt Rita had handed him. There was no fighting that, even catching the black horse wouldn't straighten it out, not to his liking. All that would do would be to show her, like for spite, and he felt it'd need a heap more than that to wipe away the uselessness he figgered she seen in him. What all he done wouldn't wipe it away. Nothing would, only a show of strength and confidence, and while he was setting still.

It was in that way that Tilden often thought of Rita, like as if she was a judge and tallying up on his worth. But she hadn't given him much of a chance, and according to that last visit his worth wasn't much as yet. He'd only pestered her, and he would never try to see her any more. That was why he felt stumped when his thoughts was of her, and why he couldn't make a stand for himself there. She wasn't giving him the chance. She'd played absent, and, no matter how high he might tally up, the only thing there was for him to do was to keep away and with no hopes of his hurts ever easing. None, only with time and work and the proof that he'd won out.

Time went pretty slow, but work was a plenty. More stock had to be brought in every day and fed, more riding had to be done, and when night come, Tilden was glad to hit for his soogans and a rest. He'd took on most of the work, and one time, when Old Joe took sick and had to stay in bed for two weeks, he took on *all* the work. He played nurse to Old Joe and then went out and played nurse to the cows. There was meals to cook, wood to chop, stock to feed, and, whenever it could be managed, there was riding to be done.

He didn't have time to think of his problems much in them two weeks, and when Old Joe got up and begin making himself useful again, he went on keeping busy and leaving them problems behind. In the meantime he was fitting himself to meet 'em. He was steady fighting his helplessness, the helplessness he'd been given to believe was still with him. But if Rita or Moran or anybody had seen him tear around Old Joe's place, and seen how he took care of things and all as well as anybody could, they, specially Rita, might of congratulated him on what a hand he'd turned out to be. But nobody was there to give him a hint of that, nobody but Old Joe, whose good words he was so used to. And so, he kept on a trying to kill that helplessness, not at all realizing that he'd left that far, far behind.

January blowed and froze itself out. And then, with February, came a long spell of bright warm days, such days that makes a feller want to try and jump over a nine foot corral and stomp the earth and snort. It was in one of them days that Tilden, while out riding for weak stock, run acrost a little bunch of Old Joe's horses. One of the geldings in the bunch had caught his eye, a mighty likely looking gelding it was, and, being there was no weak stock for him to bring in that day, he brought the bunch of horses instead.

Old Joe wondered at that as he seen Tilden corralling the horses that afternoon, but he had a hunch, and he begin to grin as he went towards the corrals.

"I kind of figgered you would," he says, as Tilden told him his reason for bringing in the horses. "He's a mighty good colt that roan, and a good age too, coming five this spring. But," here Old Joe humped his shoulders and grinned at him, "but," he repeated, "I can't let you have that horse to break, Bert, not as much as I'd like to. I've already promised him to that feller Moran when he goes on round-up this spring. Moran is a good hand with a colt and being I'm perticular about this one I wanted him to break him. But," he hurried on to say, "you could sure have him anyway, if it wasn't for that."

"All right," Tilden grinned, "I'm sorry to've run 'em in."

But if Tilden grinned when he said that it was only to hide his feelings, for he sure didn't feel like grinning. And, as he took the horses on out the last gate to turn 'em back on the range, the full meaning of Old Joe's words more than hit him.

Even Old Joe had lacked confidence in him. That'd been a sudden and hard blow, a blow that brought back to mind such other happenings. Old Joe knowed him as well as he did himself, and the hurt layed in the fact that, knowing him, he was afraid to trust him with breaking one of his good horses. A proof that Moran could and that he, Tilden, couldn't.

Here, just a little while ago, he'd felt so pleased with the idea of breaking one or two horses for Old Joe. He realized it would of been a tough job but that's what he wanted. The roan colt would of acted as a sort of primer for when he caught the black stallion, but being so took up with that idea, he never thought that he might spoil the horse by just not being able to handle him. Old Joe had made him realize that, and he felt now that his help-lessness was still riding him sure enough.

The good February weather had no more effect on him during the rest of that day. All the energy he'd had in wanting to better his ability was pretty well gone, and he kept a thinking over and over how even Old Joe had lacked confidence in him.

Of course he realized that Old Joe didn't know what a blow he'd handed him. Maybe he'd only done him a big favor and saved his neck by not letting him handle that colt, but such thoughts didn't seem to help much, and Tilden found it mighty hard to act natural as he came back to camp that evening. He tried to whistle as he chopped wood for the night, but his lips was dry and the whistling didn't go well.

It was many days before Tilden was himself again. Long days of wondering if he wasn't on the wrong trail, if after all there was any use. He'd banked his life on Old Joe's opinions always. It was sound, and now that old feller had judged that he couldn't do a certain thing, not that that certain thing mattered so much in itself, but Tilden wondered. If he'd misjudged his own ability there he'd misjudge it in other ways, and that all knocked his confidence for a loop.

He'd been all shook up over it, but as he begin to get over the blow and thought back on the subject he remembered how he'd decided to tackle this because it was hard, because it seemed impossible for him to put over. This went with what he'd tackled. It was part of it, and, now that he'd worked hard and got a footing, was he going to turn tail and quit? Was he going to let a few snags keep him from getting there? . . . Where was his religion?

It took quite a while for them questions to raise up out of the tangle of the disappointment he felt, and quite a while longer for him to find an answer to them, but when he did it seemed like a powerful lot of spirit come to the top and as if to swamp down all that had aggravated him. There was only two things for him to do, that was to quit or go on and win. He couldn't quit, so he grabbed onto this disappointment as one more reason in making the winning all the bigger. And being strong now, and full of fight, he got to feeling as if he welcomed it and could take on a few more. . . . Tilden had made another stand.

The only thing now, with the fresh stand he'd took, was to start some action. He craved to get going and doing. And there was another hard part for him to buck up against, because there was nothing he could do right now, nothing but wait, wait for the time to slip by till spring break up, and that didn't at all go well with him.

Old Joe was made to wonder a considerable at Tilden during the month that followed. That feller had seemed to take charge of the ranch and right out of Old Joe's hands, and as much as that old timer tried to interfere he found he was nothing around there but just a cook and bottle washer.

"By golly," he says one day, as he seen Tilden tearing around the corral and roping a fresh horse, "the way he's hogging all the work, you'd think he was disappointed in love or something."

But Old Joe was wrong, for Tilden wasn't disappointed no more, not in anything. He'd only got a craving for action and he was just stirring up some, any kind just so it would hold him to earth.

He kept stirring up action that way till spring break up, and on some more till the grass begin to shoot up some, and then one day, right after an early spring storm, he run in the three horses he'd used the summer before and begin to grain 'em. He was getting prepared.

"If the black stud ain't already caught," says Old Joe one evening, "and if he comes back to The Basin, why I've got a hunch he's going to be yours. And say," he went on, "better try out that big blue horse of mine sometime. If you want to use him you're sure welcome. He's a mighty fast horse, and that's what you'll need."

"Thanks, but," Tilden was about to refuse, then he thought better of it. "All right," he says, "I'll be glad to take him if you don't need him. I'll more than have use for him, if the black is not already caught."

"If the black horse is not already caught," Old Joe had mentioned that too, and Tilden had often thought of the same. He'd tried to forget that such could be, and, as he rode out on Old Joe's big blue horse one day, that thought came back to him and he had a hard time shaking it. It was the same thought that had kept him on the jump ever since Skip had mentioned the horse at the Ox Yoke camp two years before.

But the horse had still been free just a few months ago, even after so many riders had tried over and over again to catch him. Tilden rode on and begin to wonder on the possibilities of anybody ever being able to catch that horse. His freedom seemed took care of by some power other than plain horse instinct and wisdom.

Even the trap Tilden had built hadn't fazed that freedom. For, by some streak of luck, the horse had gone thru there too. Like as if something had been watching over him and managed to have a loophole for his escape.

"But there won't be no loophole the next time," says Tilden to the breeze as he rode that day. And that was a fact, because, right at the time he spoke them words, he was riding towards the trap to see that it was right up and in shape. He went prepared to stay and do a good job too, for he was leading a pack horse that carried his bed and two "paniers" full of grub.

Yes, Tilden thought, as he visioned his trap and the lay of the country it was in, if that trap don't catch the black stallion, no trap ever will. And Tilden's judgment could be banked on as to that now. The proof of that was how and where he'd built his trap. Most fellers who didn't know so much about catching wild horses would of picked on a blind, or box, canyon as the most likely place to run a wild horse into, not knowing that a wild horse worth getting is always mighty wise, too wise to run into any place where he might get cornered, and twenty riders wouldn't be enough to drive such a horse between the stone rims of any box canyons.

Tilden soon learned that, and to his surprise, for, as he'd read a few stories describing catching a wild horse in such places, he'd also thought at first that a blind canyon would be the natural place. There was lots of blind canyons in that country, miles of 'em, and he noticed that the black horse never went in one, not even while feeding, and he knowed that, rather than be drove into such a place, that horse would turn on the closest rider and run over the top of him to get away.

Tilden, in his trailing around in the wild horse country, all the while watching and studying and figgering, had got to know the wild horse and his ways as nobody else ever got a chance to. There was no other work to disturb him. Nothing else mattered. He had plenty of time, and with only the one idea in mind. It wouldn't be but just a matter of keeping on the trail and the black stallion would be his. That is, if no other rider caught him first.

But there wouldn't be any cause for worry as to any other riders for a long time now, and if the horse wasn't already caught Tilden would have clear sailing. All the cowboys, including Moran, was now busy topping off their ponies for the spring round up, and right soon, they'd be joining the Ox Yoke wagon. That work would keep their ropes aimed at range calves instead of wild horses, for two months at least, and in that time, Tilden figgered strong in having the black horse safe in his trap.

But wether it would take two months, six months or two years, Tilden wasn't going to let up on trying to get that horse. Nothing would stop him now, nothing short of some other rider beating him to the horse. But he had a big lead on the other riders, more than an even break, because he had the time and they didn't. And now Tilden had got to be such a rider that few pinnacles ever was so

*All the cowboys, including Moran, was now busy*
*topping off their ponies for the spring round up.*

steep and rough as to make him check his horse when he hit out to haze the wild ones, and if he was well mounted the black horse himself would have a hard time leaving him behind.

So, with all he'd learned, with being the good all around hand he'd worked so hard to be, and all, and determined as he was, it looked as tho the horse would be his sooner or later. Maybe later, but sometime, sure enough.

Figgering things out, Tilden felt happy at the big chance that seemed to loom up for him. He would sure make the most of it, and now that he was at least in action, after a long winter of waiting and worrying, his spirits shot up again and his hopes came up according.

With his spirits soaring up that way he got to feeling somehow that the horse was still free. If he was caught, he figgered, he'd heard about it, for that horse was too well known and too many would of scattered the news. No, he couldn't be caught. He'd come back to the Big Basin before long again, and, if not, his hiding place would have to be found, and regardless of where that was he, Tilden, would find it. He'd keep on searching till he did.

Tilden kept his horses on a dog trot and jogged along. His thoughts was on the black horse steady, and only one landmark did he keep track of. That was the flat topped butte near which the trap was. If he kept on riding he'd reach the spring near it by sundown. Ahead and to the left of him was a little bunch of horses. His thoughts was hardly checked by the sight of 'em. There was lots of horses in that country and none interested him right now. For he figgered it was still too early in the year for the black horse to be back and amongst any of 'em.

But, natural like, he kept his eye on the bunch as he rode along. He would pass to within a quarter of a mile of 'em, and as he rode on closer and closer he kept a looking at 'em, just to be looking. He was riding pretty well out of sight, amongst the junipers, and as he got into a thick patch of the trees he right away forgot about the bunch. Then, when he was about to ride by, he got another glimpse of 'em, and this time he stopped his horse and took a good look.

In the glimpse he'd got of that bunch thru the junipers, he'd recognized the bunch the black stallion had run with the summer before, and that's what had made him stop to take the good look. He'd never seen 'em at such close distance, and now he wanted to make sure of their numbers and colors so, from now on, he'd know 'em as far as he could see 'em. There was two grays in the bunch, they'd be good "markers." Then there was a light roan, and eight dark ones, bays and blacks, making eleven in the bunch.

The horses hadn't seen him as yet and he thought some of riding closer to 'em, but there was no use in doing that, and being he still had a long ways to go there was no time to waste. He took another glance at 'em, and was just about to start riding on, when one of the horses in the bunch caught his attention and caused him to stare. That one animal, which before had been feeding, had of a sudden raised a head, sniffed the air, and then begin to circle around the bunch like as if worried about something. Tilden noticed the jet-black and shiny hide of that horse, the long flowing mane and tail, and, as he started the bunch to move, Tilden stared on, unbelieving. But there was no mistaking the action of that horse. . . . It was the black stallion.

# Chapter XIV

Tilden rubbed his eyes and stared. Then, wanting to make sure that his imagination wasn't getting the best of him, he pulled out his field glasses and thru them he stared some more. And even then, as close a look as he got of that horse, he had a hard time making himself believe that it was none less than the black stallion he was staring at.

He couldn't believe that here, within a quarter of a mile of him, was the horse he'd worried about for so long, worried of his being caught, worried of ever seeing him again. The horse that everything seemed to depend on and which he'd figgered was so many, many miles away. Tilden had primed himself for some tall riding and a heap of hunting before hoping to ever set eyes on that horse again, and now here he was like as if he'd just dropped from above and as you might say, right in his hands.

The black stallion had quit circling around the bunch, the breeze had shifted and didn't carry no more scent of any human around. But the horse, being wise, was watch-

*The horse, being wise, was watching.*

ing. He was out in the open and he knowed where to hit to if a rider showed up. That would be up the long ridges towards an open pass.

Tilden thought that's what the horse would do, that being out of The Basin as he was, and if a rider took after him, he'd now hit towards the juniper ridge rather than back to The Basin again. He felt mighty thankful for such luck, that he'd started out on this day, and that he was mounted on such a horse as the blue. All this happening at once was a chance that seldom ever comes twice. Only it all happened so sudden and when least expected that Tilden wasn't fit to take advantage of it, not for quite a spell. He just stared, done a lot of wild wonderings, and couldn't at all get his thoughts to lining out. The sudden sight of the black horse and so close had left him plum helpless to act, and it wasn't until the bunch grazed on out of his sight that he begin to think clear again.

Nobody knows what a feeling the sight of a wild horse gives to a man, nobody but them that's experienced it. It can't be told about in any way, only of the craving a man gets to just be able to touch the animal. But there's more, a heap more, and specially for a man who sights a wild stallion, such a wild stallion as Tilden sighted. That feeling was all the stronger with Tilden because he'd been two years in preparing to catch him, and there was so many reasons why he should catch him, too.

So it wasn't no weakness of his that made him shaky in the knees when this big chance of catching the horse popped up so sudden. It was just what all the horse meant to him, and it was a wonder, at the time, that he didn't ride right out and try to catch him with his hands.

After a spell, and feeling less shaky, he got down off his horse. He kept his holt on the saddle horn and steadied himself, and then he begin to get his mind to working.

"Now is my chance," he kept a saying, "now is my chance, and I can't spoil it."

And sure enough, now was his chance, a chance that would hardly ever come his way again. But as big a chance as it was, there was also many ways of spoiling it. Everything would have to be done just right, and no one realized that any better than Tilden did. He wanted to get the horse in the trap, *now,* and he'd have to do considerable figgering and maneuvering to do that. He couldn't just bust out after the bunch and start chasing 'em towards it, for the black horse would get suspicious then and go some other way in spite of him. No, he'd have to let the horse think he was getting away all the time, and there's where the ticklish work would come in.

His mind was working mighty good again when he climbed on the big blue horse, and one mighty good plan was decided on. His blood was up and his heart was beating mighty furious as he took another look to make sure if the horses was out of sight, and then leading his pack horse he bent low over his saddle and eased out of the patch of junipers and down a long draw. Once in the draw he jogged along at a pretty good gait for he felt safe of not being seen in there. He wished he didn't have the pack horse to bother with, but he couldn't leave him just yet because that horse would nicker soon as he rode away on the other horse. The black stallion would hear and that'd be more cause for him to get suspicious.

Tilden rode on down the draw for a couple of miles and till he figgered he was well below the bunch of horses. There's where he'd start from, and there's where he'd leave the pack horse. He picked out a stout and shady juniper, tied him there, and took the pack off of him.

That pony might come in handy as a relay in case the black stallion turned back to The Basin.

Shaps' and all weights that could be got along without was took off and left with the pack, and when Tilden came out of the draw he was stripped down for a hard race. It was no trouble for him to locate the bunch again. They'd just grazed on, and now they was right between him and the trap, just where he wanted 'em.

He didn't try to hide no more as he rode towards 'em. He wanted the black horse to see him now, and as he jogged along slow and straight ahead that would give the horse plenty of chance to see him and take his natural way out without being crowded, just like he was getting out of the way of another rider, and Tilden hoped mighty strong that that way would be towards the trap on the long juniper ridge.

Tilden was near a mile away when the black horse spotted him, and there was no guessing that he had, for there was a commotion in the bunch about then that sure left no doubt. It was like as if a bomb had exploded in the middle of 'em. Tilden stirred his horse into a lope, so as to be nearer in case the bunch headed the wrong way, but he didn't want to get too near, for he knowed that a wild bunch can be handled easier at a distance than close, and another thing which he figgered on was to try and keep the black horse from leaving the bunch he was with. He could maybe be turned easier then and there'd be no need for real hard running. The only trouble there was that the bunch he was with might be too slow for the wild horse. They was range stuff and herd-broke and could be corralled, and if they run it was only because they felt that way and not that they was so wild.

But Tilden knowed that if he could keep 'em going fast enough and still keep his distance the black horse would be apt to stay and even if he left he'd most likely come back, if he wasn't crowded. It'd take a lot of maneuvering, but if the bunch could be used to draw and hold him, it'd save a lot of useless running and there'd be more chance of getting him.

Tilden had long ago figgered these things out, and as he rode he was now going over 'em again. He hoped the horse had never been decoyed with a "parada" (herd). If not that would be new to him, but this bunch was better than a common parada, because this was the bunch he'd been running with, it was his bunch.

It looked promising too, for, as Tilden rode on, the black stallion didn't seem to want to leave 'em. He'd circled around to start 'em on, and when they finally did, he'd dropped behind 'em and come near half the way back to get a look at the rider, the same as if to make sure it was a rider and that he'd better be going. He'd bowed his neck as he come, then stopped, whistled and snorted, and, as the rider had kept a coming, he'd finally turned and high-tailed back to the bunch and started hazing 'em on up towards the long juniper ridge, and trap.

Tilden's heart beat mighty fast at the sight of him once more, and then, noticing the direction him and the bunch had taken, he prayed that none of the gentler bunch would slow down, that they'd keep a running as they'd started to and fast enough so the black wouldn't get nervous and go to quitting 'em.

The run all started so fine that Tilden felt it couldn't last. He thought all sorts of things, that the black was wise to the trap and would turn some other direction, that the trap might be down in many places on account of the winter's heavy snows. He wished he'd had a chance to look it over first and make sure, for as it was now, if the horse got in the trap and then got away again, it would never be of any more use, and that horse couldn't be got in there no more.

He thought of many other things which might queer his getting the horse. But there was no letting up now, this was the biggest chance he ever had and he'd have to gamble on it.

But this all which might happen didn't keep him from putting his heart in the run. He went at it like as if he was sure everything was okay at the other end. And if he wondered about this or that it all helped in a way, for he sort of prepared to meet up with any happening and he would be on the spot at the right time to queer 'em.

The run kept up in great shape for a few miles. Tilden just no more than kept track of 'em in that time and he was mighty hopeful when he seen that the black was staying with the bunch, at the tail end of 'em and keeping 'em going. The bunch was feeling good and wanting to run, and it wouldn't be no trouble to keep the black horse with 'em so long as they felt that way. But, Tilden wondered, what about when they had their run out and got a little tired? It'd be some job then to keep the black from hitting out by his lonesome.

Of course he could be caught alone, maybe, but it'd be a heap harder run, because, when the horse would find himself alone and being chased by a rider he would go twice as fast as he would when with his bunch. He'd be more apt to turn and go the wrong direction, and once he did turn there wouldn't be a rider in the country who was so well mounted as to be able to catch up with him and turn him back. Then again, one lone wild horse is mighty hard to hold in any trap, and if the black horse was caught alone that way he'd be apt to risk his hide to get his freedom back. But with a bunch to mill around with and keep him company he might be pretty easy to hold.

So, Tilden figgered, a whole lot of the success of the run depended on keeping the bunch going and right with the black. It'd be more work, and would need considerable scheming so as to pull that off well, but, if that could be done, it would be the surest way.

The bunch hit a thick patch of junipers, and soon as they went out of sight in there, Tilden called on the big blue horse to do his best. Now was the time to do it, for the bunch couldn't see him come, and then again, it's at such times, when a wild bunch gets out of sight, that they do their best too. They seem to know that a rider will take advantage of being under cover to ride up on 'em.

But these wasn't wild horses that Tilden was running, only one. And instead of fearing that they'd give him the slip amongst the junipers he was more afraid that they'd stop and go to grazing there. And sure enough, they'd slowed down, and, if it hadn't been for Tilden riding into 'em a purpose to scare 'em up, they would of stopped to graze.

But Tilden had been mighty careful of his ground as he swooped down on 'em that way. He'd first made sure that the black horse wasn't amongst 'em, for, as he'd figgered, the black would take advantage of being hid to make distance, and, being the bunch was tired of running so fast, he'd left 'em behind and gone on to open territory.

This proves that Tilden had got to know a lot about horses, and his scaring the bunch into a fresh start showed that he knowed a lot more, for most riders, not wanting to fool around, would of gone on the trail of the black without even glancing at the bunch. Tilden knowed that the black wouldn't run far, that once he got in open country he'd wait a spell for his bunch to catch up with him. If they didn't he'd go on alone, and that's what Tilden didn't want to have happen, and why he spooked the bunch into a tight run and on the trail of the black.

He spooked 'em up that way twice. And at every little hiding place where they'd be apt to stop again, allowing just enough time for the black horse to be out of sight, he'd swoop down on 'em some more. Then he'd stay back out of sight and keep that way, and no time did he get anything but far away glimpses of the black horse. That horse couldn't know the rider was still on his trail, only by the actions of the spooked up bunch which always caught up with him when he waited. At that he'd start again, and for a spell he'd haze the bunch the way he was headed till, getting too slow for him, he would leave 'em behind again.

But as long as he seen no more of the rider and being the bunch was never far behind him, he didn't start on at his usual get away speed, and now he was just ambling along instead of running. Of course he was hitting for his big circle, but that was natural because for the last year or so he'd wanted to range there beyond the tall summit, and this seemed to be the first time his bunch seemed to want to go there with him.

Tilden helped him on that way, and unseen from the black, who always waited at some high spot, he'd stir the gentler range mares to catching up with him. This was a case of where the stallion takes the lead, but in this instance it was the wild horse's nervousness which wouldn't let him drag along at the speed his bunch would set. If these had been as wild as him some wise mare would of been the leader and the stallion would of been keeping guard from the rear.

But things wasn't going so bad for the black stallion now, even if his bunch did lack a leader, and if it wasn't for them spooking up so often he'd been traveling on a walk and not so much on a trot or lope. But even at that, watching and making distance as he was, it wasn't at all like the times he'd already come up on this trail, hitting out all by his lonesome, and knowing that a rider with a long rope was close to his heels. His bunch had a lot to do in keeping him at ease and from kettling away at that great speed of his.

Tilden worked on and figgered mighty hard to stay out of sight and still keep the bunch a coming up after the black. And if Old Joe had seen him maneuver around he'd been mighty surprised, for the boy, as ticklish a work as he was doing, was handling things in a way that proved him a master horseman of the range. It was surprising, sure enough, but, considering how hard he'd worked to be that, how sincere he'd been in that work, along with the staying qualities that was his, it was no more than natural. He'd put so much of his heart into the game that he'd learned as much in the two years of it as most men would in three times two years. Then again he seemed to have a bred-in knack for the game. Maybe that was why he hadn't found no lead in his home territory, and why he took on to this hard game so serious.

But Tilden wasn't thinking of that, nor patting himself on the back, as he dodged around junipers on the trail of the black that day. His eyes and mind was all for that horse, sometimes smiling with satisfaction and often holding his breath a wondering what he'd see on topping every knoll and ridge.

But his hard work and figgering wasn't for nothing. He was getting results for it, and pretty soon, after a lot of that, he glimpsed as great a sight as a human can experience. A sight that Tilden had sweated, froze, and starved to see. Less than a mile ahead of him was the black stallion, with the bunch, and going up the lower point of the long juniper ridge. Two miles further on was the trap.

Tilden was hardly able to hold his horse still at that sight. His heart played a tattoo and his breath came short. But it wasn't from fear that something would go wrong, it was more from excitement, for the black horse acted quiet and the mares seemed to be willing at last to go the way he was wanting to haze 'em, up the long ridge.

As hard as it was to do, Tilden waited till the bunch got up on the ridge and out of sight. He couldn't afford to show himself now, and he done his best to spend his time seeing that his saddle was set to stay and that he and his horse was ready. This would be the most ticklish run, and the hardest. The run that Tilden's life seemed to depend on, for now, if he failed, he would maybe never have another chance. None such as this.

Finally the last rump disappeared over the point of the ridge, and then Tilden left the spot where he'd stood. He kept his horse at a trot and easy lope, for soon now he'd be needing all the speed that horse had in him, and at the gait he was now going he could easy catch up with 'em in time to do the good work.

The bunch was less than half a mile from him when he rode up so just his head showed over the point of the ridge, and they was still going just right. Making sure of that, he skirted along the edge and kept in the thick of the junipers that growed along there. Only short glimpses of the horses did he get from then on, but that was all he wanted. He put his horse in a long lope, and the half a mile between him and the bunch was shortened to a quarter. The trap was now less than a mile away.

Another half a mile, Tilden thought, and he'd bust in on the bunch for the last run into the trap. They was all going fine and straight for it. And then, . . . all at once, the black horse broke loose, like as if a bolt of lightning had shot up from under him, over the brow of the ridge he went and out of sight.

Tilden stopped his horse, the like as if another bolt of lightning had struck him in the heart. He sat there in his saddle, stiff and unable to move from the sudden happening. Then he heard a long whistling snort from the canyon below, and that of a sudden brought him to life.

The horse had run down there and turned and snorted at whatever scared him off the ridge. And, with the sound of that whistling snort, Tilden knowed that the horse hadn't gone on. There was still hopes, if he acted fast enough.

The hopes came with the bunch of mares that was standing still on top of the ridge. Tilden knowed he couldn't turn the horse back by riding after him, the only chance was to skeedaddle the mares the way the stallion went, let him come back to them, and then maybe he'd haze 'em back up on the ridge again before the trap was passed. The horse was too wise to follow along the canyon for very far, and Tilden figgered he'd want to come back on the ridge again, after going around whatever had scared him. But the main trouble was there; would the horse try to come back on the ridge before passing the entrance of the trap, or would he come back on the ridge at all?

This was no time for guess work, and the way Tilden busted in on the mares and shoved 'em over the edge of the ridge went to prove that. The mares skeedaddled like regular mustangs and fell in on the way the stallion had took like as if they'd been shot along. Then Tilden pulled up his horse. There was nothing he could do now but wait, for he realized that the worst thing at such a time would be to show himself to the stallion or try to turn him back. That horse would of knowed there was something wrong then and nothing could of got him back but a three-eighths whaleline. But it'd been proved often that the loops of them whalelines always fell short, and in the brushy canyon the horse was in, a man wouldn't have the least chance.

It was many long minutes, they seemed like hours, when the sound of a sharp nicker was heard. From that, Tilden knowed that the black horse had waited, and even tho that didn't promise much, it was a great relief. And also a little hope came up again when low soft nickers followed on. The black horse was coming back to his bunch. Maybe he'd quiet down now and, after a while, haze the bunch back up on the ridge.

Tilden waited some more and broke little twigs off the juniper where he was hiding and was steady chewing on 'em. All was so quiet down below him that he begin to get mighty nervous. Then come a time when he couldn't hold on no longer and he rode over the edge to look down.

No horses was in sight there and no sound of 'em came to his ears. He put his horse on a lope, and staying on the edge of the ridge so he could look down in the canyon he rode up towards the trap. He hadn't gone far when he seen a sight that chilled him thru, for within a hundred yards of the entrance of the trap was the black stallion and his bunch. They was still in the canyon, and would pass right by the trap, missing the entrance only by two ropes' lengths.

Tilden wasn't thinking no more at that time. He didn't stand there and gawk, instead he went into action. There was only one little slim chance left, that he had to see at a glance, and as slim and little as that chance was, he sure wasn't letting it go by.

The horses was going along in the canyon on the left side of the trap. Tilden put his horse at top speed and fell in the canyon on the right side. His intentions was to go around the trap and meet the horses at the point on the other side and scare 'em into turning back. Of course he knowed that there was no way to keep the horses from hightailing it straight back to The Big Basin if he did succeed to turn 'em, but he didn't believe the black horse would want to do that. He banked on his knowledge of wild horses and the wisdom of the stallion there, for he figgered, if he got at the head of the canyon before the horse did, and showed sudden, that pony would be scared into turning and then hit for a high spot where he could see. The only close high spot there was the ridge.

The ticklish part wouldn't be over even then, not half started, but Tilden seen where it was his only chance, and he'd figger the rest out when the time come.

He chassayed on. His horse was going along in long powerful ground-eating strides and Tilden remembered what Old Joe had said about him, that "he'd most likely be needing a good fast horse to get the black stud, and here was one." That sure all proved true, and Tilden was mighty thankful to be riding such a horse on this day.

The big blue horse carried him around the head of the trap at top speed. He was still breathing light. The highest point was reached, and then it was all downhill and down the canyon where the horses was coming up in. A glance around showed Tilden they hadn't passed as yet, and he fogged on down that canyon like the devil was after him.

So did the horses when he lit into 'em. They turned tail and forgot which way they wanted to go, they just went. And, as Tilden had figgered, the stallion begin hitting for high ground. That was the ridge.

He was halfway up it and the mares was all close seconds when Tilden pulled a stunt which, to anyone not wise to the wild horse and his ways, would of been thought of as mighty foolish. He'd edged his blue horse in between the bunch and the trap, just exactly as if he wanted 'em down the canyon and not at all on the ridge. He had two reasons for doing that. One was that he didn't want the horses to run up against the side of the trap, that would turn 'em from the entrance. The other was that by his acting as tho he wanted the horses down the canyon the black horse would get suspicious of that place and never let himself be drove there. So, Tilden edging in as he did answered two purposes, and he done it mighty well. Missing the side of the trap, the black horse beat him to the top of the ridge and the whole bunch, all spooked up, was right close behind.

The next thing, now that the horses was on the ridge, was to turn 'em and have 'em head back for the trap again. But Tilden, nor no other man, could of ever figgered a way to do that, not unless he could of transplanted himself on the lead of the bunch and at once, and no rider could ever got the lead on the black horse now.

It looked more than hopeless. But Tilden wasn't for quitting, not even then, and he would follow the black stallion all the way to The Basin if necessary and try to get him back again.

He rode at an angle so as to get the black to crowd him as he had when making the top of the ridge, but the horse wouldn't crowd, he was on top now and his speed would do the rest.

Tilden fogged on after him, half crying at his helplessness, for he seen where, with the speed of that black stallion, all the chance he had now was to see his dust off and on, for a ways.

He was watching him vanish that way and doing his best to keep up when, with a quickness that Tilden himself couldn't account for, not even afterwards, he reined his horse to one side and he dropped out of sight over the edge of the ridge. The black stallion had turned, the

*The black stallion had turned.*

whole bunch had turned with him in a flash, and all was coming up the long ridge again at the same speed they'd started down.

They stampeded past where Tilden was hid and straight on towards the trap. Tilden didn't stop to wonder about the change of events, not just then. He fell in right behind 'em instead, stirred his horse to his best, and a couple of minutes later, the black stud away in the lead, and the rest of the bunch doing their best to follow, filed on thru the entrance into the trap.

# Chapter XV

There was no moon a shining that night. Soft filmy clouds was in the sky and hid the stars. It was dark, mighty dark, and that's why, when the last light of day went on to other worlds, Tilden stirred and started to walk away. He couldn't see no more in this darkness, no more till the light of a new day came up again, and now he'd have to rest his eyes till then. But his eyes wasn't tired, for they'd really only been feasting, feasting on the sight of none less than the black stallion.

He'd really caught that horse at last. It was hard to believe, and that's why he'd kept a using his eyes so. If they kept on seeing him he'd finally get to believing. It had been a long hard day, a day full of wondering, figgering, quick thinking, and fast riding, then disappointment and, at the last minute, success. Success just when he'd given up all hopes, and so, it was no wonder that he begrudged darkness coming on him. He wanted to stare at the proof of his winning, winning at something he'd been least fitted to tackle, besides winning something in flesh and blood, a horse that was the prize of the range, but which, to Tilden, was a heap more.

Now he had him, and where there wasn't the least chance for him to get away, but it was hard to believe, and, to make sure that he'd still have him as proof for the next morning, he had run him and the bunch in the small corral and roped the gate tight. A mouse could hardly crawl thru that corral and even a herd of stamped- ing buffalo couldn't of pushed it over.

From a little distance, on the side of the hill, he'd stared at him in there, taking in every part of him for the beauty that was his. Also, wrapped in that slick hide he seen all the principles that led to the catching of him. He'd sat there and stared, and forgot that he might be tired and hungry. Rest was the last thing in his mind, for the sight of the horse was the kind of rest he'd been wanting. And as for food, he'd never thought of that.

It wasn't till darkness come that he thought of other things, things that'd need to be done. Back on the trail, fifteen miles or more away, was his pack outfit, there was a horse of his tied to a tree there, and there'd be no time like this night to tend to things and get all set for the next day. He didn't want to sleep now, he'd had plenty of that the winter before, and more of it could be caught up on some other time.

That night's ride was no strain on him. His heart was too full of what it'd hungered for, and it was pounding strong. Of course, he thought, as he rode, he'd played in luck some, because what was it but luck that'd made the black horse turn back up there on the ridge? But as he rode back early the next morning, leading the pack horse, he seen what had been the cause of the black turning back. It had been the same thing that'd turned him off the ridge in the first place. So, instead of luck being with Tilden it really had been against him, and it was only thru his hard riding and figgering that he'd won out.

What he seen up there on the ridge, and plum acrost it, was a streak of black coals. Dry junipers had been stacked and burned there, and for reason only to turn the black horse off the ridge and away from the trap. That had been somebody's work, somebody who wanted to queer him in getting the horse, and Tilden had a strong hunch who that somebody might be. Whoever had done that trick might of figgered that Tilden wouldn't know how signs of a few burned trees would turn a wild horse. In that way it was better than tearing a hole in the trap, because Tilden would be sure to notice that and fix it up again. The scattered coals might not be noticed, they would queer the trap, and the black horse would never come up on the ridge again, for with such a wise and suspicious animal as the black horse was, them coals was the same as a ten foot stone wall, only worse, because they was signs of humans, and humans hinted of a trap.

That's why the black horse had turned off so sudden when him and the bunch was heading for the trap so straight and unsuspecting. And that's why he'd turned back again, when, getting around and above the scary place, Tilden had turned him up on the ridge.

That streak of coals had caused a lot of hard riding and suspense and was no good luck. They'd been just a snag which come nearer queering everything. But, as Tilden rode on over 'em, he held no hard feelings against whoever had done that trick, that was just another proof that he could win in spite of odds, another feather in his cap, and making the winning all the more worth while.

He rode on and by the trap. The black horse and his bunch was still there in the small corral. He wanted to linger a while and look at him some more, but there was a little work to be done. There was a horse to unpack and turn out to graze, another to unsaddle, and a bait to cook. Tilden was beginning to feel hungry, and after that he could look at *his* horse all he wanted to and figger ways to take care of him.

Taking care of him was going to be quite a problem, he thought. He wouldn't dare take the horse out of the corral to feed for fear of having him get away. The grass was still short and scarce, and it'd be quite a job to gather enough to make a day's feed. Then there was the water, the wild horse would go mighty thirsty before he'd drink out of a bucket, if there had been a bucket.

He could of course take the horse to Old Joe's place by breaking him to lead a little and then tying the rope around the pack horse's neck. He couldn't run away that way and the pack horse would sure take him on in. He could be well took care of there in one of the high corrals, there was plenty of good hay and grain and there'd be no need of rustling feed for him. But Tilden didn't want to take the black to Old Joe's place. Not yet, not till he had him broke to ride. Then, setting on him, he'd ride up there and surprise that old boy.

But there was a lot to do yet before that time come, and a ticklish part of it was started on soon as Tilden was thru straightening up his camp by the spring. He took his rope off the saddle, picked up a hackamore, and started towards the corral. The bunch jammed on one side as he came near and he was greeted by the stallion's loud whistling snort. Tilden's intentions was to step in the corral, simply rope the black by the front feet, throw him, slip the hackamore on his head, and tie him up while he let the other horses out to go back to their range. But as he started to climb over the corral he found that stepping inside wouldn't be so safe. The black had a look in his eye that hinted to anything but a welcome, and the way he worked his ears would of warned even the most ignorant.

Tilden more than knowed that the black was no ordinary horse, and he was reminded of that fact once again.

He stayed perched on top of the high corral, and studying the horse, he wondered how he ever caught him, and now, if he ever would be able to break him. The battle was only half won, seemed like, and now the real fighting was about to begin. But there was one thing about this half of the battle, he now had something to fight with.

But in this case, Tilden's fighting would be towards understanding. He meant to take his time and get the horse used to seeing him around before he'd ever try to put a hand on him. With a cowboy hired out to do such work, that horse would be throwed and saddled and rode within an hour. In a week's time he'd be gentle enough so any good rider could go out and do a little work with him. With the cowboy there's always work to be done, and as much as they think of a good horse, he's got to be used for that purpose. But work is what makes a man or a horse good. The cowboy never gives a horse too much of it, and when he turns a fighting bronk into a well broke cow horse, that pony's spirit is just as intact as the day he was first caught. If it wasn't he'd never turn out to be a cow horse, and a man that breaks a horse's spirit in gentling him is not a cowboy.

If Tilden was hired out to break horses he'd have done his best to handle 'em as Moran or any other cowboy did, for he knowed the range horse now, but he wasn't hired out by anybody. He had all the time he needed with this horse, and it wouldn't matter if it

And when he turns a fighting bronk into a well broke cow horse,
that pony's spirit is just as intact as the day he was caught.

took one or two months before he could even put his saddle on him. He'd enjoy every part of it with him, and enjoy seeing that fighting instinct die out of his eyes to be gradually replaced by a show of trust and then friendship.

But how he did hate the thought of starting in. Starting in meant a choking loop around that slick neck and, for a time, marring the velvet of his hide. The horse would fight, skin himself here and there against the corral, and a dead fear would be in his heart for many, many days. He thought some of letting the horse go. He'd won in what he'd set out to do, and now he was only taking his freedom away. But when he thought of that freedom, with other riders always after him, sooner or later to be caught again, after all, he felt that he could give him a better chance, and the horse would be as free as possible again, once his confidence was won.

The horses was steady milling around in the corral, but the black stallion, fire in his eyes, long foretop hanging over 'em, just stood while the bunch milled, watching, and like as if waiting for a chance at the human that'd trapped him.

Tilden looked at him and shook his head. "Too bad, little horse," he says. In his hands was the rope, a little loop was hanging on the inside of the corral, and then, without warning, that little loop split the air and sailed over the black stallion's head.

The bunch spooked at the hissing sound of the loop, and Tilden braced himself while taking a couple of turns around the stout juniper post, but, to his surprise, no jolt come, and when he looked at the black after making sure his rope was well fast, he seen the black standing there, still, and watching him, like as if he'd never knowed a loop had slipped around his neck.

In the time Tilden had been in the cow country he'd seen many horses handled. He'd handled a good many himself, but no time had he ever thought of running acrost a horse like this. He didn't know what to make out of him, for that horse didn't seem to be scared, and if anything he seemed to call him on to do his worst, like he was challenging.

Could the horse have already been caught and tamed? But, no, not with that look in his eyes.

If Tilden had followed the trail of the bronk fighter for a few years he'd knowed what this horse was. He'd knowed that here was a killer, a horse that when corralled would go after a man like a cat goes after a mouse. Only worse, for such a horse as this would never stop to play with his victim before killing it.

But it wasn't very long when Tilden got a mighty strong hint of that. Without ever tightening the slack on the loop around his neck, the horse had stood, watching him. Then, all at once, that good looking head of his was transformed to look like one of these dragons that's seen in pictures. The glimpse Tilden got of his mouth and eyes and nostrils more than reminded him of one, and the only difference was there was no flame or smoke out of neither the mouth nor nostrils. But the look was sure there, and as that head appeared above the nine-foot fence at him, and the weight of his body shook the whole corral, Tilden didn't want to see more, he just made sure he fell off on the outside, and when he hit the ground the front of his shirt was missing.

He sat where he was for a spell sort of dazed, and once he shivered, for he could still see that head a glaring at him. It had been quite a surprise and a shock. This horse he'd admired and wanted so, and which he'd planned to do so much for, had turned on him as tho he'd been his worst enemy.

That was a disappointment that could be healed only by handing back the same that'd been handed him. But he was mighty careful as he stuck his head over the corral a second time, and then it was only for a second. He just wanted to make sure the rope was fastened so it'd hold. Then, after a glance at the black, he came down again. That glance told him plain that he was still being challenged.

That was well for Tilden in a way, and the way he felt at that time. He would call him on that and start in right now. He didn't feel sorry for the horse as he went around the corral and with intentions to open the gate and turn

And as that head appeared above the nine-foot fence at him, and the
weight of his body shook the whole corral, Tilden didn't want to see more.

the mares loose, and all he worried about as he went to do that was to see that the stallion was well fastened and couldn't break away. But if the stallion was anyways fretful about his mares leaving him he sure didn't show it. He fought the rope and tried to break away, but all he had eyes for as he done that was Tilden, and as disappointed and peeved as that boy still was, he was mighty glad that the rope holding that horse was new and mighty strong, and glad again to close the gate when the last mare had run out.

Feeling pretty hurt at the horse's actions towards him, Tilden didn't care for the time what happened to him. He knowed there was danger of the horse choking himself, there was a tightening loop around his neck, and the other end of the rope was tied hard and fast with two half hitches around the top of the heavy corral post, but he wasn't worried any of that happening. The horse fought the rope, pawed and bit at it and tried his best to break loose, but the rope held and his fighting only went to tighten the loop around his neck. His breath was coming short, and then he begin to sway back and forth, to fall flat on his side, choking.

It wasn't till then that Tilden got into action, but when he did he wasn't at all slow. He kind of flew over into the corral, up the post the rope was fastened to and loosened up the half hitches, and then, before the horse could stir again, he'd fell on his neck, grabbed one ear, held up his nose and slipped on the hackamore. When the horse got up again, feeling kind of shaky, he was tied solid once more, but there was no choking loop holding him this time.

He was tied shorter too, and now there was room for Tilden to stand in the corral without fear of being reached by his hoofs or teeth. Tilden stood and watched him, and after a while the horse looked over his withers at him and watched him back. The same fighting look was still in his eye, and went on to tell a lot of what would happen if only he was free for just one second.

Tilden sort of shivered at the thought of that, but somehow he wasn't feeling peeved at the horse no more, nor disappointed. He just felt sorry, for he'd come to realize that here, this horse, was the spirit of wild freedom, and he, Tilden, had took that freedom from him, separated him from his little bunch, enclosed him in a jail-like contraption, and slipped a choking loop around his neck. Now he stood there like as if to torment him some more, and considering all that, considering the brain and thinking power that horse had often proved of having, Tilden didn't wonder at the stand he'd took, for, so far, he'd only showed himself as a mighty harmful enemy, one that should be pawed to pieces on sight.

Then again, there was the wild animal's natural instinct against man. Man was the most feared and hated, and that instinct had been inherited for ages of generations, ever since man put a hand on the first horse. He'd been cruel, not to be trusted. He'd run the wild ones till they dropped, took their freedom away, broke 'em to pack or pull all for his own selfish needs, and when they got too numerous many was killed from long distances. The wild ones was in the way and they had no right to live if man didn't see fit.

So, as friendly and kind as Tilden wanted to be to the black, that feeling was all wasted. The horse only seen a man standing there close, and his instinct was to fight him, his worst enemy.

But Tilden, in a man's way, was now figgering on how to handle the horse, how to get the best of him, and have him in some way so he would stand the touch of his hand. But first, and the main thing now, a credit to some of the breed that's man, was to get feed and water for him.

There was only one way, and that was to rustle for it. Tilden eased out of the corral, went to his camp, took one of the paniers from his pack outfit, and went to looking for grass to fill it with. It took him over an hour to do that, and when he came back to the corral with the grass, and throwed it over the fence, the horse only reared and pawed at it. He wouldn't take anything that man would give him. He'd always rustled his own feed, and in all ways he could be mighty independent of man.

Tilden wasn't surprised that the horse wouldn't touch the grass, he didn't think he would, and figgered it'd be a day or two before he'd even sniff at it. But, anyway, he felt better to have some there for him, and now, the next problem was to get the water.

That would have to be packed over, but the snag there was that he had no bucket nor anything big enough in his pack outfit for the horse to drink out of. He figgered on that for quite a spell, and then he happened to notice that the spring was quite a bit higher than the corral, and with some work he could have the water run right down into it. That would beat any other way, for with fresh water running under his nose always, that would be a sure medicine against the horse ever getting the lock jaw, that ailing which, from a sweating and lack of water afterwards, causes the jaw muscles to tighten, to never loosen again if treated a day too late.

Tilden spent over half the day at digging a little ditch from the spring to the corral. An old shovel which he'd used while building the trap the year before came in mighty handy, and he was pleased to at last see the water run into a little pool at one edge of the corral.

The horse never let on that he seen the water or cared for any of it. And while Tilden worked in the corral, making the little pool, he had eyes only for him. By now he'd quit fighting the rope that held him, and he stood, like always waiting. Tilden then went on the outside of the corral, and loosened up the rope a few feet so the horse could reach the water. But never a move did he make, and only his eyes followed the man.

If he drank it was during the night, but never while Tilden was anywheres near, and the grass hadn't been touched. His pride wouldn't allow him to touch anything man gave him.

It was with a sorry feeling that Tilden noticed the gaunted look of the horse the next morning, and once more he thought of turning him loose, and again decided not to. He'd try hard, and if he couldn't do it, he'd know that it was because the horse was a hopeless outlaw, as man calls 'em.

He brought over some more fresh grass that day, and the horse pawed at it and ignored it the same as he did the day before. Always he stood watching and never missing a move that Tilden made. He reminded him of a big cat waiting for a chance to pounce at a victim.

Tilden worked in the corral that day, sometimes going to within a few feet of the horse's reach. But the horse never budged, he hadn't come close enough as yet.

Many strong juniper posts was cut and brought in the corral, and Tilden was busy making a small chute, or narrow stall, at one side of it. Each post was put in the ground about two feet deep and close to one another. The posts stuck up above about four feet, and at the head of the stall was a manger and a mighty stout post to tie to.

It was what's called a bronk stall. A place where a wild horse can be tied into with just enough room for him to stand. Once a horse is in such a place he can do nothing but snort, and a man's hand can be placed on him as is wished without fear of getting bit or kicked. It's a gentling place for the bad ones, and which is used at most ranches, specially where many horses are broke to work in harness.

The cowboy seldom uses that rig. He does his gentling in the middle of a bare corral or wherever he happens to be. But with this horse, and Tilden wanting to take his time, the bronk stall would be a mighty handy thing. He could touch the horse on either side then and show him there was no claws on his fingers.

It was high noon the next day before the stall was done, and up till that time, all the while Tilden worked in the corral, the horse had stood like a statue, still ignoring the fresh grass that'd been brought him. Something would have to be done or, as Tilden figgered, that horse would starve himself to death. He'd heard of wild horses doing that after they was caught. But that was caused from being heart broken, and sure this horse wasn't that way, not with that fighting spirit that was sticking out all over him.

Maybe it'd be best if he stayed away for awhile and give the horse a chance to forget him and to notice the grass hay that was at his feet. Then, as he built the manger on the stall, he thought of another thing. If there was

*He does his gentling in the middle of a bare corral or wherever he happens to be.*

a little box on that manger, and a little grain in it, maybe the horse would get to nibbling at it in time. Of course he knowed that grain is a mighty strange thing to a wild horse, but once one of the breed gets to tasting it, a little handful once in a while goes a long ways towards gentling even the wildest.

So, while Tilden thought it'd be best to stay away from the horse for a spell he'd figgered it a good time to hightail it to Old Joe's place and get a couple of sacks of the grain. He'd get 'em at night so that old feller wouldn't get suspicious of his reasons, for Tilden wasn't wanting to answer any questions as to what he'd wanted it for. He wanted to keep his secret a secret.

Making sure that the corral gate was well fastened and that all other parts of it was up to stay, he went on the outside of it and unfastened the hackamore rope, letting the horse free in there. With the forty feet of rope he'd be dragging, it'd be easy to reach in with a stick and get the end again from outside the corral.

It was early in the afternoon when Tilden, riding the big blue horse and leading the other to pack the grain back on, started towards Old Joe's place. He took another look at the black horse to make sure that all was okay, and then hit out on a fast trot.

By noon the next day he was back again, and not only with grain, but he'd brought a box to put it in at the manger, and then he'd raided Old Joe's store room for all he'd need to last him three weeks or a month. And he was mighty careful that there was plenty in granary and store room so that what he took wouldn't be missed, for he didn't want Old Joe to get suspicious.

All was fine when he got back, the horse was still in the corral, and the fact that he was much alive as yet was proved by the whistling snort that greeted him as he rode towards the corral. Some of the grass hay was missing and there was no sign of the lock jaw taking holt on the horse, so it was plain to see by that that he'd been eating and drinking.

But his fighting spirit was still all there. That Tilden seen when he reached with a stick to get the rope that afternoon. It was a good thing, once again, that there was a strong corral fence between him and the horse. But to-morrow, Tilden thought, as he dodged away, there might be a difference in that spirit. It might get to reason and understand once he got the horse in the stall and where he couldn't do no harm.

He drawed the rope up to a strong post and tied the horse so he could also go in that corral, and then he finished his work on the manger. He nailed the little box to it, put some grain in there, and then, seeing that all was ready, he went out and untied the rope again.

He pulled out a fresh supply of grass, throwed it over into the corral, and seen the horse glare thru the fence at him. He smiled, like in sympathy, then he says:

"Starting to-morrow, old boy, we're going to get acquainted, and if you will give me the chance, I'll show you how much I want to be your friend."

## Chapter XVI

The sun was just peeping over the ridges when the hated man showed himself at the corral. In his hands was more of these snake-like coils which had proved useless to fight against. To the horse, these coils was as the man's touch, always holding, and cutting to the heart.

The man didn't come inside of the corral. He worked his coils from the outside, and the horse watched him reach for the rope he was dragging. That rope wasn't fastened to the top of the tall post that morning, it was switched over to the other side of the corral instead and slipped around another post at the head of the narrow and suspicious looking enclosure. Slow and easy the horse's head was turned towards that. He felt a pull then, a steady pull, and wanting to relieve the pressure against his neck he took one step and another towards the narrow place.

But he was quite a ways away from it yet, and he could take them few steps without getting too close to the thing. Then, when the pressure of the rope was still on his neck and he feared to make another step, was when the man appeared in the corral. The horse, in surprise, jumped forward and when he tried to jump back he found that, as usual, the rope held him there. The man was behind him holding one end of it, and then another bunch of coils appeared and part of 'em settled on his rump in a loop.

What can a wild animal do in such a case but fight? The black horse fought. He wanted to fight the man, but the ropes was part of him it seemed like. So, not being able to get to the man, he fought them. He struck and kicked at all of them that was around him, but always, with every bit of slack he gave as he fought, he felt himself drawed towards the narrow place. And then, as he found himself near inside of it, he made a desperate jump like as if to clear it and the corral all at once. But he no more than got half ways up when his head was pulled down, and the first thing he knowed he was right inside the narrow place and his head was pegged down so he could hardly move.

But that wasn't all. A half a second later a heavy timber came up behind him and held him there. He couldn't even pull back then, and he couldn't jump out of the enclosure either, because as he tried that he felt a rope just back of his withers and which held him right where he was. All he could do was to stand. He had

*A half a second later a heavy timber*
*came up behind him and held him there.*

plenty of room to do that in, but right then that was the
least thing he wanted to do.

It was the first time in his free life he'd been held by
anything and so close, the first time he'd felt so helpless,
when he wanted to fight the most and could do that the
least. He'd been glad to bunt his head against a log right
then, for death was better than this. But he was power-
less to hurt himself in any way, and the most he could do
was to beller his rage and stomp the earth.

Wild eyed, he chewed at the heavy timbers and ropes.
His body was covered with sweat and his every muscle
was a quivering. And there, not over ten yards from him,

was the man, like as a wolf grinning at the helplessness of his victim.

But the man, Tilden, wasn't grinning. Instead he felt mighty concerned at the way the horse carried on, and, realizing the fear and hopelessness that was in that pony's heart, he'd kept away from him, knowing that his coming near would only make him more desperate.

For that reason he stayed away from the horse all that day, figgering that the animal had enough to contend with without aggravating him with his presence. Towards the afternoon the horse seemed to be quieter, like as if he'd resigned himself, but there was a murderous look in his eyes, and Tilden wasn't happy when he got a glimpse of it.

He went back to his camp then, and that camp being well out of sight from the corral he started to busy himself to doing little odd jobs which all he'd neglected ever since he'd caught the horse. He didn't want to think about the horse nor what that pony was going thru just then, and being busy would be good medicine against that.

He put on a stew to cook, of what all he had that'd go in such a combination, and after that he begin sorting out all the shirts and such which needed washing. There was a considerable amount, and they needed that treatment awful bad.

He was in the thick of such work, and keeping his eye on the stew at the same time, when a surprising sound, awful near, made him drop his bar of soap. It was a voice, a clear tuneful voice, and it'd said, "Hello stranger."

Tilden turned, starey eyed, and there, to within a few feet of him, was Rita Spencer setting on her horse.

She smiled at the surprised look on his face, but she didn't notice that there was a little fear in that look. Fear that she could maybe see the corral from the back of her horse, and see the black horse in there. If so, his secret would be out to one.

"I guess I wasn't expected," she says, still smiling, "but I seen the smoke of your fire, and I wanted to find out if it was you camped here."

"Yeh," says Tilden, sort of getting back to himself. "Won't you get down from your horse? I'll tie him up for you."

"He won't need tying, thanks, and I don't think I should stay to talk to you at all. Not since you make such a stranger of yourself."

"Why, I didn't know I had," Tilden stuttered. "I didn't . . ."

"But you did," she interrupted. "You haven't been over to visit us since early last fall. That's nearly seven months ago."

Tilden was surprised. She'd even counted the months, just like he had. But with him, he was mostly counting the time when he could show her, whereas with her. . . . He didn't know what to think.

*Tilden turned, starey eyed, and there, to within a few feet of him, was Rita Spencer setting on her horse.*

"The last time I went over to see you," he says, feeling like he should offer some excuse, "you weren't home."

"Yes, Moran told me about that. He said you didn't have the time to wait, and I was sorry to've missed you. But you couldn't guess where I was that day . . . I climbed up on the flat topped butte and to see if you had moved to The Basin."

"And you wasn't playing that you wasn't at home then?" Tilden, caught by surprise, had blurted this out before he could think.

The girl stared at him, wondering. "Why, what makes you say that?" she asks.

There was nothing for Tilden to do but go on. "Well," he says, fidgeting around, "I was afraid that I may have been pestering you. You see," he hurried on, "there's so little to me, and I couldn't see where my company could be tolerated only thru sympathy for my uselessness. I don't want . . ."

"Are you talking seriously, Mr. Tilden?" . . . The girl got down off her horse, and coming a little closer, pointed a finger at him. "Just for that," she says, "I'm going to make you take me home, and you're going to stay for supper when you get there."

Tilden didn't at all find them orders hard to take, and while he straightened up his camp, pulled the half cooked stew off the fire and made away with the washing, he went on a trying to talk so as to lead off from what he'd just said. He went to catch and saddle the blue horse, and all the while he wondered at himself being such a fool as to call on and pet this hurt of many months past. If he'd had the gumption, and had investigated instead of letting Moran put something over on him there wouldn't of been no such a hurt as what he'd put up with. He'd let himself slip and feel bad all on account of imagining things, that he was no man or anything else much. And now he seen where there was a whole lot in backing what all he was wanting to be. He'd have to live that and let nothing shake his confidence. He'd have to believe in himself.

The ride over to Miss Rita's home, and the supper there, with a little talk afterwards, done a whole lot to stir that belief and give it strength. There was some talk about the black stallion, and Rita and her father passed their opinion on how doubtful it would be for any man to ever be able to catch him. Tilden's secret was still a secret, and when he came back to his camp that night and tended to the horse, he felt mighty pleased at the thought of surprising another party, a party even more important than Old Joe, by some day straddling the stallion and riding him up in plain sight.

He didn't think of what the object would be in doing that. It wouldn't be that he'd want to show off, for all he thought of from that happening was visions of two fair hands clasped in wonder and glad surprise a shining in bright eyes.

Them visions done a whole lot to cause cheerful whistling tunes to be heard at the trap corral the next morning. The black stallion fought some more when he was hazed into the narrow stall, and he still meant to do harm to the man that hazed him there. But that morning Tilden hardly seemed to notice the fiery look that was in that pony's eyes. He put him thru the ropes like it was all in the day's work, and it wasn't till the horse was in the stall to stay that he gave a thought to what all was ahead.

There was a lot ahead yet, a lot to be considered in handling that horse, and the way it was starting it looked like the horse would educate the man as much as the man would educate the horse. Tilden left him alone in the stall all that forenoon. He wanted him to get used to that, and it was in the middle of the afternoon before he came in the corral and begin to get close. Stepping slow and careful he eased towards the horse. He talked a bit and whistled low, and as he came nearer he gradually raised a hand, for with a few more steps he'd be able to touch him.

The horse, wild eyed, crouched in the stall and shivered. He'd long ago realized the uselessness of trying to get out of this place which held him in at all sides, but, as Tilden's hand was about to touch him, he tried to break loose once more. Crouching as he'd been, he shot up and the stall creaked and shook, but it held. And then, in a desperate way, he squealed and tried to reach the man's hand with his teeth.

But all them efforts was for nothing. Steady and without hesitating once, Tilden's hand kept a getting nearer till finally it touched the horse's quivering side. There was another squeal and a snort, striking hoofs hit the side of the stall, and for a second it looked as if the horse might shrink to nothing and slip away. Terror and rage both had a holt of him at once, and being so helpless to fight made that seem worse. He didn't feel no pain as the man's hand touched him but at that touch it was as if an electric current went thru him and his heart was beating so the thumping of it could be heard.

"Steady boy," Tilden was saying over and over again, and he kept his hand on the horse's side as he talked. After a while he moved the hand, and in rubbing motion brought it nearer the withers. The horse tried to reach him once more then but his head was tied short and all he could do was try. Tilden never seemed to notice the action, the withers was passed over, and fingers was run thru the long strands of the black mane. And all the while the horse quivered and crouched and fought.

Tilden went from one side of the horse that way to the other and back and forth. Sometimes he'd leave him a few minutes to sort of give him a chance to think things over and when he'd come back again the hand would always feel the same quivering hide. It didn't seem that the horse would ever get used to the touch of the human hand, for when late afternoon come there was no sign of any change.

He turned him loose in the corral again that night and as usual let him drag the long rope. He then brought him a lot of grass hay, and as the next day come he sort of hoped to see some change, for the horse had et quite a bit of the hay and he'd seen him drink out of the little pool once. That all was at least a show that the horse wasn't sulking, and if he could keep him from doing that, there was a chance of sometime getting him to reason how the man wasn't so much an enemy as his instinct would have him.

But that day didn't bring much change. The horse was hazed into the stall as usual and it took the same amount of work and figgering to get him in there as it did on the first day. And after that, when Tilden's hand touched him there was the same quiver run along the horse's body, the same fighting, the same wild look, and often Tilden was reminded of the danger of getting to within reach of his teeth.

But Tilden, even tho feeling hurt at the stand the horse had took, never let up in his trying to win the horse's confidence. That seemed impossible to do, and often he wondered if the horse wasn't too much of a killer at heart to ever accept a man as a friend.

Two days went by and with very little change in the horse. He'd got a little quieter and didn't flinch so much after the hand had once touched him, but that little amount of quietness was replaced by a waiting look on that pony's head which Tilden didn't like. It was as if instead of fighting so much he'd resigned himself to wait for a chance when he could put in a lick that'd count.

From then on he seemed to get quieter every day, but that waiting look was still in them eyes of his. He'd started to chew some grain by then. He'd tasted it once, when mad clear thru he'd stuck his nose in the box fastened to the manger and took on a mouthful. At first he'd chewed it just to be chewing something, in the place of a stick or a post or anything. But one time after that Tilden seen him stick his nose in there and chew on some more of the grain when he wasn't peeved. Then one noon, when he'd left the horse to go cook a bait for himself, he seen on his return the box was empty.

Tilden put a little more grain in the box. The horse ignored it then, but the next morning the box was empty again. The horse had come up to the manger of his own accord during the night to get that grain, a proof that the stall had got to be less feared.

The sight of the empty grain box stirred Tilden's hopes up a considerable that morning. He knowed what a failing every horse has for grain, and it was thru handing out little handfuls of that once in a while that he figgered on getting a start at getting a holt on that pony's heart strings. That was the only way, just now, that he could prove his friendship for the horse. Nothing that he'd done so far could prove that, for, getting the horse in the scary and narrow contraption, then crawling up on him when he was helpless, wasn't what could be called a show of friendship. But with a little grain now and then, and with the horse getting a craving for it, he could maybe get him to perk his ears at him instead of laying 'em back. He could then, in time, handle him in the open corral and with no fear of them hoofs of his, or teeth.

But such a happening seemed a long time off, for even with the grain that was handed the horse, he never touched it till Tilden was out of sight and he seemed to want to let on that he'd never seen the grain, that he wouldn't touch the stuff if he had seen it, and how he was entirely independent of man for anything he could give him.

He kept on fighting the touch of Tilden's hand, but every morning the grain was missing, the box kept on being empty. And then one night Tilden didn't put no grain in the box. He missed doing that again the next night. And when he rattled the grain in a pan the next day the black stallion perked up his ears, and nickered.

It wasn't many days later that Tilden could run his hand along that pony's neck without him flinching. That pony had got to looking for his grain by then, and as Tilden kept feeding him little handfuls now and again, he'd got so he didn't seem to mind being in the narrow stall or having a hand touch him.

The taming of that horse progressed on a considerable from that time, and come a day when Tilden could lay both arms acrost his withers and rest them there without a quiver being felt. The murderous look begin to disappear, and instead of being greeted by snorts he was now nickered at, like as if he was welcome.

It seemed as tho the horse had given in at last, and even tho he wasn't at all tame as yet, there seemed to be a big change of heart in him. The man-killing instinct had gone, and, outside of a few little man actions that still spooked him up, he acted as tho he would now give that man a chance.

That was a mighty pleasing surprise for Tilden, and he felt as tho he couldn't do enough for the horse. He brought him fresh hay twice a day now, mornings and evenings, and he'd got so he hated to put him in the stall for the daily taming, but he wasn't sure of his ground as yet and the picture of that fighting pony's head was still in his mind. Then again, the horse didn't seem to mind going in the stall no more, and there he could feed him his grain and crawl over him as he pleased.

But he hadn't got to crawling over him much as yet. He wanted to give the horse time and not bring on too much at once. And so, after waiting a few more days, he finally climbed up on the stall, and slow and careful brought a leg to rest over the slick black back. There was a commotion about then, and it was a good thing the horse was pegged down in the narrow stall or there'd been a scattering of something sure enough. But Tilden, steadying himself with a foot on both sides of the stall, held his position, and while the horse fought under him he got a mighty strong hint that it wouldn't do to set on him while he was free, not for quite a spell.

And he didn't try, not as much as he wanted to, but every day he brought the horse in the stall and sat on him there. Every day the commotion from such doings got to be less and less, and come a time when, as Tilden fed the horse a little handful of grain after each setting, that he could climb up on the round back without hardly being noticed. But Tilden knowed enough about horses so as not to be fooled by the possum acting. He knowed that the horse would more than take him on if once he got the chance, for he seen that even tho he seemed to get used to him he was still mighty neutral as to any hankering for his friendship. He took the grain and nickered for more, and thru the craving he'd developed for it and knowing it was the man who brought it, he'd stood the company of one so he could get the other.

If Tilden had proved himself the master, and showed the horse that he could be handled in the open and regardless of what he done, there might be a different story to tell. The horse would either been made to behave and do as was wanted, or else he'd kept on fighting till he dropped. That last would of been the most likely, for that horse wasn't wanting no man for a master and he'd only went from bad to worse and stayed a killer. But Tilden didn't try to master him, he only wanted to be a friend and have the horse recognize him as such, and if he did corner him in the narrow stall it was only to that end, to get a hand on him and stir a little trust.

And Tilden was winning, slow but sure enough winning. The proof of that was how the horse had seemed to forget to want to kill. Of course he might still be biding his time and waiting, but by not giving him the chance there would come a time when it'd be safe to come near him when he was foot loose and head free. He would keep him in the stall and handle him there till he was sure of that and till a spark of friendship showed. That's what he was working for.

Every day he was with the horse, talking to him, giving him little handfuls of grain now and again, and setting on him. The horse had got so he didn't seem to mind what the man done with him no more. He'd got so he didn't even watch him nor cared when he sat on him in all ways and from rump to withers, but that was all there was to it. He just didn't care, and he didn't as yet show that he liked the man's company.

Then one day, like as if there was no end of scary happenings for the horse, Tilden came in the corral packing a saddle. There was some more commotion as that rig was brought close, and more fighting to break out of the stall. But Tilden didn't rush things, he let the saddle lay to within sniffing distance of the horse all that forenoon and it wasn't till the sun had passed the highest point that he begin to ease it up on his back. There was more flinching and quivering as that was done, but Tilden noticed with a glad feeling that no bad look showed in the pony's eyes. He put the saddle on, let it rest there a spell till the horse got used to it a little, and then took it off again, and put it on some more till, with a little handful of grain being handed out once in a while thru that performance, the horse finally got to accept that tool, in a neutral way.

The saddle was slipped on again the next day, and cinched up, and then Tilden sat up on it, stuck his feet in the stirrups and worked 'em back and forth. There was more muscle quivering and flinching but it wasn't for long this time, for with Tilden's talking, which sounds the horse had got to perking his ears at, and with more handfuls of grain and so on, that all had got to fit in with the man's doings. And it was getting so that that man's doings didn't call no more on that fighting instinct of his.

He was getting to even welcome the feeling of the hand now, for it seemed like there was a relief with the touch of it. There was raw and sore places on his hide, places that'd been nicked off while he'd fought the stall and tried to get away, and it seemed, with the touch of that hand, that the soreness was gradually leaving and the raw sores was healing. Then again the pestering flies, which was now beginning to come, swarmed away as it came near. The sores was covered with something cool and soothing, and even the itchy places, like at the back of his ears and along his neck, was relieved with the scratching motion of it. And now, instead of quivering at the touch of the hand or trying to reach for it with his teeth, he leaned over to meet it and it was with a mild look in his eyes.

But still, even tho he seemed to've lost all hankering to do harm, Tilden kept on putting the horse in the bronk stall every day and to getting him more and more used to the saddle. It was near three weeks now since he'd first set hands on the horse, and if another three weeks brought on again as much results, why, that was all he could hope for.

The only thing now, while it was taking so much time, was that some rider might drop by any day, see the black horse, and spread the news of his being caught. Old Joe himself might come up at the trap, and then Miss Rita too. Them was the two people Tilden wanted the pleasure of surprising, and he wished he could rush things a little so he could pull it off before anything happened that'd spoil the surprise.

Since that day Miss Rita had dropped in on him at the camp, he'd been to see her twice. One reason was to keep her from coming again and finding out about the black horse, and the other reason, the biggest one, was just to see her.

He'd been made mighty welcome, both by her and her dad, but as he thought on that welcome he couldn't see where it was any better than any other they'd always greeted him with. It only seemed better, and the reason for that was he felt more fitting to their company. The catching of the black horse had done wonders for him, wonders which he didn't realize, for, with the catching of the horse, he'd proved a whole lot to himself which he'd long wondered about. That all had kept a stacking up in him as he went to breaking the horse, and right along he felt a strong backing which kept a pushing him up and up.

From then on, the way he went at things, it seemed as tho all trails was blazed for him. There was no snags that could stop or make him hesitate, and like that day, when he'd apologized to Miss Rita and said how he amounted to so little, that he was afraid his company was tolerated only thru sympathy for his helplessness. He'd said them words only because that had been the reason for his not seeing her the fall before, but he didn't mean them at the time they was said, because, somehow, he didn't feel that way no more.

Every visit at the Spencer home done a whole lot to clinch that belief in himself, and that was proved one evening when, as he and Rita was riding side by side, he reached over and touched her hand and said, "Rita, you're beautiful."

It wasn't so very long ago when Tilden wouldn't dared pay such a compliment to such a girl as Miss Rita, because then them words would of sounded like as if they'd come from a beggar to a queen, and what would they amounted to? But as he spoke that evening he knowed them words would be heard.

They was heard, heard better than he might of expected, for as he went to start back for his camp a while later he felt Rita's hand on his. And he heard her say, "Bert, you're wonderful."

The ride back to camp was another time when all was bright and no stars or moon was in sight. The sun come up behind dark clouds the next morning but it was still bright, and when he went towards the corral he greeted the black horse there as an old pal and friend, someone to share good news with.

From that day on the black horse got to hear a lot that no horse could understand. But the sound of the voice went well, it hinted to friendliness, and that it was, for now it seemed mighty important, more so than ever, that the horse would accept him as a friend. He needed him now more than ever it seemed like. He forgot how much he'd needed and wanted him before. He forgot that the horse had been his lead, that he'd suffered to follow him on and on. Now he'd caught him, and all he remembered was that he wanted to be a friend to him, a pardner, both to drift towards the Spencer home some day, and stand under the light of Rita's eyes.

# Chapter XVII

Of all animals, the horse is one what can nearly know the thoughts of man. Of course there are many horses that don't seem to fret any about such, the same as there is many men who don't care what the to-morrows bring, but amongst most wild horses there's an instinct that makes 'em want to watch and figger out the man. He's a strange crethure to 'em, to be feared, and it's thru watching his every action that they get to feel the gumption, or failing, or love of him.

Horses are very different one from the other. No two are ever found alike, excepting maybe in color and size. And there's as big a variety of actions and spirit amongst 'em as there is amongst humans. The cowboy is always reminded of that mighty strong as he runs in a bunch of the wild ones and starts handling 'em, and that same cowboy will always find a few in any bunch that set out to test him. Each will have their own way of doing that and each will make the cowboy prove himself, and it stumps the man on how the horse can tally up on him, figger him out, find the weak or strong points, even up to the mind of him, and with more sureness than another man could.

As to brain power and instinct that way the black stallion ranked up to the top. That was proved by the way he'd kept out of loops and traps for so long. Then again, when he was finally caught, by the way he wanted to destroy this man who had took his freedom away. He'd realized the loss of that freedom and looked at the man as his worst enemy.

He'd felt that way towards him till time sort of healed his hurt. And then, with getting used to the man and finally receiving attention from him that was to his liking, he begin to take an interest and to see him without feeling the craving to kill. He got so he didn't mind his being around, and then come a hint of friendship. He stayed neutral as to that, and the reason for that was the man didn't trust him. Every day he'd been hazed into the stall, and even tho that was necessary for the first introduction it wasn't a place where a horse could get to liking a man from.

But he'd got to know the man from that place. He'd got to know him better than the man knowed himself, and there's where his brain power and instinct came in at, again. He knowed from the first that the man was scared of him (but who could blame the man there), and what's more he could tell at the touch of his hand, afterwards, that he was trying to be friendly. He didn't appreciate that because he didn't want to be the friend of no man, and when he did finally forget his hate there's where the horse had it over the man, for the man didn't know.

But it wasn't for long. Tilden came back from a visit with Miss Rita one evening and the horse got a strong hint of a change the next morning. He wasn't hazed in the stall. Instead, the man walked right into the corral, picked up the long rope and came up to him to rest a hand on his neck. The horse didn't see no fear in him no more, only a strong friendly feeling which made him stand without flinching. He got the hunch he was needed, that he was trusted, and that, without doubt, he was expected to return the friendship that was handed him.

It took some steady nerve for a man to handle the black horse the way Tilden did that morning, but he had a considerable amount of that. He was sort of hazed along by the vision of a fair face under a broad brimmed hat. Under that spell he failed to notice any danger in the stallion. He only seen him as a powerful pardner, one to remind him that any lead can be caught up on if a feller has the will. Now he needed him to catch up on another lead, and no king in a chariot of gold could ever been as proud as Tilden when, once mounted on the black, he'd ride up on the tall pinnacles to complete what all he'd set his heart to doing.

There'd still be considerable to do yet tho. The horse wasn't quite ready to throw in with him that way. But Tilden wasn't stumped by that, none at all. He took him on and without once wondering as to how his wide open actions would be received. He took it for granted that they'd be received well, and he talked to him, laughed, run his hands along the powerful shoulders and neck and up to the short ears and long foretop.

The horse stood like a statue, sort of puzzled at the show of the man's feelings. They was new to him and strong, and it seemed like there was nothing he wanted to do but stand there and take 'em in. Once, when the man first walked in the corral, his old spirit of wanting to pound him in the dust sort of flickered up to the top. It had been his first chance at him, a chance he'd long waited for, but somehow, with the man's actions and all, the lack of fear in him and the show of friendship, the bad light that come to his eyes was smothered with the first words. He'd been set back at the sound of 'em, like as if he'd bumped up against a wall of blue joint grass.

A good half of the day was spent by the man and horse getting acquainted again, this time with no stall or anything to keep the horse from using his hoofs or teeth. But with this meeting out in the middle of the bare corral that day there seemed to be no reason for any fear of them, and not only that, but the new freedom of that meeting only went to give the horse more confidence in the man.

A good proof of that was how the horse stood when Tilden slipped the saddle on him that afternoon. There wasn't a twitch of the hide as it was slipped on and off and on and off again, and the horse acted as tho he was wanting to make good for the way he was trusted. Tilden, mighty pleased at such a showing, often talked as he moved around him. Once in a while he brought him a handful of grain and held it up, in his hand, to the head that not so long ago had been the living image of a fire belching dragon.

There was no hint now that that good looking head would ever be transformed into such a way again, and even tho the eyes was watchful, it was thru interest, and the light in 'em was mild.

The foot-loose acquaintance went on again the next day. The saddle was slipped on and then, grinning and talking, Tilden eased one foot in the stirrup and climbed up in the middle of it. The horse only looked back at him and stood, stood quieter than when in the stall. Tilden let him stand and rubbed his hand along the smooth neck and talked the while. Then he got off, talked to him some more and climbed on again. That was done many times, and then some fresh action was brought in. From then on the horse was led a ways every time Tilden got off. That was as much as to let him know that he was allowed to move, and to get used to it so he wouldn't spook while Tilden was in the saddle.

It was late in the afternoon when Tilden pulled his hat down tight and climbed on the horse a preparing to ride. He was going to move him while setting in the saddle. That was ticklish work, because, as Tilden knowed, then's when a horse is apt to "break in two" and make riding interesting. But it seemed like he pulled his hat down tight and felt of his saddle for no reason, for, as he pulled on the hackamore rein, the horse just leaned to it like as if it was to his liking and followed the lead of it without once showing signs of wanting to kettle or fight his head.

But that was no sign he wouldn't sometime, and sudden. And now according to the way Tilden figgered, was the time to keep him from the notion. With the cowboy, he'd want the horse to spook up and have it over with right now. But Tilden was working different, and according to the way he'd passed the ruffle in other testing events he had a good chance of winning. He was more for studying a thing out and preventing a happening, if he could. And he'd rather take a chance on that happening coming along later than right now, for, with time, it might never come.

And it didn't come. That is, not that day, nor the next. He moved the black horse out of his tracks and while he was setting on him, and taking it easy with him he teached him to answer to the pull of one rein and then the other.

As a bronk fighter, taking horses to break for five dollars a head, and working at the speed he was, he wouldn't of been able to afford the papers for the making of a smoke, but Tilden was wanting to be a bronk fighter only to be able to catch and tame the black horse. That had been his first high ambition towards doing things, but he hadn't got into the game, and he didn't need to, for he had time, time to figger things out and with no interruptions as to following his lead, and he'd singled that lead out so that his plans changed and nothing was kept track of excepting that lead.

He'd hit straight for one mark, and realizing how hard that mark would be to reach he hadn't took on any more than was necessary. He'd won out by doing just that. And now he'd win out again in breaking the black horse, even if he'd have to get in and learn the bronk fighting game. But, so far, that hadn't proved necessary. He knowed enough to keep things a going, and he wasn't letting any side work interfere with his getting there.

But he had a big advantage now in breaking the black horse. There was two leads, one on the trail of the other, and either one was a plenty to stir him to doing his very best. The black horse was sort of doubled up on that way and he had no chance, no chance to do anything only what was wished on him. He was sort of swamped down by a lot of determination and a flood of reckless friendship, and there was nothing for him to do but float along and bathe in the coolness of that. He found, as he drifted on that way, that he even wanted to help, and he wasn't letting any snag spook him up into queering things.

From then on is when a big change begin to be noticed in the horse, and it was thru his knowing the man so well that the change come. His instinct sort of told him of what layed deep in the man's heart. It was of two loves, the strongest of which wasn't for him, but he felt the effects of that one too, like as if he was needed to carry it thru. Of course there was no understanding of them feelings, only the power of 'em, and they controlled him the same way as they controlled the man.

To see the man and the horse out there in the corral, one that had been brought up amongst all that's shut in, bustling, and civilized, the other a wild spirit of freedom from the rough open range, a feller would wonder where the tie came in at between 'em. But a tie there was sure enough, and mighty strong. The sprouting of that was only of a week. But now, the way the black stallion followed the man around the corral, it looked as tho he was dependent on him for air and life.

For the last two days, Tilden had been riding him around in the main trap and out of the little corral. There was more room now, many acres of it, and there, on the ridge where his freedom was lost, the black stallion was teached how to answer at the pull of the rein, how to stop, and start, and turn, and stand. All of that was along with many resting spells. The teacher was lenient and patient, the pupil was mighty willing, and even tho the pupil was often the teacher, neither ever sulked or slacked down on the job.

This training went on that way for many days, like as if preparing for a big event. And a big event it would be, that day when the man and the horse lined out *together*.

Finally that day come. The entrance of the trap was opened wide, and they started away, neither seeming to be of the earth. The horse took on with the spirit of the man, and at that time that man's spirit was more with wings and not so much with steps. The black flowing mane of the horse was as the plumes of a powerful bird that was taking him to the high point of his goal, and when the main gate of the Spencer ranch was reached, it seemed queer that it was opened and not sailed over.

That day was a day of events for Tilden, events that's remembered thru lifetimes without the need of marking down. Astraddle the proud black stallion, the prize of the country, he rode by the Spencer corrals on up to the house. And there on the porch, and like as if in tune to make that day's happenings perfect, was Rita.

Tilden had had visions of this day's surprise for her, of clasped hands, of shining eyes, and glad smiles. But, as he rode closer, he seen where them visions had been, after all, just that, and mighty weak as compared to what he was now taking in.

*And there on the porch, and like as if in tune
to make that day's happenings perfect, was Rita.*

She'd jumped down off the porch, a regular apparition of joy and wonder, and she seemed about to want to try and hug both the man and the horse right there on the spot. Tilden's thoughts was soaring sky high about then, away up amongst the heavens, and it looked like they was due to soar on and on up there. For as he dismounted and came to her, he seen, mixed in with the proud light in her eyes, man's biggest reward, love.

Out in a country of blue grass, pinion, and aspen, and in the shadiest spot of that country, where the cool summer breeze was most free to blow, stood a little bunch of horses. To spot 'em there a feller would think they was just another bunch of wild ones, for they was on the wild horse range, but on getting closer and seeing how they all tallied up in size and color, all trim of built and showy of pure breed, they'd be stared and wondered at, because as straight and clean a looking bunch of ponies is seldom seen anywheres.

But there was more to wonder at along with the sight of them horses. The country they was in was fenced, fenced with expensive six foot woven wire and put up so as to turn and hold any hoofed animal. Thousands of acres, the cream of the territory, was took in with the big fence that way. The finest of summer and winter range, pure water from many springs, and shade galore, not mentioning the tall blue grass which ranks so high towards building up horseflesh, bone, and muscle.

Enough range was took in by the fence to run a couple of hundred head of stock the year around, but there was only a privileged eleven head for all that space and feed, ten bay mares and one black stallion.

The black stallion, a sire mighty worthy to stand at the top in horse kingdom, was a little ways from the mares, under a shady pinion, and close to the tall gate of his fenced-in range when a big automobile, following the dim wagon road that run along the fence, came to a stop there. A man got out, then a girl. The two opened the big gate, walked on into the big pasture, and as the man talked, something sort of hard to believe happened. The wild looking stallion had started to run away but, at the sound of the man's words, he'd turned back, nickered, and came to rest his powerful jaws on the man's shoulder.

Man and horse and girl had a confab there for a spell, one that might not of had much meaning to an outsider, but it was sacred to them three and a fourth party couldn't of fitted in just then. The way the three men waited in the car sort of hinted as to that.

"Mighty expensive idea of Bert's to fence up this land just for one little bunch of horses," says one of the men.

"Yeh, mebbe so," says another, "but there's one horse in that bunch that's a heap more to him than just a horse, and I'm mighty glad for that. Glad because that horse will call him back to this country again. . . . You know, Spencer, it ain't often that an old sourdough like me gets any such company as he's been to me, and I'll sure miss him."

"I savvy how it is, Joe, and I'll want to see my girl again too. But I won't begrudge her leaving, not with that boy, and now that he's so all-fired enthused to catch himself another black horse in financial and civilized worlds why I sure wish him luck. He'll win there too, and as far as company is concerned you and me can sort of pitch in together Joe. I'll try and stand you if you can stand me."

The third man never said a word as the two talked. He was busy with thoughts of his own, and while he sat at the wheel he didn't once turn his head to glance at the man and girl out there with the horse. When they finally came back and took their seats he kept a staring straight ahead, the same when, as he was told that all was set, he started driving.

The car was put up and down pitches that looked unfit for anything but a high geared wagon to go over. The dim road was followed on and on for a few hours to finally run into a long stretch of graded highway.

It was the middle of the afternoon when the telegraph poles of a railroad was sighted. The highway had curved and soon was running right alongside the steel rails, and then, away off ahead, an object was spotted. It looked like it was moving, but the one man in the car who thought of that had got to know better. He knowed that that object was a little red building. It was right alongside the track, and the same one he'd wandered away from early one morning more than two years before.

After considerable more driving the car was brought up alongside of it to a stop. He walked nearer to the little building, and, sort of wanting to go over all that'd took place since the train had left him there, he went around the corner of it, to be by himself for a spell. But he didn't get to thinking on any of the past for long. A hand touched him on the shoulder and he turned to face the man who'd sat at the wheel of the car.

"Well, Spats," says that man, grinning and holding out his hand, "I've cornered you here, to congratulate you. . . . This all might sound sort of queer after the way I've treated you, but I had two reasons for doing that. One was how you'd started out to get all that I wanted, and the other was to see if you'd be man enough to deserve that, to see if you'd let a snag turn you back. You haven't and now I want to congratulate you and wish you luck. Shake."

He gripped the hand for all he was worth. "I'm very glad to hear that, Moran," he says, "and . . . come to think about it all now I realize you helped more than you interfered. I want to thank you, and I only hope always to see you at the ranch every time I get back there."

The two would of went on talking some more, but they was interrupted by a woman's voice calling, "Bert. . . Gilbert, the train is coming." There was biddings of good byes and best wishes. The man helped the girl up on the train, and, as it begin to move, he placed an arm around her, pressed her tight, and took a long look at the country he was leaving. It was the country that'd made him, where he found himself, and love. Away off in the distance was the hazy outline of the flat topped butte. The black stallion, his lead, was in the shadow of it, and as he looked in that direction a happy, grateful tear came to his eye and he was heard to say:

"Yes, Rita, we will come back again, and often."

The train speeded on, the tear dried away, and then a glint appeared in his eyes, a glint of mighty strong confidence and purpose, for now, with another proof of his winning held close to his heart, he was headed to another country and where there was more for him to conquer.

*The black stallion was in the shadow of it.*